Prai[se]

"Poignant, diverse, and enthr[alling, the latest] Menagerie series evokes the majesty of sirens, from the [...] deep sea variety of Greek mythology to those that entice sailors of deep space to ones who scan modern dating sites with wistful hopes for a good match. I could not stop reading."
— Beth Cato, author of *The Clockwork Dagger*

"Like its titular subject, *Sirens* drags you in with promises of beauty and mystery and then refuses to let go. You tear yourself away from the pages just long enough to note that it's two in the morning before deciding to read just one more tale…Sirens is a fantastic voyage that tosses the reader up on many a strange-yet-familiar shore. Listen to the unique voices of each story. They're worth the risk of drowning."
— Amber E. Scott, author of *Chronicle of the Righteous* and *Siege of Dragonspear*

"The call of SIRENS is quite powerful indeed. With a variety of stories, crafted with care, you will delight in the tales that the many authors weave throughout this fantastical anthology. It will lure you in and not let go."
— Tara Platt, author *Zartana*

"The moment Rhonda Parrish announces another anthology—especially *Magical Menageries* installments—I get grabby hands. She always cultivates an amazing selection, and this group of maligned and misunderstood sirens is my favorite of all her books so far, displacing FAE (which I will continue to heartily recommend)… Get this anthology. Do it now. You won't regret it."
— S. L. Saboviec, author of *Guarding Angel*

Titles in the Anthology Series
Rhonda Parrish's Magical Menageries

Fae
Corvidae
Scarecrow
Sirens
Equus

SIRENS

Edited by
RHONDA PARRISH

Rhonda Parrish's Magical Menageries
Volume Four

World Weaver Press

SIRENS

Copyright © 2016 Rhonda Parrish.

All rights reserved.

This is a work of fiction; characters and events are either fictitious or used fictitiously.

"Siren Seeking" Copyright © 2016 by Kelly Sandoval
"The Fisherman and the Golem" © 2016 by Amanda Kespohl
"We Are Sirens" © 2016 by L.S. Johnson
"Moth to an Old Flame" © 2016 by Pat Flewwelling
"The Bounty" © 2016 by Gabriel F. Cuellar
"The Dolphin Riders" © 2016 by Randall G. Arnold
"Is This Seat Taken?" © 2016 by Michael Leonberger
"Nautilus" © 2016 by V.F. LeSann
"Siren's Odyssey" © 2016 by Tamsin Showbrook
"Safe Waters" © 2016 by Simon Kewin
"Notefisher" © 2016 by Cat McDonald
"Experience" © 2016 by Sandra Wickham
"Threshold" © 2016 by K.T. Ivanrest
"The Fisherman's Catch" © 2016 by Adam L. Bealby
"One More Song" © 2016 by Eliza Chan
"Homecoming" © 2016 by Tabitha Lord

Published by World Weaver Press, LLC
Albuquerque, NM
www.WorldWeaverPress.com

Cover layout and design by Jonathan C. Parrish.
Cover images used under license from Fotolia.com.

First edition: July 2016
ISBN-13: 978-0692687208

Also available as an ebook

Dedicated to Sarena. Thank you for doing the right thing.

Contents

Introduction
Sara Cleto and Brittany Warman – 1

Siren Seeking
Kelly Sandoval – 4

The Fisherman and the Golem
Amanda Kespohl – 14

We Are Sirens
L.S. Johnson – 35

Moth to an Old Flame
Pat Flewwelling – 58

The Bounty
Gabriel F. Cuellar – 78

The Dolphin Riders
Randall G. Arnold – 85

Is This Seat Taken?
Michael Leonberger – 94

Nautilus
V. F. LeSann – 118

Siren's Odyssey
Tamsin Showbrook – 140

Safe Waters
Simon Kewin – 162

Notefisher

Cat McDonald – 172

EXPERIENCE
Sandra Wickham – 184

THRESHOLD
K.T. Ivanrest – 198

THE FISHERMAN'S CATCH
Adam L. Bealby – 217

ONE MORE SONG
Eliza Chan – 226

HOMECOMING
Tabitha Lord – 240

CONTRIBUTORS
258

ANTHOLOGIST
277

RHONDA PARRISH'S MAGICAL MENAGERIES

MORE GREAT SHORT STORIES

SIRENS

INTRODUCTION
Sara Cleto and Brittany Warman

Sing to us, oh Muse, of the tales of the sirens. Sing of the beautiful, deadly creatures, half-bird and half-woman, who haunt the sea and lure men to their deaths with their irresistible voices. Sing to us of their lives, their loves, their fears, and their victories. Tell us why they sing.

We've all heard of sirens, but their song remains elusive. We look for them where waves crash on jagged shorelines, at festivals where smoke hangs like a veil and women whisper into microphones on makeshift stages, on the subway when we hear a husky laugh. Their song still enchants us and, in Rhonda Parrish's latest anthology, we hear sixteen new melodies.

The siren is a figure from Greek mythology that appears in many stories, perhaps most memorably in Homer's The Odyssey. Odysseus, intrigued by their notorious and deadly song, plugs his sailor's ears with beeswax but ties himself to the mast of his ship so that he may hear them without jumping to his death in the sea. Having ordered his men not to untie him no matter what he says, Odysseus becomes the only known man to survive hearing a siren's song. In some later stories, it is said that the sirens were so distraught over their failure that they sought their own deaths beneath the waves.

According to Ovid, the sirens were once the companions of Persephone. After she is kidnapped by Hades, the God of the Underworld, the sirens beg for wings so that they can search the world for their lost friend. Perhaps their song, then, is a song of grief, and a punishment for all men because of the cruel actions of one god.

Sirens are also connected to mermaids, fellow temptresses of the sea, and one need only to look to Hans Christian Andersen's "The Little Mermaid" to note the similar emphasis on voice that both figures share.

The enigmatic, enchanting siren has served as inspiration for countless stories, songs, novels, poems, and other works of art. Indeed, some view them as being related to the Muses themselves. From John William Waterhouse's eerie painting "The Siren," to the Starbucks logo, to Disney's The Little Mermaid, sirens and their kin saturate our culture, reminding us what it is to sing, to listen, and to yearn.

In this collection, a group of talented authors each tackle the mythological creature from very different perspectives, though certain currents emerge and repeat through their tales.

Silence is a particularly potent theme throughout the anthology—from sirens who have lost their voice or are discouraged from using it, to those who cannot tell their own stories to themselves or others. From these voiceless, unstoried sirens, we learn the power of speaking and the importance of knowing and telling your own tales and histories.

Of course, love and desire are foregrounded in many of the stories, sometimes with compassion and tenderness but often with a violent edge. Refreshingly, love takes a variety of forms in Sirens; the tales here speak of romantic love across genders, and even species, but also explore the love between friends, siblings, and even strangers.

Addiction, self-destruction, and rejuvenation also cycle through these stories. We wonder at the opiatic properties of siren songs and marvel at how they can serve as the conduit for healing. In addition, we explore the limitations and incredible power of sirens' hybrid bodies and celebrate their resilience in their oceanic homes and on less familiar terrain.

INTRODUCTION

Dive beneath the waves, look into their eyes. Listen. Perhaps even now you can hear their singing—they are calling you, tempting you. Turn the page, they sing, turn the page.

Further Reading:

Austern, Linda Phyllis and Inna Naroditskaya, eds. Music of the Sirens. Bloomington, IN: Indiana University Press, 2006. Print.

Heiner, Heidi Anne. Mermaid and Other Water Spirit Tales from Around the World. Nashville, TN: SurLaLune Press, 2011. Print.

Lao, Meri. Seduction and the Secret Power of Women: The Lure of Sirens and Mermaids. South Paris, ME: Park Street Press, 2007. Print.

Takamiya, Toshiyuki. From the Deep Waters. San Francisco, CA: Chronicle Books, 1997. Print.

Bio:

Sara Cleto and Brittany Warman are PhD candidates in English and Folklore at The Ohio State University. They both specialize in the intersection of folklore and literature—Sara is currently exploring the implications of disability in fairy tales, while Brittany is working on fairy tales, fairylore, and the Gothic aesthetic. Also creative writers, their co-written poems have appeared in Niteblade and Ideomancer and are forthcoming from Liminality and recompose. You can find them online at saracleto.com and brittanywarman.com, respectively, and teamcatawampus.tumblr.com together.

Siren Seeking
Kelly Sandoval

The morning after her date with Kreskin, Thelia came home to find her apartment covered in flower petals. They drifted out the door when she opened it and she had to wade in, ankle deep, through the fragrant, colorful intrusion. She'd never been much for flowers, and could only name a few. Rose petals, yes. Snapdragons and daffodils. But what were those slender blue ones, the little white ones, the red ones that smelled of pepper?

She found the bouquet in her living room, twelve perfect stems in a crystal vase. The stems budded, bloomed, wept petals, and began again. There was a note tied with red ribbon. Kreskin's words were poetic and eager. He compared her to the moon, to the sea, to sunlight. She was fairly certain she couldn't be like all three. For a few minutes, she let herself sit, quiet, the note in her hands, while the flowers bloomed and died and bloomed again.

The carpet of petals grew deeper every minute, and the air was so thick with perfume she stopped breathing just to avoid the smell. Eventually, she gave in and took the stems outside to the compost bin, where she left them with the banana peels and coffee grounds.

She called Meda for cleaning advice.

"Oh, just leave them," Meda said. She didn't sound nearly as offended as Thelia had hoped. "He's a fairy, right? They'll be gone by morning."

"Easy for you to say." Thelia picked up a handful of petals and started tearing them into slivers—they left purple stains on her skin, like wild berries. "I can't even walk in here."

"Well, at least he's making an effort?" Meda had that tone in her voice that said she was searching for something nice to say and coming up blank. "What'd you say his name was?"

"Kreskin," she answered. "He was nice enough on the date. But this is all a little, well, ridiculous."

"Wishing you hadn't signed up for the Elsewhen membership?"

"Maybe?" Thelia picked up the vase and turned it so it caught the light and cast rainbows on the wall. "I don't know. Sometimes, it seems like the old ways were easier."

"Singing sailors to their deaths, you mean?"

"Well, when you put it that way…" Thelia smiled despite herself. "But at least we all knew where we stood. They didn't send flowers after."

Meda laughed, but Thelia could hear no humor in it. "Neither did mine, for that matter," she said.

"I'll send you flowers," Thelia said, disliking the chill in her friend's voice.

"Nevermind. Tell me more about this Kreskin. What's he do?"

"He's a fairy, Meda. I think he reclines in sweet-scented meadows and writes poetry."

"Oh, come on. He must do something. Collect teeth, maybe?"

Thelia nudged a petal with her toe. Something purple. Lavender? "Well, he'd make a lovely florist."

They chatted until Meda's son came home, and then Thelia was left to wade through the mess. She had to shake out her sheets to clear the bed, and the petals left behind a rainbow of stains. That, she decided, was crossing the line. Kreskin had a lovely accent, like bells ringing. She'd liked his sense of humor, too. But she couldn't possibly date a man who didn't respect her sheets.

That night, she dreamt she was being eaten by rosebushes. When she woke, the flowers were gone.

Kreskin texted her three times that day, but instead of replying Thelia logged onto Elsewhen and scrolled through her messages, looking for someone with a profile free of romantic inclinations.

The Grashe were beautiful, startlingly so. Thelia was fascinated by their hands. Long, dark fingers, square at the ends, and pink nail polish. She liked the fluid way they moved. Still, there was something a little disconcerting about the way the Grashe's personality changed each time one of their communal consciousness took control. She liked the one she thought of as Bird, who fluttered those lovely hands when they spoke. But there was another, silent as a tripwire, who made her skin itch. Thelia'd known her share of multi-deities, but she'd never dated one before.

"Of course, we're out of the deity business," said Bird-Grashe, as they pushed a slice of potato around their plate. "We work in investing. Appropriate, don't you think?"

"Do you enjoy it?" Thelia asked.

"Very much. We've always been fond of patterns."

"I suppose all fates are."

They shrugged. Tripwire-Grashe glared at their plate, letting their full fork drop. The silence stretched for minutes, and Thelia wondered if she might simply leave. Maybe they wouldn't notice, or care.

"And you work in marketing?" asked a Grashe that was neither Bird nor Tripwire. They smiled, and kept smiling, long after the expression should have been allowed to fade.

"Jingles, mostly." Thelia didn't like talking about her work. She enjoyed it, but sometimes wondered if she should. It was so easy to hook a heart with a well-placed rhythm.

"That sounds fascinating," said Smile-Grashe. "Sing for us?"

The request would've been too intimate even if they hadn't been in a crowded restaurant. "Some other time."

That brought Tripwire back.

By dessert, Thelia had named five entities, and she was worried she'd missed a few. She liked Bird and one other. Less than 50% didn't seem enough to justify a second date. And while she liked the idea of taking Bird home and getting to know those fingers, she didn't want to wake up next to Tripwire.

"I'm just not cut out for polygamy," she told Meda the next day. She was on her lunch break. She'd called Meda from the roof, for privacy. "At least, not without a comprehensive list of partners."

"Gods are out, then," Meda replied. "They've all got a bit of that. I think it comes from being too many things to too many people. Once you're the god of sex and medicine and kittens it all starts to get a bit messy."

"You ever date one?" Thelia asked.

"Of course. Some of us can't afford to be picky. Used to be my criteria was 'hasn't turned to stone.'"

"Except certain parts of their—"

"Don't even start," Meda interrupted. "You think I haven't heard that one?"

"Fine, fine. No gods. No fairies."

"No fairy florists, anyway."

"Right. I give up." Thelia leaned against the roof ledge and stared down at the distant pedestrians. "Who needs it anyway? I'll be a crazy fish lady. I'll have an army of, I don't know, sturgeon."

"I think two dates might be a little early to declare war on all landwalkers," Meda answered. "At least finish out the month. You already paid for it."

"Well, I did get a message from a mermaid, yesterday."

"Perfect. You can be a crazy fish lady *and* keep dating."

Thelia and Lusha agreed to meet on the beach, where they'd both be in their element. Thelia arrived early and paced beside the ice cream shop where they'd agreed to meet. When Lusha arrived, wearing a shimmering green sundress, Thelia couldn't help but stare at her legs.

They were too perfect. Long, hairless, gleaming. Muscular calves and delicate feet. They had the same quality as Meda's hair, a sort of over-definition that hinted at magic.

They shook hands, bought their ice cream separately, and started along the beach. At first, the conversation stumbled, but once it turned to days long past, it came easy. Lusha talked about her family, and her words tasted of wind and brine. She was as familiar as memory and Thelia only wanted her to keep talking.

"The best days were the ones where the ships came. We'd all climb out of the water and stretch out on the rocks. That's all it took. We'd just smile, and the sailors would start diving overboard. Sometimes, I hated them for making it easy. But they brought such lovely presents."

Thelia thought of her own sisters, standing beside her on the rocks. She could feel the shape of the old songs in her throat. A smile, a song, a promise, and the sailors would treat the rocks like the arms of a lover.

They finished their ice cream and sat side-by-side at the waterline, where the waves could roar up over their legs. Thelia covered Lusha's hand with her own, and Lusha leaned closer so their arms touched.

"You remember what it was like," Lusha murmured, her voice soft with longing.

"Funny, how good it felt back then," Thelia said. She watched the water. Near the shore, children played tag with the waves. Further out, beyond the pillars of rock that defined this part of the coast, she could see sailboats and jet skis. The mortals were free from the old fears. The water was their toy. "I guess everything was different. Men don't tie themselves to the mast for me, anymore."

"I bet they still would." Lusha turned her hand and intertwined their fingers. "I bet we could drown a battleship, the two of us."

A wave, larger than the others, crashed over them. For a moment, with the water still swirling high around their shoulders, Thelia saw through Lusha's glamour. Her tail, sleek and silver, stretched well past her feet. Her teeth were long and white and very sharp, and her eyes were black pools, like lakes on moonless nights.

The wave retreated, and Lusha sat dripping in the sun. Her dark hair stuck to her sun-brown skin, and she was almost as beautiful as she'd been beneath the wave.

"What do you say?" she asked. "Want to find a Navy base?"

And Thelia realized, having seen the truth of her, that Lusha wasn't kidding, not really. For Thelia, the hunger was a sort of nostalgia, but Lusha still felt it as a need.

"Some other time," she said.

"Sure," Lusha answered, the joy gone from her.

They kissed when they said goodbye. Lusha was soft against her, and her lips tasted like salt. Thelia wanted to hold onto her, wanted to feel those teeth, the ones she'd seen for only an instant, against her skin. But Lusha was quick to pull away.

What came next wasn't a surprise. Tepid responses to eager messages. Careful avoidance of second date plans. Thelia had done it to others often enough to recognize the brush off. There'd been a test and she'd failed. Lusha wanted her hungry, wanted her as she had been.

After a few days, Lusha stopped responding to messages at all.

"But what did she expect?" she asked Meda. She was back at the same beach. It looked gray and lifeless under the late afternoon sun. The day was clear, but chilly. No children played in the waves.

Meda sounded tinny and distant. "Well, you *are* a siren. A certain amount of drowning comes with the territory."

"Sure, and if I run into any demi-gods, I'll get to work." Thelia picked up a stone and sent it spinning into the waves. "But this is now. I'm pretty sure there's a law against singing people to their death."

"Oh, I bet you'd get off with manslaughter. It's not like you hold them under." Meda's voice went soft, which only made her sound further away. "You okay?"

"Yeah. But I liked her."

"We can find you another mermaid. A less murdery one. Someone more in the Ariel mold."

Thelia laughed, as she was meant to, but she couldn't help thinking that she'd liked the murdery bits. Lusha still held pieces of a self Thelia had almost forgotten she'd possessed.

"I can't hear a thing you're saying," she told Meda. "I'm gonna go for a swim."

She left her phone and shoes in a pile and started walking toward the water, until the waves came to meet her. The water was cool and clear. The waves tugged at her ankles, pulling her in deeper. When the water reached her knees, she dove. Within a few strokes, the local fish surrounded her, their scales slick against her fingers. When she was young, she'd plucked them from the water and sucked their flesh from their bones while they were still wriggling in her hands. She only watched them now, naming them as she couldn't name flowers—shining salmon, dark bocaccaios, blue-green blacksmiths, and long, grinning eels.

She swam until she reached one of the rock spires. The stone was covered in anemones, and she let them explore her skin with their tingling caresses as she climbed. There were sailboats on the water, white sails against a darkening sky. She watched them and thought of Lusha. Lusha stretched out on the rocks with her sisters. Men diving to their deaths for her, bringing bright knives and shining rings as their courting gifts.

Maybe she did miss it. Maybe she'd only forgotten how good it felt.

She lay on her stomach, waiting.

It was a small boat that finally drifted her way. Only one man onboard. Young, tan, with blond hair as fine as a baby bird's. She didn't sing to start, only watched, waiting for him to notice her. When he finally glanced up, he met her gaze without hesitation. There was no awe in that look, no reverence. Just surprise and an amused, almost possessive desire.

She kept her gaze locked with his and began to sing.

It came easily, as if she'd never stopped. As if she'd stood on the cliffs with her sisters only yesterday, making bets on who could wreck the most ships in a week. The words were old, in a language long past memory, but he didn't need to know the words. All mortals understood longing, and sorrow, and a woman reaching out her hand.

He dove from his boat, and she admired his grace and the confident way he swam toward her. He couldn't know the ocean itself was on her side. The waves knew their part. They let his outstretched fingers graze the rock before they pulled him under.

She watched him turn to shadow, disappear, then come up sputtering and startled. His face was red, his eyes wide, and he got one good lungful of air before the waves had him under again.

Longer this time.

As long as she liked.

His fingertips clawed toward the surface without breaking through. Thelia kept singing, waiting for it to feel good. But it only felt desperate. It'd been centuries. She didn't even eat meat anymore.

Nothing with a face, she'd told Meda. She could see his face, through water too clear to be called wine-dark. His eyes were open, a thin circle of brown around a pupil huge with panic.

She stopped.

The waves let go, but they'd had him too long, and when he surfaced, it was only to gasp, sucking in as much water as air, and submerge again. Not her problem now. But she dove in anyway.

It was easy to get her arms around him. He was bigger, of course, but barely fighting, and the water was eager to assist. She got his head above water and kept it there while he coughed and choked and finally started to breathe. When he started swearing between coughing fits, she figured he'd be all right. She dragged him back to his boat, and after a few failed attempts he managed to climb onto it.

"You saved me," he said, and now he had that awe she'd been looking for. He had the wrong end of the story; she could tell by the way he was reaching for her.

"Don't trust strangers on rocks." She turned away and started swimming for shore as fast as she could manage.

Meda was waiting by her shoes. She was dressed for the office, in a severe black suit, but she pulled Thelia, dripping, into a hug. Her hair brushed over Thelia's face, tickling like serpents' tongues.

"You sounded like you needed company," Meda said, stepping back.

"Thanks." Thelia let Meda tug her down onto the sand. The boy was too distant to see now, just a red-faced memory. But his boat was growing slowly closer.

"So, you decided to try singing?" Meda asked.

"Only a little."

"Feel better?"

"Not particularly." But Thelia knew the words for a lie as soon as she spoke them. The questions Lusha left her with are no longer filling her thoughts with noise. "Maybe. Some."

"If this becomes a coping method, we'll have a problem."

"One-time thing," Thelia promised. It felt true.

The sun, nearly setting, stained the water red. The boat grew closer. Soon, she'd be able to see the boy. They'd have to leave before he tried to promise undying devotion. But Meda was cool as stone and serpents beside her, and the water was bright as wine. For the moment, Thelia didn't want Lusha, or Grashe, or Kreskin. She didn't want a stranger, song drunk and lost to the waves. She wanted a friendship that'd lasted centuries. She wanted the memories of her youth, without the weight of its hungers.

"What'll we be next?" she asked. "One hundred years from now, will we still meet on this beach?"

"We'll meet somewhere," Meda answered. "And we'll be different. And we'll be the same."

Thelia's phone chimed from her shoe, and she ignored it.

"Not going to answer?" Meda asked, picking up the phone.

"I'm done."

Meda studied the screen. "How do you feel about bondage?"

"Done, Meda."

"You're sure? She's a jorogumo. You've never been with a spider before."

Done for the moment, anyway.

The Fisherman and the Golem
Amanda Kespohl

As Ged passed through the market on his way home, he paid no heed to the sellers hawking their wares. Eggs and flour were all he'd come for, and so eggs and flour were all he'd leave with. Even as the merchandise shifted from fruit and wine to spell components and worker gremlins, he kept his attention on the road, his mind on the chores to be done when he arrived home.

Despite his best intentions, a flicker of gold caught his eye at the edge of the market. He turned his head and saw a pen of vacant-eyed maidens milling around like grazing sheep. In their midst, a blue-robed wizard extolled their virtues to passersby.

"Lonely, are you?" he crooned to a freckled teenager who stood gaping at the wandering women while his mother haggled at a neighboring stall. "My golems make for pleasant company."

Before he could answer, the young man's mother rounded on him with a swat, scolding and hurrying him away while his ears blazed crimson.

The wizard sighed and turned to a harried housewife hustling her two children past. "And you, miss? Need an extra hand with your housework? Golems excel at simple tasks!"

"As if I had the coin to spare!" the woman huffed, hardly sparing him a glance.

The wizard reoriented on a fat, balding man in a butcher's apron standing nearby. "How about you, sir? Their bones may be wood, their flesh clay, but they're real enough to your hands and eyes to pass. That's the beauty of illusion, dear sir—all the charms of a real woman without all the fuss!"

THE FISHERMAN AND THE GOLEM

The butcher hesitated, eyeing a buxom brunette who was meandering around the limits of the pen. Then her skirt got hung up on a post and she fumbled, baffled, to free herself. Scowling, he went on his way.

The wizard shook his head and walked over to disentangle the brunette. While he was preoccupied, Ged sidled nearer, his gaze fixed on a golden-haired golem standing at the edge of the pen. While the others shifted and rambled, she was still, her hands resting lightly on the wooden slats that kept her caged. At a glance, her face was as empty as any of the others, but there was something almost wistful in the set of her lips.

"Ah, you like that one, do you?" the wizard crowed, swooping in like a buzzard to a corpse. "She's new! Just turned up in the pens yesterday. I assume my associate did the work. The craftsmanship is unquestionable, yes?"

Ged pursed his lips, more embarrassed to be seen eyeing golems than if he'd been caught with his pants down in a whorehouse. "She doesn't look like any of the others, certainly. She almost looks…human."

"Pish posh." The wizard waved that off. "I looked her over, myself, with the eyes we both have and the eyes the magic gives me. She's empty inside, just like the others. But some of them learn to emulate emotions quite well." He opened the gate and came out to put an arm around Ged's shoulders. "Come on, what do you say? By your clothes, I take you for a fisherman. It must be lonely out at sea. How nice would it be to come home to such sweet company waiting by your fireplace? And should you meet a nice flesh and blood girl, all you have to do is say the counterspell I'll give you and she'll dissolve into dust. No one will be the wiser."

Ged made a face. "Right, no one except for all of the people who are staring at us right now."

"They're just jealous of the deal I'm about to give you," the wizard concluded nonsensically. "I'm willing to give you this masterful work of art for a mere fifty silver."

"Fifty silver?" Ged exploded. "I could buy my own milk cow with that money!"

"Why would a fisherman need a milk cow?"

"Why do I need a golem?" he countered. "No. No, I haven't the money to spare." And truthfully, although he had enough coins in his purse, he was saving them to buy a new boat. His old dinghy was nearly ready to give her brittle wooden bones to the ocean.

"Very well, then. Thirty silver," the wizard sighed, as if the words were being dragged out of him by one of Ged's hooks. "And then you'd best run off with her, for you'll have robbed me blind and left me to my tears of regret."

For a moment, the fisherman stood there, staring into light green eyes in a soft, heart-shaped face. Then she smiled at him and he heard himself say, "I won't pay more than twenty."

He walked out of the market twenty coins poorer, trailing a silent, golden-haired girl that drew eyes the way flies collect on honey. His ears burned at the bemused murmurs he left in his wake. Grabbing the golem's hand, he hurried her down the road out of the city, travelling four miles to the rocky shore.

His cottage was perched beneath a sheltering copse of beech trees, close enough to the shore that the lullaby of the waves pounding the coastline sang him to sleep each night. Inside his tidy, thatch-roofed home, he set his basket of eggs and flour on the rickety table and turned to inspect the girl.

Golem, he reminded himself, not girl. She wasn't real, no matter how sweetly shaped she was, or how prettily the bow of her mouth quirked at the edges when she studied a passing butterfly or a lizard sunning itself on a rock. Now that he had her, he wasn't quite sure what to do with her. Obviously, there was one option, the option that his fellow market-goers assumed he'd had in mind. And yet, Ged realized that it wasn't in him to treat a woman like a thing, even when she *was* a thing. He hesitated a moment, ruffling his fingers through his dark hair.

"Do you bake?" he blurted foolishly.

The golem blinked her pretty eyes at him, pulling at a handful of her skirt and worrying it between her fingers.

"I was going to make some bread. It's my mother's recipe, you see," Ged went on, deciding that if he was going to be a fool, he may as well embrace the label fully. "She used to make this thick black bread that tasted so rich and earthy you hardly needed any jam or butter. I haven't had it in years and I've been pining for it of late."

Her eyebrows quirked. She wandered over to the table and picked an egg from the basket. Curious to see what she'd do, Ged rifled through his cupboards for a bowl, then brought it to the table. To his delight, she cracked the egg neatly against its side and let the fat golden yolk slide inside while she scooped off the bits of shell in her hands.

"You know how to cook!" Ged exclaimed. "Or at least how to crack an egg, which is a start. That's marvelous. Here, let's put those shells in the garden. My carrots will love them."

Looking bemused, the golem wandered after him as he showed her where to dump her handful. Then they returned to the table and began adding new ingredients.

He spent the next hour or so trying to teach her his mother's recipe, going so far as to shape her fingers into the dough until they began to knead of their own accord. When the bread was ready, he took it from her and loaded it into the oven beside the main hearth. Then, seeing her examine her sticky fingers, he brought her over to the pallet along the wall and sat her down so he could wipe her hands with a wet cloth.

Studying her small, slick hands as he wiped away the last of the dough, his movements slowed. He raised his eyes to hers. "I was lonely, you see. My father was lost at sea when I was a child. After that, I looked after my mother for as long as I could, but at last, she grew old and weary, and she left me as well. It's just been me here for a long time." Flushing under that puzzled green gaze, he added, "I wanted someone to talk to. Someone who can garden with me and help clean my catch, when there's anything to be cleaned. I don't want anything more from you. I just don't want to be alone."

She tilted her head, studying his face. Almost, she seemed to be trying to speak. He sat utterly still, wishing he could hear the voice that went with that lovely face. Then her restless lips stopped their shifting and relaxed, her eyes dropping back to her hands.

Ged sighed, feeling ridiculous. "I should give you a name, I suppose. Even the old one-eyed cat I throw fish guts to has a name."

She looked back up at him and he took in the golden ringlets clustered around her face, the creamy hue of her skin, and the gentle green of her eyes.

"Lucette," he decided.

She smiled at him again and, God help him, his heart melted.

The next morning, someone knocked on Ged's door just after sunrise. He shuffled out of his room to answer it, rubbing the grit from his eyes as he went. Casting a nervous glance to where Lucette lay curled up on a pallet by the hearth, he opened the door to find his friend, Edward, standing there, beaming with a cheerful exuberance that had no business existing at that hour.

"Rise and shine, beanpole," he trumpeted, shoving his way into Ged's house. "The fish are jumping today, I could see 'em from the path to your door. I thought we'd go out together, perhaps take a bottle of rum and make a spectacle of ourselves. Maybe you can practice talking to something that doesn't have scales for a change." Then he stopped as Lucette sat up to blink at him with confused green eyes. "Oh. I didn't realize that you had company. And *female* company, at that. You dog, you." He frowned. "Why is your female company sleeping on the floor? Is she a relative?" Both of his

THE FISHERMAN AND THE GOLEM

eyebrows rose. "Is she married?"

Ged hesitated, glancing at Lucette. He put a hand on Edward's arm and steered him outside, closing the door carefully behind him. "Edward, she's…she's a golem."

"What?" Edward opened the door, peered around it, then closed it again. "There's no way that's a golem."

"She doesn't talk, she can't process very complicated instructions, and I have a spell in my pouch that will turn her to dust. She's a golem. I bought her from a wizard in the market."

"I don't know, that kind of sounds like my younger sister, except I only wish I could turn her to dust." Edward frowned. "Why on earth would you buy a golem? You know, you could probably get a real girl if you wanted one, what with those big brown eyes of yours. Even a beanpole like you has his charms."

Ged flushed. "I doubt that. I never know what to say to a woman unless she's old enough to be my grandmother."

Edward snorted. "Well, what do you say to this one?"

"Everything that crosses my mind," Ged admitted. "And she listens."

"She doesn't know what she's listening to, Ged, she's just wood and clay."

Ged fidgeted. "I don't know. She learns things. She smiles. I think she tried to hum while we were baking yesterday, but then that scared her, so she stopped."

Edward sighed. "What's your plan here, Ged? Are you going to marry her? Craft clay children together and have the wizard animate them as well? She's a doll, a toy. It's a fine way to pass the time, but don't start thinking like she's a person."

"I…I know," Ged lied. "I won't. Anyhow, I could use the company today on the water. Just let me tell Lucette I'm going and I'll meet you down by the boats."

"Lucette? You named her?"

"Well, what else was I supposed to call her?" Ged asked crossly.

"Just hold on a minute. I'll be right back."

Walking back inside and shutting the door, he found Lucette opening the shutters to look out at the sea, her eyes widening at the roar and dazzle of the waves. He addressed the girl awkwardly. "There's leftover bread on the table. I think someone told me that golems don't get hungry, but they can eat if they want to. For appearances. So, you know, you don't have to, but if you want to, it's there. I'm going fishing, but I'll be back before dark. I'd prefer it if you didn't leave the house. I don't want you to get hurt."

She nodded, then turned her face back to the sea.

"Goodbye," he called softly.

She never looked away, mesmerized by the restless dancing of the ocean.

He came back that evening with only three smallish flounder to show for his day and found Lucette still at the window. Her elbow was propped on the window sill, her cheek in her hand as the sea breeze played in the waves of her hair, making it dance and shiver like spools of gold thread. It was the only brightness in the room as the last of the sun's light began to fade.

Ged lit the lantern on the table and hung it on its hook, setting his fish on the counter. After he washed their smell from his fingers, he walked over to stir Lucette from her trance.

"Lucette?" He put a hand on her arm when she didn't move. Then he startled. "Oh, your skin is like ice. You shouldn't stand in this wind without a shawl!" He ushered her away from the window to sit in his favorite chair, snatching a blanket from her pallet to tuck it around her shoulders. Then he bit his lip, studying her sweet, puzzled face. "You don't get cold, do you? And you probably don't get sick." He heaved a sigh. "Edward was right. I'm treating you like a person. I can't help it. You seem like a person to me."

THE FISHERMAN AND THE GOLEM

She smiled at him, which she seemed to do sometimes when she was confused.

"Stay warm, anyhow," he said, patting her arm. "I don't know if the cold will hurt you, but I don't want to chance it." He rose from his crouch, returning to the counter to clean the fish. He almost jumped out of his skin when he turned around to find her standing in his shadow. "Oh! Lucette, what are you doing?"

Clasping the blanket around herself like a cloak, the girl walked past him and took up his knife, shooting him a hesitant look.

He smiled. "You remembered what I said yesterday, didn't you? About wanting someone to help me clean the fish? Edward would say I'm crazy and you're just doing as I do, but I like to think that you remembered. All right, don't do anything yet. Let me grab a bucket and I'll show you how."

They passed a pleasant night as he showed her how to wash and gut the fish. They cooked it together, then ate it with leftover bread and a cup each of the honey mead he kept stashed in his cabinet. Even though she never said a word, as he sat across the table from her and basked in the soft light of her green eyes, he felt contented for the first time since his mother died. Then she went to lie on her pallet and he crawled back into his own bed, and they both pretended to sleep.

For two weeks, Ged enjoyed the gentle company of his golem. He taught her how to patch a sail and work in the garden. They planted seeds together while he told her stories about his dashing father, who braved the summer storms to bring fresh fish back for his family. He even took her into the market to buy her new clothes, so busy chatting with his silent companion that he hardly noticed how people stared. She smiled at the brightly colored blouses he put in her hands, her lovely eyes brightening when he bought her a shawl embroidered with red and orange flowers. He was so delighted to see such life in her that he added a skirt the color of the waves to their parcels, though he was chipping away at the funds he'd saved to replace his boat.

On the fifteenth day, as he went out on Edward's boat to fish, they both glanced back to the shore and saw the glint of gold in Ged's window.

"She's always looking at the ocean," Edward noted. "Every time I've seen her, she's at that window, watching the waves. What do you suppose she's looking for?"

"Maybe she just likes the way the waves look when they come foaming into shore."

Edward frowned. "I didn't think golems liked things. I thought they just sort of…were."

"I did, too. But I swear, she likes a lot of things. She likes the way it tickles when a lizard crawls across her hand, and she likes embroidered flowers and my mother's bread. She likes it when I hum while I cook, and the smell of the lavender tea I brew when my throat is sore."

"She's not real, Ged."

"She's real enough to me," he replied.

That night, as Lucette helped him clean his catch, he distracted her from her task with an explosive sneeze. Seeing her wince and the well of blood on her finger, Ged sucked in a breath and grabbed a cloth, putting pressure on the wound as he led her over to the table to sit down.

"I'm sorry, dear girl, I didn't mean to startle you. I got a tickle of dust in my nose and—" He froze, his eyes dropping to the cloth. Carefully, he unwrapped her hand and inspected the cut above the joint of her finger. It wasn't deep enough to need stitches, but it was bleeding freely. He wrapped it back up and took a deep breath. "I'll get some fresh water to wash it with."

He rose to his feet, counseling himself to stay calm. When he came back with the bowl and pitcher, he poured the water, telling her, "Golems don't bleed."

She blinked up at him, holding the cloth around her finger until he took it from her. Watching her face change as he gently cleaned and bandaged her wound, he added, "Golems don't feel pain, either."

She inspected her newly bound finger with interest, flexing it experimentally. He grabbed her wrist to get her attention. "Who are you? Where did you come from?"

She lifted her eyes to his, gazing at him steadily. Her lips did not so much as twitch in an attempt to answer.

"Do you know who you are?" he asked. "Are you sick? I don't understand how the wizard could have made such a mistake. He said you were empty. I wonder what he meant by that. We'll have to go back to the market and ask. Maybe he'll be able to find your family. There must be people looking for you."

She shifted restlessly beneath his touch, rising from the chair and going to open the shutters. He sighed and hopped to his feet, snatching one of her shawls from the back of the chair and wrapping it around her shoulders as she propped herself in the window. His hands lingered on her arms as he watched the waves with her.

"I'm…I'm appalled to find that I bought a human woman for twenty silver," he told her. "My mother would be ashamed. But I'll make it right, I promise." He closed his eyes against the sting of tears, adding, "I will miss you, though."

She spun beneath his hands to look at him, her attention caught by the rogue tear tangling in his stubble. She touched it with light fingers, her brow quirking in sympathy. It was all he could do not to kiss her.

Instead, he stepped away with a shaky breath and went back to the fish, leaving her to watch the waves in peace. He did not want to miss her any more than he already would.

On the next clear day, he took Lucette back to the market, returning to the pen of aimless maidens. The wizard was propped against the fence, studying his fingernails with a furrowed brow. As he worried the edge of one nail between his teeth, Ged stepped forward and cleared his throat.

"Excuse me, sorcerer."

The wizard glanced up, spitting out a piece of nail. Catching sight of Lucette, he frowned. "No refunds. I don't care what bits of her fell off, I won't be held accountable for rough use."

Ged shook his head. "No, it's not that. I, uh, I think you made a mistake with this one. She appears to be an actual human girl."

The wizard snorted. "Don't be silly. If she was human, I'd have charged you more." He guffawed at his own joke, then sighed at Ged's expression, putting an arm around his shoulders. "I know you want to believe that. I see your type here all the time, lonely men who think they can make a real woman of a doll. But they have limits, you see. She's never going to be everything you expect."

"Well, I certainly didn't expect her to bleed," Ged said wryly.

"What's that?" The wizard's voice went flat.

"She cut herself yesterday helping me clean fish. She was in pain, and she bled."

"You imagined it," the wizard ventured.

Ged drew Lucette near and unwrapped her finger to show him. "I didn't imagine this."

The man sucked in a breath, inspecting the wound. Then he shot a nervous look around and put a hand on each of their shoulders, steering them into the shade of his tent. "Listen, there has to be some kind of mistake. I looked her over, just like I told you. She's nothing but an empty shell." He paused, staring into her eyes. "Or…she was."

"What do you mean, 'she was'?"

"She's changed since you bought her. She's…Well, she's still empty inside, but she's haunted by little echoes of feeling. It's quite strange."

Ged turned to Lucette, rewrapping her finger so the cut wouldn't get infected. "Where did she come from?"

"She just turned up in the pen. I work with a partner who helps me craft the golems. I thought he made her. I can ask him about her, if you like."

"I'd appreciate that." Ged met Lucette's eyes, his heart twisting inside him. "Do you know of any spell that could do this to a person? Make her mute and empty like this?"

The wizard snorted. "If I knew spells like that, I wouldn't be peddling golems in a shabby little coastal town. No, that's big magic, the kind you get from much more advanced sorcerers than I, or inhuman things that are innately magical."

"Well, I'll come back tomorrow and see if you have news for me," Ged said. "In the meantime, perhaps I'll ask around the market and see if anyone knows her."

"I wouldn't do that," the wizard cautioned. "Whoever did this is incredibly powerful and obviously meant her harm. If you let them know she's still alive and that someone has taken an interest in her, they may decide to finish the job."

Ged sucked in a breath. "I've put her at risk by bringing her here, haven't I? I'll take her straight home, and leave her there when I come back tomorrow."

"A sensible notion." The wizard frowned. "Listen, I'd appreciate if you'd keep this to yourself. It's really not my fault, and I don't want to get a reputation."

Ged raised an eyebrow. "You're telling me that you don't already have a reputation?"

"Not one this bad."

"Fine, I'll keep quiet."

"Good man." The wizard clapped him on the shoulder. "Now get that girl out of here before someone smites her and hits us both with the debris."

Ged made a face at him and led Lucette away.

Though they made it back to the cottage without incident and had a pleasant dinner, Ged was still too troubled that night to sleep. He lay in his bed, staring at the ceiling and listening to the waves pound while his mind roamed in restless circles. When he couldn't stand it anymore, he heaved himself up and crept out of his room to check on Lucette.

She was standing at the open window, her eyes fixed on the sea. The moonlight made her skin blaze silver, her hair a crown of light spiraling around her delicate face. Hearing his footsteps, she glanced at him and went to retrieve her shawl from the back of a chair before resuming her vigil. Ged smiled, coming to stand behind her and watch over her shoulder.

"My mother used to stare out of the window like this," Ged murmured. "Even after my father disappeared and we all knew he must be dead, she never stopped watching for him to come home. Sometimes, I find myself still watching, picturing his dark head bobbing up over the beach, his weathered face breaking into a grin to see me in the window."

She shivered, hugging her shawl close, and Ged absently put his arms around her to keep her warm.

"There is something in the sea that speaks to you. I wish you'd speak to me. If I take you out there in my boat, do you suppose it would jog your memory? There must be some reason why it fascinates you so."

She leaned back against him, seeming comforted by his embrace. He closed his eyes and tried very hard not to smell the jasmine scent

THE FISHERMAN AND THE GOLEM

that clung to her hair. At length, he sighed.

"Wait here for a moment, dear girl. I'll prepare my boat."

His shabby little fishing boat leaped among the waves like a minnow as he steered them out to sea, shivering to and fro until they passed into calmer waters. Once the water was as smooth as a looking glass, Ged shifted his attention to where Lucette sat in the bow. Her face was turned to the west, her hair fluttering around her body like a heavy cloak. Feeling his gaze upon her, she looked at him with the spark of something in her eyes. She made an urgent noise, lifting her hand to point. Obligingly, Ged steered his boat in that direction.

As they traveled through the still waters, Lucette came up on her knees in the bow, looking like a gold and silver figurehead in the moonlight. Then, as he slowed, her fingers gripped the sides, her gaze on the water just beyond the boat's nose. Ged stopped, wondering if they'd arrived, and what exactly they'd arrived at. As he opened his mouth to ask, Lucette rose to her feet and dove into the water.

Ged cried out in horror, dropping anchor and lurching to his feet to follow. He leaped over the side without bothering to remove his boots, straining for a glimpse of her bright hair in the murky waters. The salt stung his eyes and the currents tried to lead him astray, but he stroked deeper into the sea, ignoring everything but the throb of panic in his heart.

Something along the bottom caught his eye, shining like a beacon in the dark waters. It gleamed on a rocky shelf just before the ocean floor dropped off into the crushing depths where God only knew what existed. Mesmerized, Ged kicked toward the light. As he drew closer, he found a glowing shape, like a soft red stone, caught among the rocks. He reached out to take it and nearly dropped it as it pulsed in his hand.

In a moment that was a lifetime, he saw the world around him change. He was still in the sea, so deep down that the world was little more than shades of gray and green and black, but this darkness was speckled with the white, bare limbs of young women, swimming round and round with their long tresses trailing, their voices singing like the waves against the rocks. And from the sway of their bodies and the gossamer flutter of their hair, ripples passed up to the surface and turned into a mad frothing that thrashed against the sky, roaring its anger into the howling wind.

Ged kicked toward the light, feeling the tickle of silk against his bare back as his head broke the surface. He listened to the storm singing around him, the wind whipping against his skin, the clamor of gulls seeking shelter. Above the din, distantly, he heard a man crying out in fear.

"God have mercy! Undines, have mercy!" he cried. "I've a wife and son waiting for me at home. I woke before dawn and tiptoed out so as not to wake them. If I'd have known you meant to kill me, I'd have kissed them goodbye. Don't let this be the day that I don't return to them. Let it be a day when I at least told them goodbye."

Ged's heart stirred in pity. He hadn't known there was anyone near when the maids of the sea began their dance. He hadn't meant for anyone to get caught in the storm. He swam through the pounding waves, bobbing up on a swell that towered like a glass mountain before it slammed back into the ocean. Just before his high vantage point collapsed in on itself, he caught a glimpse of a little boat, shattered into ragged chunks of wood in the middle of the raging sea. There was a flutter of dark hair receding beneath the surface. As the wave came crashing down, Ged raised his white arms above his head and dove after him.

There was confusion beneath the surface, with the sea grasses thrashing and the currents ripping savagely along the rocky bottom. Strain his eyes against the darkness though he might, he could not find the man in all the chaos. He surged forward with powerful movements of his arms and legs, his hair streaming out behind him,

THE FISHERMAN AND THE GOLEM

his lungs filling with the sweet coolness of seawater. Then a surge of movement caught his eye. He turned in time to see the man slammed against a coral reef, a crimson halo blossoming around his head as he floated among the rippling waves, borne along as limply as a child's ragdoll.

Ged's heart twisted in his chest, then withered as hope faded. Too late, he knew, even as he swam to where the fisherman lolled among the shadows. Too late.

Carefully, he cradled that limp body in his arms, smoothing back the dark hair, and whispered a promise in his ear. Then, regretfully, he let the man go, watching him fade in a flutter of clothing and a shimmer of hair like a ghost evaporating in the light of day.

He turned and swam away from the others, leaving them to pause in their dancing to stare after him in puzzlement. He heard their words burbling after him, calling, "Sister, sister, where do you go?"

He ignored them and swam toward the shore, where the water grew so thin that it hurt his lungs to breathe it, and the fish gaped at him without recognition, having dwelt too long near the mortal shore to know him for what he was.

Then he raised his head above the water and took an uneasy gulp of air. It seared along his throat like a swallow of winter, freezing his insides and making them feel dry and withered. The breeze tickled across his skin, teasing away every trace of moisture, taking even the scent of the sea. For a moment, his purpose faltered. Then he lifted his chin and walked across the sand on shaky legs, looking for some sign of the place the fisherman might have launched from.

He came, at last, to a little cottage sheltered under a copse of beech trees, close enough to let the ocean sing its inhabitants to sleep. But there was no sleeping in that home on this night. A face gleamed in the window, dark eyes hunting through the sea foam that came tumbling ashore for some hint of the bow of a little boat.

Ged knew her, and his heart sank as he tried to think of what to say.

The gleam of his white flesh caught those restless, roving eyes, and the shutters banged closed, the door opening. A dark-haired woman came striding out onto the beach, the wind ruffling her green cloak around her, her face pale beneath its dusky hue.

Nervously, Ged cleared his throat. "Lady," he called, his voice rough with disuse. "Lady, I bring you a message."

"Nothing I'm like to wish I'd heard, undine," the fisherman's wife replied, her arms crossed tightly beneath her cloak. "Is that your storm I hear singing over the ocean, keeping my husband from coming home to me tonight?"

Ged's fingers worried at a lock of his bright hair. "Your husband wished he would have said goodbye to you this morning before he left. It was only that he didn't want to wake you."

Tears prickled at the hardness of those black eyes. Her chin tightened. "And what say you about why he cannot tell me this himself? And what would you have me say to the little boy inside who'll weep to find him not in his bed in the morning?"

His throat tight, his heart dashed to ribbons against the sorrow that strained every bone in the woman's body, he whispered, "I would say that I'm sorry. I never meant for him to come to harm. I only thought to sing in the summer storms."

"A lot of good that does me," the widow snapped. "A lot of good it'll do the boy. Is that all, undine? I've a mourning feast to plan, and me with no grave to tend after."

"Lady," Ged called after, his voice breaking. "Lady, I would give you a wish. Any wish that you would ask of me."

The stiff form stood huddled in the doorway, head bent. Over her shoulder, the woman asked, "Can you bring him back to me?"

"I cannot take from the sea what it has claimed," he whispered. "Anything but that. Ask something else, please. Whatever you wish."

"Whatever I wish?" the widow raged, whirling on him. "What else would I wish, you fool of a sprite? What else in this world could I have left to want?" Then her eyes narrowed. "Perhaps, though, there

THE FISHERMAN AND THE GOLEM

is one thing."

Ged, who had swum, unbothered, through a forest of icebergs, felt himself shiver at the coldness in her eyes.

"I would have you know what it is to lose your whole world," the widow told him. "I would have you know what it is to have your heart ripped out and cast into the sea. That, undine, is what I wish."

With a sigh, Ged lifted a hand to his breast and pushed his fingers beneath the skin. His hunting fingers found the soft, warm pulse that hid in the shell of his rib cage, and he gently withdrew it, holding it in the palm of his hand like a sleeping dove. Then he heaved it into the ocean, watching it sail above the leaping, frothing waves and vanish into their darkness with a last red gleaming.

An emptiness settled inside him. He looked into the widow's eyes and saw a confusion of joy and regret, warring together like the wind and the waves. He turned his back on the sea and began to walk across the dry, gritty ground toward the glint of sunlight on the horizon.

He heard the scuff of footsteps behind him, felt the softness of good wool against his skin. In his ear, a ragged voice said, "One day, I will be sorry for you. But not today. Not yet."

Clutching the cloak around his neck, he nodded without raising his head. Then her shaking hands released him and she let him walk away.

Something throbbed against his fingertips. Ged opened his eyes to the trickle of silver bubbles between his lips and the cold gray shivering of the world around him. Disoriented, he could not tell which way was up and which way was down, only that his lungs ached with the strain of holding his breath for so long and that he must find the right of it soon. Closing his fingers around the soft, red stone in his hand, he cradled it against his chest and pushed off from the bottom.

He rose through the water, that gentle light cutting through the shadows until he caught a glimpse of Lucette's flowing skirts. He kicked harder, grabbing a handful of fabric to pull her within reach and wrapping his arm around her waist. Clinging to the girl and the strange red stone, he fought his way toward the moonlight.

When their heads broke the surface, she gasped and wrapped her arms around him, burying her face in his neck. Though the memory of what he had seen scattered his thoughts into chaos and he was shaking with fear and exhaustion, he could not help but savor the feeling of her clinging to him and the tickle of her warm breath against his wet skin.

At last, she lifted her head, her weary eyes drawn to the light trickling from between his fingers. Her eyes widened, her breath hissing as she stretched her hand toward it covetously. Ged unfurled his fingers, offering it to her. At her touch, it dissolved, the red glow pulsing up her fingertips so that her whole body flared briefly with light. Then she met his eyes with a stunned look, a different kind of light dawning in her face.

"Ged," she whispered. Her eyes filled with tears as she saw the memories that darkened his eyes. Her voice, though soft and muted with fatigue, was like the silvery trickle of small waves skipping up the shore. "I'm sorry, Ged. I'm so sorry."

"I forgive you," he replied. He tightened his arms around her, burying his face in the fall of her hair and breathing in the mingled smell of salt and jasmine. Then, as his muscles began to protest endlessly treading water, he freed one arm and swam them both back to the boat.

There was a rough blanket in the storage bin beneath his seat. Once he had her settled in the bow, he wrapped it around her shoulders to keep her warm. She didn't speak as he steered them to shore, but her head turned to and fro as they went, watching the waves as if she saw each one as a raised hand bidding her farewell. At last, he hopped over the side to pull the boat into the shallows, then lifted her out to carry her up to the beach. Her arms clung to his neck even after her feet touched the sand. She pressed her face into the

THE FISHERMAN AND THE GOLEM

skin above his collar bone, her eyes closed.

"I came back every year to check on you," she whispered. "I never came too close, because I knew your mother was still angry with me. But I liked to come close enough to hear my heart sing among the waves, and to see how you'd grown. And you'd grown into such a fine young man after a time that the song from the waves seemed brighter, and it made me feel all the colder and emptier for being denied its comfort."

"And when my mother was gone?" he asked, his lips moving against her hair. "Why did you not come back to me then?"

"I may not have had the heart to feel, but I had some little sense left in me. I did not see how you couldn't hate me for what I'd taken. And after so many years spent wandering, empty, with nowhere that would ever feel like home, and nothing that could ever make me happy...I gave up, at the last. I came back one last time to hear my heart sing, and then I wandered off into the fields and let the last pieces of myself fade into the wind."

"And that is when the wizard found you."

"And that is when the wizard found me. And then you found me, and took me back to where I could hear my heart sing again. It called and called, saying it still had some use left yet, that it had finally found something other than the sea worth loving. But I couldn't take it back with my own hands."

He drew back to look into her eyes, the pale green of shallow water, and he smiled at her. "But I could do it."

"I suspect that *only* you could do it," she whispered.

"Then you are very lucky that I came to market on that particular day. And luckier, I think, that I have my father's gentleness, and not my mother's temper."

"Very lucky," she repeated, her eyes glittering with tears.

"Having you with me is the first time I've felt at home in a long time, undine."

"And being with you is the first time that I've felt at home since I left the sea."

"Would you go back?" he asked, smoothing her hair back from her cheek.

"The sea would not have me if I could," she replied. "That part of your mother's wish still holds true."

"It is selfish of me to feel grateful."

"Then think of how confused I am to feel the same way." She smiled at him, looking weary but content. "I cannot give back what I took from you, Ged, but I can give you what your mother took from me. If you'll have it."

"I will." He leaned down and kissed the taste of the sea from her lips, her arms twining sweetly around his neck, her curls tangling between his fingers.

When their lips parted, he smiled down at her. "Your name cannot have been Lucette. I would like to know the true name of the woman I love."

"You, my dear Ged, may call me whatever you like," she replied. "But if you would like to call me as my sisters did, then my name is Melusina."

He smiled and kissed her again, then took her hand to lead her back into the warmth of the cottage while the ocean sang them a wistful lullaby.

We Are Sirens
L.S. Johnson

1.

We roll into town on a bright sunny morning, steering the Caddy around the half-dozen streets that make up "downtown." Three of us in the back dozing and the other two up front with our arms hanging out the windows, letting our fingers ride on the fall air.

We love autumn. Autumn is football and soccer and tennis season, it's harvest festivals and Oktoberfests and the last round of carnivals and fairs. We can still get away with tank tops and shorts, or we can wear our tight wool suits with their snug skirts, or our sweaters with the necklines way, way down.

It just depends on what there is to do around here.

We roll the Caddy into two parking spaces and we pile out, lounging against the car and sizing up the people, reading the flyers posted on windows and utility poles. Free movie nights, a potluck, two spaghetti feeds, a reading at the library. When we find the town fair poster we groan in disappointment: it's two weeks away.

"Hey," we call out to a passing kid. "What's there to do around here?"

The kid looks us over, his round little face intrigued and suspicious.

"Big game's tonight, over at the high school," he says, scratching at the back of his calf.

The big game. We sigh with pleasure. We love big games, and their parties afterwards. Big games are easy; we'll be spoiled for choices.

The kid squints at us. "Where're you from?" he asks.

We crouch down to study his rocket ship t-shirt and his cargo pants with bulging pockets, his oversized sneakers, his rosy-cheeked face. These boys, they're a blur to us until their voices break, nothing but sticks and snails and puppy dog's tails; we love them because of what they'll become.

"We're sirens," we say, smiling at him. "We're from everywhere."

Big games mean guys from other towns, with two, maybe three parties afterwards. Big games mean the red suitcase, not the blue or the grey. In the red suitcase we have the high school clothes: the miniskirts and tennis shoes, the t-shirts and the lipstick as red as the cherry slurpees we grab on our way to the field. In the red suitcase we have five denim jackets with a patch on the back that says SIRENS, because for the big game we're always an out-of-town gang, tough girls from some generic City that turn heads and make the adults scowl and whisper, make the mothers especially suck their teeth in disapproval and the fathers agree, though with a gleam in their eye, a gleam that remembers what it was like to be a teenage boy watching the tough girls and wondering if it was all true, what they said about tough girls.

We take our slurpees and we climb up to the top of the bleachers and sprawl there, our bare legs loose and splayed on the warm metal, the wind ruffling at our skirts. We slurp our slurpees with our pursed red lips and we hum, just loud enough for the wind to hear.

We hum the call of Hades, so he'll be ready for his new arrivals.

And as always, we pause and listen. Sometimes we'll hear an answering melody, like a shepherd's pipes, or a farmer suddenly bursting into song, or a radio starting from out of nowhere. But though we strain to hear, there is only the rumbling of the crowd and the blaring loudspeaker announcing names.

It's been a long, long time since we heard an answer.

But we are sirens, and someone has to sing.

WE ARE SIRENS

We settle in to wait as the game kicks off, scratching the bumps of our wings against the railing of the bleachers, our legs tangling pink and olive and brown as we play footsie with each other. We sing in whispers of other sunny days spent waiting, watching games being played, watching cars and horses passing, watching our meadow-grass bending in the wind or the surf crashing against our rocks.

We have been this way a long time, and some time, and not long at all, for all times are then and now and everything between. We will be and we have been and we always are, and that's all we need to know.

And damn, but we love us some cherry slurpees. One of us farts and some of us titter and we slurp until our straws are sucking air. The final whistle is like birdsong and we sing in response: *it's time it's time it's time.*

We join the crowd hanging around the school afterward, nodding to the guys as they pile out of the building, shower-fresh and slapping hands and swaggering. We love that swagger, we love the dewy hairs on their napes and their still-flushed skin. We sit on the gold-colored hood of the Caddy and poke and kick at each other and we feign boredom while we pick and choose like they're sweets in a shop.

The girls give us side-eye looks and the guys mutter and snigger and we're humming *our* song, our dangling feet kick in time with it, our fingers drum it on the warm metal. When they start to disperse we call out, "So where's the party?"

One guy walks over to us and he's already a man, filled out and stubbly, and we see the girls watching him watching us and our hum changes to a contented trill. Oh, he will do. Oh, he will do us nicely.

"Where you from?" he asks.

"The city," we say with a shrug.

"We're visiting her aunt out here. Got sent to the boondocks to straighten us out."

"It was either that or juvie."

"You guys gotta do something for fun."

"We haven't been to a good party in ages," we finish, to seal the deal.

He looks us over, appraising just as we appraised him, but we titter because we know we're assessing very different things.

"Jason's dad is out of town," he says with a twitch of his head. "We're gonna pick up a couple kegs and go out there tonight."

Two of his friends have sidled up behind him, their pads and helmets dangling from their hands; the setting sun torches their faces so we can see their very skulls.

"So you're in a gang or something?" one asks, his voice full of fake scorn, as if the thought doesn't make his heart race.

"We're our own gang," we say. "We're the Sirens. And we like to party." We hop off the car, dusting our skirts so the hems flutter around the tops of our thighs. "Give us the address and we'll meet you there."

They confer among themselves and manage to come up with a pen but no paper; we sigh and take off our jacket and hold out a bare arm. The big one, the man, writes the words in rough strokes along the soft inner skin, and while he leans in close we whisper our song in his ear, the one we love best, and he trembles and drops the pen. When he bends to pick it up we spread our legs a little, our skirt brushing against his face as he stands.

"We'll see you there," we say. "What's your name, anyway?"

"Uh, everyone calls me Big Mac," he says, red-faced.

At once we fall about laughing, we haven't laughed this hard in ages. Both a song and a meal! We feel the threads of fate close around us, we sense our meandering path become the purposeful soaring of flight. Still snickering, we hum the first notes: *two all-beef patties…*

"Of course you are," we say. "We'll see you soon, Big Mac."

WE ARE SIRENS

When we show up to the party we park the Caddy way down the road and leave our jackets behind, folding them up carefully and putting them back into the red suitcase. We like our jackets too much to risk ruining them, and there will be ruining tonight.

Instead, we put on cheap t-shirts and our special skintight pants that are as tricky as chastity belts. We do our eyes dark and our lips red. In the dim light of the streetlamp our little mirrors reflect back five bloody-mouthed skulls.

We sing the song of approval, our harmonies spot-on; we sing of longago lakes and rivers and oceans and our reflections in those waters, hollow-eyed and bloody-mouthed, and how the lapping of the waves was also the rhythm of the gods' approval.

"As if they could keep us trapped in those rocks," we say. "As if."

"Someone has to sing, I don't see anyone else doing it."

"Someone has to test their mettle." The word *mettle* makes us smile like cats.

"Big H understands. Big H lets us do as we please."

"One Big Mac for Big H, coming up!" We fall about giggling again.

We walk up the drive to the party, our arms filled with bags. We've come prepared: we've got hard liquor and weed and long pretzel sticks we can suck on, we've got our tight pants with their trick openings and our bad-girl smiles, and we're ready to get this party started. Because these parties are never like the movies, there's never shoulder-to-shoulder dancing and making out; instead, there's cliques huddled in corners sipping flat beer and smoking pin-thin joints and that just won't do, that won't do at all. We like dancing, we like groping and kissing, we like sweat and lust and nervousness all at once, we like a build-up so that when the time comes all of that energy gets transmuted into a spine-cracking terror that makes all the humours gush forth and tastes like heaven.

Everything else is just gravy.

Inside, we turn that music *up*. We start dancing with ourselves while we sneak off and spike a few bottles of soda in the fridge; we light up and smoke a little and we dance to our rhythm, which is the rhythm of pop songs. "You don't get this stuck in a rock," we tell each other, and we sing out our agreement in time with the music. Sure enough, others start dancing with us, we're moving furniture out of the way and there's more smoke in the air and bodies are sliding around us and now we're feeling it, that rush of anticipation. We can see eyes watching us and we can feel bodies moving unconsciously toward us, and we twist and shimmy in time with the music *closer closer closer*.

We are pulled aside by another boy-man who starts dancing close and we sing *yes*.

We are stumbling up the stairs with strong lips on our lips and strong hands on our hips and we open our mouths to theirs and into the beery chasm of their throats we sing *yes*.

Throughout the house our five bodies trill and we whisper, "let's go for a drive and we can really party," and we hum in unison *yes yes yes*.

And we're stumbling through a hallway, around bodies and over bodies and leading the warm sweaty hand in ours, when a door opens and a girl comes out. Her eyes are swollen and she looks like she's going to be sick, she's wearing her jacket and it's buttoned all the way up.

We know about buttoned-up jackets, and coming out of bedrooms with eyes swollen from crying.

A guy comes out behind her, looking both sated and pissed off, and we ignore the one with us and instead sing to him, this Bedroom Boy, we sing to him. For we know about swollen eyes and buttoned-up jackets and we know the sweetness of surf crashing on rock and our song is *Bedroom Boy are we gonna make you crash*. It's new and old all at once, it's a song we've sung since we can remember and it's a song about this boy, this night, right now.

We offer the girl our drink and she tries to take a sip but then starts heaving and we know about this too. We hum *girl*, we hum *swollen eyes buttoned jacket throwing up*, and our hum fills the house with a mixture of trepidation and delight and we start the crash song all over again.

The girl looks around, wiping at her running eyes. "What's that weird music?"

And then it is like a movie, because the world goes quiet as we study this girl, there's something about her, something we can't put our finger on. When was the last time a girl heard us? Ages ago, we think; ages ago, when we were four and became five, because a girl heard us.

We call out a new chorus: *she hears us*. We listen to the silence, we feel the utter shock through the house, we hear the rhythm of bewilderment. Until at last we call out our response, from five mouths at once: *then she comes with us*.

We're making out in some big van-car with guy-breath and guy-hands while we barrel along some dark road. The girl sits in the far back with us and she's finally started drinking, trading gulps from the bottle and listening to the wet smacking and grunting and our feet tapping in time. We have Bedroom Boy with us and we've promised the girl we're going to do something terrible to him. In response, the girl said her name is Sarah, but otherwise she's stayed quiet, sitting in the far back with us, a wary expression on her face.

"So you're like a gang or something?" the Sarah-girl finally asks. Her eyes have stopped running, but now she's wiping her nose over and over.

"We're sirens," we agree, taking another long swallow.

"Like the Odyssey, right?"

Odysseus.

Fear makes us convulse in a long, body-wrenching shudder that spirals out into the night, following the threads of fate that connect all the sirens we have been and will be, so that everywhere and everywhen we are shuddering, in cities and villages and open plains and rocky coasts, aloft on our black wings or still stuck in the mire of this world singing *yes come to us yes*, we all to a one shudder.

Oh, we have not thought his name in so long.

We still don't know—we'll never know—if the gods turned us into rocks because he lived, or because we tried so hard to make him die.

If there's one thing we learned from that time, it's that the gods are bastards and never, ever to be trusted.

To suffer so, for one stupid man! As if some pointless punishment wouldn't make us mad for the world, wouldn't propel us back into the world hungrier than ever, wouldn't drive us to scream our song into every corner of the world.

As if.

The car squeals and lurches around a corner and the Sarah-girl looks over her shoulder. "Slow the fuck down!" she exclaims, but we turn up the radio and drown her out and go right back to fondling Big Mac and Bedroom Boy and whoever their friend is, he's too bland to inspire a nickname.

"We're going to die," Sarah-girl says. She says it like she doesn't really care; her eyes are filling again. "What kind of girl," she asks in a shakier voice, "what kind of girl gets in a car with a guy after he treats her like shit? Not a very good one, huh?"

"A girl who wants to see him hit the rocks," we say with a grin. "We are sirens, after all."

"The way Mac's driving, we're all gonna hit some rocks," she says, and takes another drink. "So why aren't you with someone?"

"Oh, we've got all we need," we say. "We could even lose the boring one, he's just gravy."

WE ARE SIRENS

She frowns at this. "What's with the we shit? Is it like the royal we?"

The question makes us go quiet again. First a reminder of *him*, now this question; we pause in our groping and lean in close, because this is very serious. "There is only we," we explain. "We are one and all, we are in time and not, we are past and present and future. We are sirens." We lay our hands lightly upon her, wondering at that strange feeling she exudes: of something becoming, something about to burst free. "No you, no I. No doubts or differences. No family save ourselves. Only we, together, singing."

"Yeah, sure. Pick on the freak, I get it." Her lower lip trembles. "You know, not everyone like me has a shitty family, we're not all dying to join some weird hivemind clique. But no, go ahead, have your fun." She takes the bottle from us and drains it. "Hope you're proud of yourselves."

Her every word thrills us. We look at her and we see ourselves as we were before becoming this: that unknown longing, that sense of our self being an ill-fitting suit, until at last we heard our song.

How cute she would look with lovely raven-black wings, clawed at the tips, feathers stained with blood!

And then we feel it; we nod at each other across the car. It's time.

We sing. We sing the song of offering and the guys snigger and call us wannabe rock stars and we sing harder, so hard we drown out the radio. We sing *our* song, the song of *come and get it*, the song of *you know you want it*, the song of crashing against rocks and falling headfirst into waves of grass and groping us in dark van-cars, all because they're hearing the song they've longed for.

The van-car jerks left, shooting off the road and barreling into something hard with a sound as loud as an explosion. We reprise the song of offering, as beautiful as always. More explosions and the guys are screaming in time with our song, the car hurtles into empty space in time with our song. We seize Sarah-girl and burst through the glass, unfurling our wings as the car falls away below us and crashes against the rocky hillside, shattering and bouncing and then finally landing in a steaming heap below.

In our arms, Sarah-girl screams and screams, clinging to us with a good amount of strength. All things we like in a girl: this death-grip and her lusty wailing. We spiral downwards like the mighty vultures we are, our song that of flesh and appetite and the underworld. Deep and rich, this song, it comes from our bellies and makes our thighs tremble. Sarah-girl too goes quiet and we croon our thanks and settle on the ground at last; when we let her go, she curls her knees to her chest and starts rocking back and forth. And though we say nothing we hum to each other *the rocking remember* for we all rocked so in our time, just as we screamed the first time we tasted sky-air, just as we gagged the first time we bit into raw flesh.

All so long ago as to be a story.

We toss aside the remains of our t-shirts and bras and stretch our wings to the cool night air. We take a moment to pin back our hair, straight and curly, thin and thick, and then we set to work. We drag the bodies out of the wreck, one after another, bloodied boy-limbs contorted and folded, heads at odd angles and bones jutting from flesh. One's still moaning and we start with him, falling upon him with clawed hands and hungry mouths and when he stops moaning we hear another sound, a rhythmic keening that we rather like, and we all look at Sarah-girl, who stops both rocking and keening as our five faces turn to her and her eyes roll up and she falls over in a faint.

We cradle her between us, this Sarah-girl, and we take a mouthful of Bedroom Boy and we chew it into a soft pap and then we kiss our sleeping Sarah-girl, easing his warm, soft flesh into her mouth, and we stroke her throat and we sing the song of becoming until, with a jerk, she gulps it down.

WE ARE SIRENS

We coast on the wind until we're circling the Caddy, loving the starlight and the lights below, how many starlit nights have we flown so? Over mountains and beaches, pitch-black villages and cities like a million scattered jewels gleaming. Gone are the days when we can safely soar in sunlight, and we croon a soft song of regret and time before slowly returning to earth. Our wings disappear, becoming ridges beneath our flesh once more. The party is still going on, we can hear music drifting down from the house. As we drive away into the purpling dawn our sleeping Sarah-girl sprawls atop our laps in the back seat. She stirs and whimpers, baby-like, and we stroke her thick black hair and we rub her narrow back but we feel nothing.

Why are there no bumps forming?

We look at each other, confirming how it was for each of us: first the feeding of pap, then the wings, then slowly the loss of *I* and the sweet emergence into the warm mind-nest of *us*. How long did it take? We cannot remember exactly, but it doesn't *feel* long, it doesn't feel like it took long at all.

Confused, we peer at her more closely, our hands exploring. Only then do we realize that her breasts are padding; only then do we feel what lies between her legs; only then do we realize what lies nascent in our Sarah-girl is not any likeness to us but the rising question of who she really is, for our Sarah-girl is very much a boy.

We drive and we drive, all night and all day, pulling over only to piss and switch seats. We drive as if something were following us, as if we were being chased to the very ends of the earth. Or at least across state lines.

We cannot sleep. We slouch, silent and pale, watching and not watching Sarah-girl in her uneasy slumber between us, her head rolling and flopping as the Caddy sways. We whisper to each other, "it's a test, they're just testing us, she'll change or crash anytime now," but we do not believe our own words.

When she awakens, she merely looks at each of us, then turns and watches the unfolding landscape, as tense and as silent as we are.

And though we dare not admit it, we are, each of us, flexing elbows and knees for any hint of stiffness. We turn our palms this way and that way, we slide our feet in and out of our shoes thinking to glimpse any hint of cold greying. For that's how it came upon us last time, sneaking in like a chill, creeping through our bodies while we went about unsuspecting, until we realized we could neither run nor fly nor even touch one another, not even just to give a last brief comfort…

Watching Molpe's face vanish in a wall of stone, and I could not even say her name…

The Caddy lurches as we steady ourselves. But it cannot be unthought. That *I*-shaped crack in our defenses.

We make our hands into fists and keep driving.

Until at last it ends, as everything does, for we're running out of gas.

2.

In this town it's convention time: the streetlights are festooned with banners proclaiming it, the bus stops have posters proclaiming it, there are lunch specials for convention-goers and vacancies for convention-goers and cheap parking for convention-goers. There's a snap in the air and a river running right past the hotel, and there are lovely balconies with flimsy railings and blind curves of traffic and pathways that veer close to the jutting rocks of the riverbed. We look at the rocks longingly and we hum *remember*, for we long to be back where the grasses wave in the breeze and the sea sits glass-smooth and empty; we touch each other and softly sing how it was, in the cool grasses beneath the warm sun, our wings drying and our bodies drowsy, singing simply to hear our voices in the world.

We should be opening the gray suitcase which contains our wool skirts and silk blouses, we should be combing our hair smooth and pinning it in such a way that it can tumble free the moment the pin is withdrawn. Instead, we're standing around the Caddy in a deserted parking lot because Sarah-girl is huddled half-in and half-out of the backseat and we're afraid to touch her, even as we long both to hug her and break her neck.

Sarah-girl says, "He didn't deserve that." She has said this many times since we pulled off the road. It's a song we know, the one of guilt and remorse, but we never sing it because it has no end.

She says, "Okay, yes, he was a homophobic asshole, but I mean, in a way I kinda led him on, and you can't just kill people for being homophobic assholes." Then, small, "can you?"

We shrug; when she looks at us expectantly we say, "it doesn't matter what he was, Sarah-girl."

"Some hear the song and crash, and some don't. Swings and roundabouts."

"Sometimes they're nice, sometimes they're assholes."

"What is constant is that we sing, Sarah-girl. Someone has to sing—"

"So this is what you do?" She bursts in before we can continue. "I thought you were like, like temptresses or something. But you're just serial killers."

"We don't kill," we snap at her. "We only sing." It's all we can do to keep from shaking her, why won't she understand? She heard us and she's still alive and she hasn't changed; we could turn to stone at any moment. What does it matter what we are?

We are sirens. As we have always been.

We realize then that she's cringing, maybe even about to scream, so we take a deep breath and say more calmly, "all we do is sing, Sarah-girl. We sing to those who want to hear, whose fates lead them to us."

"You sing to men," she says in a smaller, trembling voice.

We sigh at that. "Women crash in other ways."

"And I heard you," she says in her smaller voice. "And I, I'm—"

"We know," we say, in perfect chorus.

"Are you just going to kill me, then?"

The vision fills us at once: piling into the car and pinning her while she screams and cries. Breaking her neck, one swift wrench and then the sudden silence. Her body in the trunk, the suitcases piled in her place on the backseat. A swift tumble in the river at nightfall.

"We only sing, Sarah-girl," we say again, but we can hear the quaver in our own voices.

She wrenches her jacket more tightly about herself and we find ourselves mimicking her, wrapping our arms around ourselves, unable to look anywhere but at her. "So I've heard you, and I'm alive, and I haven't turned into some winged murderess," she says. "So then I'm nothing, right? Not one thing or the other. So maybe I can, just, go home?"

We only look at her.

"You let Odysseus go. I mean, he heard you and he, he lived..."

But her voice grows smaller as she speaks, she can see our anger, and at the *lived* she starts to cry. We hate her now, we hate her tears and her smallness that reminds us of when we were *I*, we hate her for reminding us of *him*, we hate her for going to that party like an idiot, what was she thinking? As if they wouldn't see her as something to bully and abuse, as if the world has changed that much.

As if.

"Homer never sang what happened to *us*, Sarah-girl," we say coolly.

"He never cared about any of us. Only Odysseus, Odysseus,

precious Odysseus." We sing the name out in a whining screech.

"He didn't even bother to *count*. There were more than two of us on that ground, we can tell you that."

"Precious, crafty Odysseus who made us fail for a *joke*, for his own *cleverness*."

"Do you know what happens when you meet Hades empty-handed?"

We crowd around her now, our shoulders itching, our wings straining at our shirts and our hands balling into fists. "We're never failing again!" we yell at her. "Do you understand? We are *never* failing again!"

"Please don't!" Sarah-girl cries out, throwing her arms over her face. "Please, I don't want to die!"

Her voice brings us up short, as swift and sure as if she struck us. For those were our words, then, our single voices jangling as we fell, our limbs stiffening and our bodies suddenly so cold. *I don't want to die!* Our tears streaming down our faces, our song thin and weak from our closing throats:

All that I had left undone,
All that I wanted,
All that I hoped,
All that I longed for,
All that I was, I don't want to die!

Our body-prisons, our caged minds and their lonely calling: blindly we fling our arms out, each feeling for the other, even as we come back together in a rush of awareness that leaves us breathless.

In the back seat of the Caddy Sarah-girl is still crying, oblivious to everything but her own fear. There were others before this, others with women's souls in men's bodies or men's souls in women's bodies, others who were children of Hermaphroditus or claimed no sex at all. Every time they crashed or changed. Why now, why her?

What are we supposed to *do*?

We start to hum the song of *crash* but it feels wrong, it feels like we're singing it to ourselves.

Instead, we do the only thing we can think to do.

"Damn it all," we say. "We need a drink."

We dress from the grey suitcase, silent and grim, scraping our hair back and twisting it violently, gouging our lips into pencil-sharp bows begging to be undone. We turn our attention to Sarah-girl then, managing to prise her out of her jacket and into a cardigan, though she keeps clutching the jacket to herself.

"You're our intern," we tell her, and for once she simply nods.

We go to the convention, but in truth we don't care, we don't care about the men in their off-the-rack suits with their little name cards clipped to their jackets and their identical folders tossed about. We barely notice them drinking their beers and liquors, we wince at the din of their bellowing voices, and we go up to the bar as silent as if we're already lost.

"Six Cosmo—"

But before we can complete the phrase, we start babbling other names.

"Gimlet."

"Lemondrop."

"Glass of cabernet."

As we speak, our minds flicker in and out, so we are buffeted by moments of dark loneliness before we are one again, and we cannot meet each other's eyes.

"Martini."

With a sigh, we add, "*One* Cosmopolitan."

"Water."

At the last we all look at each other, astonished, until we realize it was Sarah-girl speaking. She shrugs, frowning at the bar. "What? I'm underage."

We elbow her and step on her foot. "You're our intern," we whisper loudly. "You can't be underage."

"I can be whatever I want to be," she retorts.

"Get her a Cosmopolitan," we say to the bartender, only to shake our heads.

"Let her choose," we say.

"She'd be better off with a beer."

"She'd be better off with a Shirley Temple."

"We could get her a coke in a little glass, like it's a rum and coke—"

"I want water," Sarah-girl interrupts, and we grumble in our irritation. "You don't have to do everything alike, you know. Do you all even like Cosmopolitans?"

Our confusion and sorrow suddenly looms large before us, even amidst the bustle and noise of the bar. One by one our drinks appear, so many shimmering colors and shapes, and do we all even like Cosmopolitans? We cannot say—we dare not say, lest we fall apart, lest our differing selves somehow lead us to fail.

What would happen if we just walked away?

Where would we go, what else could we do? We're sirens. All we can do is sing.

We take our drinks and knock them back and smile gamely. Around us, the men are looking, looking and we make ourselves return their gazes, make ourselves run our fingers around the rims of our sweating glasses and steal cherries that we bite free of their stems, feeling the sickly sweet syrup fill our mouths, tasting for all the world like the blood of a day-old corpse.

"Let's get to work," we say.

These men.

They wear cheap suits and polyester-blend ties that just-so-slightly clash; they smile at us with whitened teeth; they comb their hair over the first patches of bare skin and give themselves little bangs to hide the creep of their hairline. They drink beer and scotch and whiskey and the younger ones do shots.

The convention has something to do with leadership and millennia and these things bore us so we hunker down into a shoal of couches and wait, drinking, hoping against hope that Sarah-girl will start to change or keel over dead and end all our doubt and misery. But she only sips at her water with a big straw, her eyes darting around the room like a cornered rabbit.

"She's our intern," we tell the men when they ask about her. We hold out business cards. "Siren Enterprises. We're human resources."

The words are like code, it's just enough of an excuse, they plop down on our couches and we manage a half-hearted hum while they chatter on about their companies and their roles, their workloads and their successes. All encoded like the songs of birds. Only we cannot help wondering, now: does any of this matter? If we weren't here, would they find other ways to crash?

Through the birdshit-spattered windows we can see the sun setting, we can sense the crowd becoming drunker, sense fates sliding and intertwining—or are we imagining it all?

But we need to begin, if we're going to do this.

There are four men perched on our couches, their long arms extended behind us and our empty glasses crowded on the table; a fifth hovers nearby, his head turning at every laugh, eager for an excuse to join us. The piped-in music has gone from light jazz to something more brisk, tugging at our memories of earlier bars and filtered sunlight and hands that want to stroke our knees but aren't yet emboldened. We're wearing our stockings as strong and dense as spiderwebs and our wool skirts are tailored tight and our silk blouses are open one button too many for decency.

We try to sing, we try to find the rhythm of this offering, and we're just humming the first harmonious notes when Sarah-girl suddenly giggles. Loudly. One of the men whispers in her ear again and she bursts into a braying laugh that makes heads turn.

As fractured as we are, as faltering as we are, to a one we narrow our eyes and mutter in unison, "if she changes, that laugh will be the first thing to go."

As if sensing our irritation, one of the men says, "how about we take this party elsewhere? Friend of mine has a suite upstairs, he said to bring anyone looking for a good time."

We feel it then, we feel it at last, that sense of fates coalescing, of wind in the grass and the crash of waves on rocks, and we smile and sing out in unison *good time good time good time.*

In the elevator, the music is a tinny samba and we find ourselves singing along, we sing of hot sun and sand and glassy-smooth sea. The men smirk and one tells us "you girls should start a band" and from behind us Sarah-girl mutters "oh *please.*" Another guy whispers to his friend "what else can they do with their mouths, huh?" and now it's our turn to smirk because he's about to find out, but before we can sing to Mister Curiosity Sarah-girl says, "you are *so* the gravy, pal," and despite all our fear and misgivings we love her for that.

The music coming out of the television is all thumping synthesizers and the liquor bottles are heavy in our hands and the cocaine up our noses burns like the rising sun. The men stumble against us, laughing, they're pulling off their ties and whispering bad words in our ears as they try to dance to our rhythm which is the rhythm of late night grooves. We sing along with the mimed images on the screen, dark syrupy words about grinding and riding and whipping and shackles and thighs and wet wet lips.

The men push our skirts up and bury their snotty noses in our cleavage, and if they weren't so drunk we'd do something about that, we're wearing silk after all, but they are very, very drunk and it's almost time. We sway and watch and sing out *crash baby crash uh huh*. When the first one stumbles to the balcony doors and flings them open we sing *mmmm let's do it* and when two start yelling at each other we sing *hit it sugar* and soon they're rolling and punching and the wind gusts in and our shoulders itch with anticipation and we sing out to Hades *she wants it, she wants it all to crash—*

and then we realize we cannot see Sarah-girl.

We wedged the hallway door shut when we came in, because no one is leaving this party, and it's still wedged shut so she cannot have gone far. *Come and jump on it yeah.* We check under the bed, humming *uh-huh uh-huh*: no Sarah-girl. We check the closet *don't stop get it get it*, we check the balcony *I got it goin' on*, and then we seize the handle of the bathroom door and sigh for it will not move. We egg on the fight and we grind against a man on the balcony and we crouch by the bathroom door and whisper, "Sarah-girl."

"I'm not coming out," she says from the other side. "There's a phone in here, and if you try anything I'm going to call the police."

We glance at each other, at our loose hair and our red-smeared mouths and our blouses that we're unbuttoning to let our wings unfurl. "We can't kill you, Sarah-girl. You must change or crash—"

"I don't want to fucking change or crash!" she yells. "I want to go home!" She takes a heaving breath and we know she's crying again. "I thought you were helping me, I thought you were on my side. But you're just psychopaths."

"We only sing—" we begin again, irritated.

"So you say," she bursts in. "So why am I here? Not because of some stupid *rules*, not because someone's making you do this. I'm here because you're all *batshit*, you've all lost the fucking plot." Her voice is rising, it's drowning out the men and the music alike. "I'm sorry I ever heard you, I'm sorry I ever went to that party, I'm sorry I was ever born!"

We open our mouths to reply but a man seizes our arm and jerks us upright, his face a snarl as he tries to kiss us and we sing out *crash* but we've messed up, we lost our focus and we messed up. The men swarm around us, grabbing and groping, crushing liquor-sticky mouths to ours and trying to wrestle us onto the beds and we remember this, their hands like iron and their weight and their hot stinking breath on our skin

and then we feel nothing but our anger, pure and cold and vast as the night sky

our wings erupt from our backs and we whip the first man off the balcony, sending him sailing into the night with an echoing howl

rattling the bathroom door singing *Sarah-girl come out come out* but it's jumbling with the song of *crash* and our harmonies are jangling and sharp and we drive the next man into the mirror *crash*

lamp cord strangling the third man we bite and wrench him *crash*

there's one screaming between the beds they're everywhere like rats stomp them out *crash*

with a cry we throw our weight against the bathroom door feel the flimsy lock snap and tumble inside

Mister Curiosity falls over the balcony   good-bye gravy

thump-thump-thump from the hallway door and *wump-thu-wump* goes the television and Sarah-girl is jamming the phone buttons in time with the hallway cries and our singing *crash* and it's all messed up we messed up

and suddenly Sarah-girl sings

she opens her mouth wide and sings a song we've never heard before, a song of light and dark, of crashing and flying; she sings of sunlight on deathbeds and regrets cast aside and hands that hold yours in that last coldest hour, and from all sides there is *song*, radios and car stereos and a drunken singalong and a thousand voices belting out an anthem across town

and we're just sirens and somewhere it all went wrong.

The hall door shudders on its hinges and then my mind becomes pin-small, dark and jumbled with memories, and as the door gives way I stumble blindly onto the balcony and out into the air, my wings barely catching the current as I drag myself skyward. So many memories, all the Aglaopes I have been, so many night skies and blood-tinged breezes and, oh! I am so small! so meaningless! Around me the others are flapping, struggling to stay aloft, and though we look at each other there is no more *we*, there is only *I* and *you* and *you* and *you* and *you*

and I remember now how I found Raidne annoying and Thelxiope stuck-up, how I desired Molpe but dared not touch her, how I admired Leucosia's wit but envied her closeness with Molpe

and my wings ache, they feel heavy and stiff, and when I hold my palms up to the moonlight the skin is grey and firm, and as I begin to fall I watch the moon recede from me, the very moon is turning away from us. Great hands of earth rising to seize us, fingers of stone closing over us, and the last thing I glimpse is Sarah-girl peering down at us from the balcony with pale wings unfolding and I say *never again* but I cannot

3.

In my stony cocoon I dream of Sarah-girl, grown tall and broad and so, so strong, striding through her life without fear, her winged shadow sheltering all she chooses to love. I dream of her red lips and her death-hooded eyes and those strange pale wings, and as I dream my tears dry upon my cheeks and my fists loosen and I start to smile.

We are sirens.

And perhaps we failed again, or perhaps the gods are just bastards; perhaps Sarah-girl was nothing but a test, or perhaps she is what we were meant to be; but we will be and we have been and we always are, and we have a bone to pick with little miss *I don't want to change or crash.*

WE ARE SIRENS

Do they really think these rocks can hold us? Oh, they can cage Aglaope and Molpe and Leucosia and Raidne and Thelxiope. But we have been *we* for a long time now, and we haven't forgotten how we made the very stone about us vibrate, how we hummed and trilled and moaned and slowly coaxed from our prison walls a shuddering not unlike a song.

We're sirens, after all. We *sing*.

And when we finally free ourselves, when we finally shatter the rock around us and feel our mind once more as vast as the sky, when at last we stretch our wings and raise our fists and bare our teeth at Hades himself—

when that happens? We're coming for you, Sarah-girl. And we are going to make you *crash*.

MOTH TO AN OLD FLAME
Pat Flewwelling

Serena let the sky lark jump from her finger to a perch within the aviary. When she closed the cage, the bird tilted its head, peeping softly, and shook itself, dropping one light brown feather to the clean gravel below. *A cage within a cage*, Serena thought, peering out through the latticed window. *Ye gods, but we shouldn't be here...* She rubbed at the familiar stabbing ache in her heart. She'd meant to leave years ago. *Eros, you bloody old sod—why now? And why him?*

Outside, a rusty lorry rumbled over the cobbles, its engine roaring in the narrow street. Situated on the corner of Tennis Street and Mermaid Court in Southwark, London, Serena's Pet Emporium felt comfortably muggy with its clutter, its warm animal smells, and its myriad shades of brown, yellow, and orange. Once she had closed the shutters and blackout curtains for the night, she'd switch on the new but dim electric lamps, which would add a lovely firelight glow. The shop was a cage for Serena too, but at least it was a cozy one.

Once upon a time, there had been open meadows along the Thames, with living earth, free air, and waves of lavender blooming from deep green stems. How many sailors had she drawn up from the shore to spend their final, heavenly hours against her breast while she sang them to sleep forever? *Now the air feels like it's been boxed and shelved in neat stacks and rows,* she thought. *And it smells like tar and exhaust fumes.*

"Sleep now," the macaw squawked with an eerily human voice and uncanny timing. "Who's my sweetie? Nighty night."

The bell tinkled over the shop door in the front room and Dr. Jack Harold entered. The veterinarian wore a grey tweed cap and coat, brown woollen pants, and a bright green argyle scarf, and he carried a large, stiff leather bag. His aura smelled of mown hay and pipe smoke. Her breaking heart raced when she saw him. He was delicious, and utterly inedible. *Oh Jack, why did it have to be you?*

"Come to me," the macaw sang. "Follow me down. Come to me!" With a hand sign, Serena commanded the bird to silence. Dr. Jack wouldn't have heard it, but she didn't need pedestrians lured in so soon. Later, when shore leave was expiring and men were staggering to their boats, she would sing to draw in her prey. *Anything to dull the pain*, she thought, grinding her fist against her empty belly. She crept close behind Jack, breathing in his cologne, caressing his aura and weaving it around her fingers, craving his essence, yearning for his love.

Jack turned abruptly. Happily startled to see how closely she stood, he doffed his cap, nodded and smiled awkwardly. Embarrassed, she mumbled a greeting he couldn't hear and tucked her hands into the pockets of her cardigan. She beckoned him into the cage room where the springer spaniel puppy lay on a cushion and adjusted the blackout curtains to let in more daylight.

Why did it have to be you, Jack? she thought angrily. *Eros, I swear by all the gods—*

The birds stopped singing. They ruffled their feathers and shook themselves, disquieted while the skin across her fingers and hands drew tighter, threatening to split.

No. Think about other things.

While the veterinarian probed the dog's tender tummy, Serena checked on the kittens in their cages. She'd already finished feeding the puppies. Their impatient yapping could draw customers of all ages, boys, girls, men, women from miles around. She had trained all her animals in the ancient secrets of her people. Lonely men would come in and sit in front of the cages, listening to the meadow larks and the sparrows and the purring kittens, while a puppy cuddled up and napped in his lap. They often lost hours that way, blissfully unaware that Serena was feeding off their melancholic daydreams.

Some lost more than hours.

She drew them all in, the lost, the lovers, the desperate, the despairing. But she only kept those souls no one else wanted: the unloved, the mean, the lotus-eaters, the murderers. Sad ones she kept for days, sipping away their loneliness and giving them soothing dreams in exchange, until they passed on in peace and comfort. The wicked she drained and disposed of quickly. So far, no one had ever noticed the strange, sweet smell of the cat food, and whenever a customer asked for her recipe, she would only smile and call it a company secret. Some detectives had once come by asking sticky questions, but they had left relaxed, forgetful, and open to the wonder of nature, even if it only grew out of a window box.

But neither she nor her pets had any power over Dr. Jack. He was happy. He had a full house at home, though he was unmarried. He was well-loved by his friends at the pub, respected by his clients, even recognized on the street by politicians and bankers. He was a man of the earth, through and through. Bright green eyes, mouse brown hair, wind-tanned skin bronzed by summer holidays in the country, the smell of wood smoke and wild thyme clinging to his vest. A quiet, God-fearing son of Adam. A gentle soul. Salt of the earth. Perfect. Except for his deafness.

And gods help me, I might have loved him even without this damned arrow in my heart.

Dr. Jack stood and angled his notepad toward the window over his shoulder so he could see what he was writing. He paused for thought, then finished his note with a flourish.

He brought out a hunger in her so frustrating that it made her aura swell like the lifting of feathers. Her eyes dilated, her nostrils flared, and when he handed her the note, she cocked her head like one of her trapped birds. *How dare Eros do this to me?* she thought with such outrage that birds screeched and flapped about, casting up a flurry of feathers and making Dr. Jack's thick eyebrows lift. The dogs joined in, while the cats scrambled about their playpen. Even the sick spaniel lifted his head to howl mournfully. She cleared her throat and focused on the note in her hand, grounding herself in the mortal world. Her stomach growled.

He had written his recommendations for the spaniel: medicine, a modified diet, and tender loving care. She hid a bitter snort of laughter. *"There is no greater physic than love,"* he had written beside the cost of the medication and the fee for his visit.

No greater physic—what codswallop! Love is the disease, you idiot. And why can't you see...?

Dr. Jack followed her to the register, as eager and oblivious as ever. He glanced over his shoulder at the cacophony he couldn't hear, visibly marvelling at the flurry of feathers. When the cash drawer opened, however, he turned to accept the money and tilted his hat from his forehead.

She caught a flash of destiny in his eyes and, as he turned for the door, she grabbed him by the wrist. He jarred and blanched. Fear kept his eyes on hers, which was fortunate, or else he would have seen her hands turn scaly and her claws emerge.

There, she thought. *Let me see it in your eyes.*

She saw orange smoke and search lights, women running in all directions, children screaming, and men shambling along, unaware of the mangled limbs hanging at their sides. The air was full of the noise of industrial fans, distant explosions, and of voices pleading with pedestrians to get out of the streets and into the bomb shelters.

Fiery-headed Enyo, the goddess of wartime destruction, rode up the street on a horse that sweated blood. Enyo grew fat on civilian deaths just as Serena devoured the souls of lonely sailors. For eons, Enyo had been her father's black-robed camp follower; but now she wore a full suit of armour, and commanded the invasion.

The goddess drove a spear into one man's heart. He fell to his knees, screaming. Then, as if sensing Serena's presence, Enyo wheeled her horse about. She chuckled and pointed her spear to the ground by Serena's right foot.

There, in the rubble was Dr. Jack's head, his face fixed in terror. She saw the rest of his body two doors down.

Enyo lifted the face mask of her brazen helmet and screamed a laugh.

Serena threw down Jack's hand, breaking the spell. She felt her skin soften and her eyes shrink to their normal size.

The Adam's apple bobbed in Dr. Jack's throat. He hastily tilted his hat again and pulled open the door so quickly the bell bounced on its spring. "Wait! I'm sorry!" She hurried after him, touching his sleeve. He stopped. He was very tall, and his neck muscles were like ropes under the skin. She let her fingers slide down his sleeve to his cuff. She conjured a note and pressed it against his palm.

There were flecks of blue in his surprised green eyes.

She imagined her ancient meadow of lavender, where she and this gentle giant would recline under a willow, holding each other, watching the boats drift by.

That Arcadian world was long gone. This was a petrol world now, built up with cement, criss-crossed in iron rails, smothered in smog and coal ash. Discarded newspapers tumbled where autumn leaves should have rolled. There were no more lavender meadows on the banks of the Thames, and in the end, this man would hold nothing in his arms but the crushing cinderblocks that killed him.

Standing on the threshold between her sometime-abattoir and the death that awaited him outside, Dr. Jack opened his hand and read the letter. "*Thank you for your kindness,*" she had impressed upon the paper. "*Please, stay safe today.*" He pushed the note into his coat pocket, shook her hand delicately, and mouthed, "Good day." His coat and cap turned a brighter shade when he stepped out into the sunlight. He crossed the road, touched his pocket, then struck off up Tennis Street, likely to take his solitary afternoon walk along the Thames. She closed the door.

The shop stank of scat and wet animals.

MOTH TO AN OLD FLAME

It doesn't matter if he dies today or if he dies in fifty years! So long as this curse is upon me, I'll pine for him until the end of time. She snapped the lock shut on the door and crossed her arms tightly over her empty chest. It wasn't fair. How many angry, vicious young men had she given a serene death? Why should a kind and happy man die in horror, watching his own beheading?

She returned to the cage room—*"No greater physic than love!"*—closed all the blackout curtains, braced the windows with plywood, and rushed up through the narrow stairway to her roost above the shop. She gathered the things she would need for an urgent summoning, and headed to the centre of her sitting room, passing by a full-length mirror as she went.

She stopped.

It was no wonder Dr. Jack saw nothing in her. She was a seagull among swans. Banished by pollution from her home waters and from the air, grounded by airplanes and zeppelins, Serena had lost her siren's splendour. Her obsidian hair had turned greasy brown from years of gaslight smoke. Her skin had lost its lustre, her voluminous lips had thinned, her bosom had fallen, and her nymph's body had thickened into a column of coagulated fat.

"Come now, beloved," a sultry voice said from the corner of the room.

The figure was poorly reflected in the mouldy mirror, sitting in a tattered chair, half-hidden by shadows and a beam of dust motes.

"If you're so upset by what you see," he said, "slip into something comfortable, and we'll chat."

Serena let the summoning articles fall. Feathers erupted where frizzy hair had escaped her bun. Scales itched as they emerged from her pale arms, wrists, and hands, turning yellow and black. "*Eros.*"

"My sweet chick." Eros was wearing an opera cape and tuxedo, complete with a top hat on his curling blond hair and he blew a chute of cigarette smoke, churning the dust in the air.

"It wasn't you I meant to summon."

He cast a judging eye over the items on the floor. "And you think Mother Night would help a silly old siren like you?"

"She could suggest a good curse. Like leprosy, or syphilis."

"Such venom." He rose. "I've only come to talk."

The angrier she grew, the more musical her voice became. If she wasn't careful, customers would come knocking. "Eros, if you had wanted my love, you could have…" She pointed lamely at the crossbow lying across his lap. "You could have aimed better."

Eros said, "Ah, but that's not the kind of love we need. Desire is a pack of chewing gum, when what you need is a good steak dinner."

"Then make him love me," she said.

"Sing to his soul. You can do that. He wouldn't be the first deaf man you've lured to his doom."

"It's not his doom that I want! Why are you doing this to me? You've punished me enough."

"You think this is about punishment?" he asked.

"Eros, what happened between us was four *thousand* years ago. Take this from me," she said, pointing to the place where his bolt had struck home. The arrow appeared like a shaft of blue illuminated smoke.

"Oh hush, darling, and listen. I came to ask a favour of you."

"And what of Psyche?"

Eros sucked in his cheeks and pursed his lips. Anger did not become him.

"You do remember your wife?" Serena asked. "She went to Hades and back to save your life. I've gone to Hades and back to *avoid* you. Why…me? And why now?"

"Yes," he snapped. "Why you." He removed his top hat. "I mean, look at you. You've become weak. Cowardly. Can you even manifest your wings? You're starving, my little eater of souls."

"And yet you've never been more…"

"Robust?" he asked proudly.

"Lively."

MOTH TO AN OLD FLAME

"I like to keep up with the times. Hollywood, Burlesque, pin-up magazines…They keep me young and playful. You know, I've been working on this new repeating crossbow. Really quite a fantastic innovation, based on the Gatling gun—have you heard of it?"

"Eros. What has happened to Psyche? I read the newspapers. I've seen millions sacrifice their own conscience to the will of madmen. Where is the Spirit of Mankind? What has happened to her?"

"She left me years ago, and I haven't any idea where she is, not for a lack of searching nor for all my pleading for forgiveness. The last I saw of her, she was bawling about exhaustion. Let her sulk, wherever she is. Forget her!" he said again. "It's you I need. You are the Siren of the Channel! The Doom of Dover!"

"And I have a bloody arrow in my chest pointing to the wrong man."

"Thelxinoe." Eros began. New, shining feathers sprouted at the mention of her ancient name. "You should never have fled from Anthemoessa to hide from me—you're no more English than I am."

She couldn't explain why she was so drawn to London, especially now that the whole Continent was rich with the luscious aroma of hopelessness and desolation. Maybe it was the Brits' maritime inclination and their brash pride—"Britannia rules the waves" and all that—or maybe it was their optimism and spirit of adventure. Greek or not, she simply felt like she was meant to be in London, as if the Fates had commanded it.

"These Londoners are not your people. The English do not worship you. Who were you to the Celts, the Angles, or the Saxons? Who are you to the Christians? But *I* still love you. Thelxinoe, *I* can restore you to your former glory."

"What do you want, Eros?"

"We need to repopulate." The horror must have been plain on her face, because he rushed to take her by the arms and explain himself. "We need a new army to stand against Ares and my siblings. See how they're devouring this entire mortal realm!"

She wriggled free. "Eros, you are Desire, as am I. What can we do but create new obsessions? Addiction, Jealousy, Betrayal, Hunger for Power...How will *they* help to tame the world out there?"

"If I took you forcefully, yes, we would only create evil. But if we worked together, in love, we could create a new Philosophia or Harmonia, a new craving for knowledge and peace."

She raised her clawed hands and said, "Eros, I cannot love you. I did not love you when I was a mortal virgin and I cannot love you now. Love is not in my nature!"

"Liar!"

The arrow in her heart flared, making her gasp and lurch into his arms.

"Tell me, luv, when you dream of your Dr. Jack, is it his body you crave, or his companionship?"

His mercy, she thought. He'd spent nights on end nursing one of her sick kittens to health. She'd seen him bring new shoes and hot soup to an old homeless man sleeping on the banks of the Thames. She had even seen him drop everything and rush to save a yelping dog after it had been hit by a tram, and seeing it too gravely wounded, he had put it out of its misery with his own strong hands. *His compassion. Understanding kindness. That is what I ache for, and that's what I deserve least of all.*

"This is why you stung me?" she demanded. "Shoot me, and remove the bolt only if I agree to bear your children? Of all the inhuman—"

"I stung you to prove that you *are* capable of love. I made you fall in love with a man, in order to make you fall in love with *mankind*, so that you would help me!"

"Eros," she said with a long, weary sigh, "Enyo is coming. I can already smell death in the air. And thanks to your arrow, I must find a way to stop her *now*, or I will die of grief."

"That's why we must change, Thelxinoe. Adapt, regroup, *repopulate*, rally the new gods against Enyo and my other siblings!

MOTH TO AN OLD FLAME

Without an army of our own, she will bomb your city into Tartarus." His eyes were like cold brass buttons fixed in ivory settings. "And then where will your Dr. Jack be?"

The arrow burned. Feathers lifted. Blood boiled. "Get out of my nest."

The floor was shaking, and the windows rattled.

Eros pursed his lips as if to toss her a cruel kiss. "Think on my offer, before you have nothing but corpses to feed upon." His opera cape shredded into strips. Strips became feathers. Feathers joined to make wings. A moment later, he was a golden oriole and gone from her window.

Serena kicked her black ceremonial bowl across the room, shouting, "Bollocks!"

Eros was right. Nyx would never stoop to help a faded and pudgy siren resolve her romantic issues. There was only one being who could remove the arrow from her heart, and that was the same god she'd commanded out of her home.

Downstairs, the macaw repeated the curse word, adding, "Who's my sweetie? Bollocks! Nighty night. Bollocks!"

Her feet felt like they were buzzing from the vibrations in the floor.

Eros wasn't the first lonely god to seek her out. She drew all the forlorn to her, mortal and otherwise. She was a beacon to them, the moth's favourite old flame. *So...he's lonely? Because Psyche has left him? But where on earth could she have gone that Eros couldn't find her? And why?* The couple had had their spats over the millennia, as all married couples did, but ever since she had become immortal, Psyche had devoted herself to her husband. And though inciting infidelity was Eros's job, he was the dictionary picture of faithfulness in his own marriage. *So why would she leave him?*

And why now, when mankind needs her the most? The more she considered this new mystery, the more Serena worried. After all, of the whole pantheon, it was Psyche who gave a damn about humanity, building hope, inspiring compassion, pulling survivors out of death's grasp. And yet, for the last ten to twenty years, mortal kind had fallen into misery. Even before the rise of the Axis Powers, there had been global starvation, unemployment, civil uprisings, military coups, and xenophobia. Warmongers had industrialized genocide. Once-mighty nations were bowing before fascist regimes with only a meagre show of resistance. *Why is the human spirit so weary and ready to surrender?*

Has Ares done something to Psyche?

Minutes had passed since Eros left, and yet the rumbling noise was still there. On quiet days, Serena could hear the trains pulling into London Bridge Station, but they never rattled the floorboards like this.

In the distance, through the brick walls and thick curtains, she heard the opening note of a gigantic metal wolf, tuning up for an ear-piercing howl. *Cerberus,* she thought. *He's howling for his dinner.* As a second and third alarm began to sound, she heard a triumphant, scathing voice join in.

Enyo. She's already here!

Dr. Jack spent his afternoons walking and sitting on the banks of the Thames, watching the boats. If he was alone, he wouldn't know the bombers were coming until they were overhead. He wouldn't get to the London Bridge Tube station in time.

At the sound of Enyo's voice, the dogs began to yap and the birds to screech. Serena ran downstairs as an air raid siren near the Southwark Cathedral whirred up its wail. She would have mere minutes to cut through Kings College on the way to the Tube station. If the animals survived the raid, she would call them back, but she would not let them die in their cages. The cats had already broken out and were running amok. She opened the macaw's cage and he flew in her face before bashing against walls, crying, "Bollocks! Bollocks!" She opened the last of the cages, then stooped to pick up the sick puppy, who squirmed in her arms. She glanced at the cash register but decided Dr. Jack was far more valuable than any mortal riches.

She opened the door and recoiled from a pair of women running in high heels, one breathless, the other shrieking. The gasping one took her friend by the elbow and tugged her along, up Tennis Street toward Kings College. The puppy whined and wriggled.

Serena heard an eerie, subhuman laugh overhead.

There was Enyo, as tall as Big Ben, armoured astride her bleeding horse. Enyo sang, "To fire! To death! To war!" to the tune of the disharmonious sirens whirring from eight or nine poles around Southwark. Every time she opened her mouth, students and teachers ran from their campus buildings with their hands over their ears, some dropping to their knees, many praying to a newer god.

Dr. Jack can hear no siren. I need to get him to safety. I need to sing to his soul, draw him down with me into the underground. But, the rest of these people—

Paralyzed by indecision, Serena stood like a boulder in a stream of panic-stricken foot traffic. One young man tripped. Another stumbled over him, and two more ran by without stopping to help.

"And where are you running off to, little nymph?" The gigantic goddess's voice was as big as mountains.

Serena held the puppy close to her chest.

Enyo tilted back her meteoric head and laughed.

"What have you done to Psyche?" Serena shouted.

Enyo lifted the face plate of her helmet, blinking languidly. "I learned a new song from you, pigeon, and I sang it for her! I drew her underground and made her sleep forever!" Her voice rose in pitch and then broke up into that chaotic, shrieking laugh.

New pin feathers grew from Serena's temples. "Then I'll just have to rouse her."

"Then you had better run, tiny siren, run!" Enyo tipped her spear point to the ground, and with lightning speed, struck the courtyard. The spear struck again and again, sometimes clipping Serena's heel, once cutting through her sleeve.

"*Rouse her?*" Serena thought, bewildered at her own bravado. *I'm the opposite of "rousing".* She was a siren, created to lull men to fatal sleep.

Yes, but I was a woman once, and I know: if you want a woman up and swinging, you need to make her angry.

Serena ran the last block to the Tube station doors, where people crammed in from all angles. Enyo struck again, this time stabbing a woman through the head, causing her to faint and fall against the human press. She struck a man next; he reached for a weapon inside his coat, but he didn't have elbow room enough to draw it out. With her siren's voice, Serena sang, "Move aside, please!" And people moved aside.

She rushed down the stairs, past the reach of sunlight and Enyo's spear, past the helmeted volunteers pleading for civility and calm, and into the glare of electric lamps. The puppy's ears flapped like limp wings with every step, but he was quiet, and no one complained of him. She nodded her thanks at a volunteer, who directed her down the platform into the deeper, rounder recesses of the Tube itself. She rushed beyond the shouts and screams until her breath echoed off the shadowy carved walls. *Find Psyche. Wake her up. Get her to appeal to the pilots' sense of humanity. Make them defy Enyo. Stop the bombs. Save Dr. Jack. But first, find Psyche!*

She stopped in the dark, let out her feathers, dropped her vocal register and sang a modern song far outside her regular repertoire. Bessie Smith she wasn't, but she could sing with just as much soul and frustration as any jilted lover. She was halfway through "A Good Man is Hard to Find" when she added notes of scorn and derision, honing them, targeting them on memories of Psyche, and sending the song around the world and deep into its bowels. For the first time in history, Serena would draw someone *up*.

"*Just when you think that he's your pal, You look and find him foolin' round some old gal,*" she sang. "*Then you rave, Shall you crave, You wanna see him in his—*"

MOTH TO AN OLD FLAME

Her voice clogged with surprise.

Standing in the glow of a flickering safety light was a cross-armed woman wearing a colourless kerchief, a dirty yellow sundress, and a stained apron. She wore a butterfly hair clip in her tired, sweaty bangs and looked like she had come from a long day on the job as everyone's least favourite nanny. She turned to Serena, lifting her knobby chin and narrowing puffy eyes. Judging by the scowl on her face, all she needed was a rolling pin and one good excuse to use it.

Serena scrunched her nose. "Psyche?"

The woman uncrossed her arms, strode over, and socked Serena in the mouth with a broad, calloused fist. Serena stumbled and dropped the yipping dog.

"Bloody hell!" Serena exclaimed.

"I know what you've been up to, you filthy *strumpet*. Four thousand years later, he's still *my* husband. Slattern! Hussy!" Psyche pursed her eyes and lips. "You dirty *hooer!*" She was missing teeth, and the ones that remained didn't seem healthy.

"And you can keep the bloody bastard!" Serena pointed to her heart. "While you're at it, count his arrows."

"You will not have him, you repugnant Lorelei—try it, and I'll—Wait, what?" Psyche looked impatiently puzzled. "And what's all that racket?"

"See for yourself."

Psyche closed her eyes. Her nostrils flared, as if she was getting a good whiff of the strife in the air. "Enyo," she growled.

"She stole a song from me and used it against you. The *witch!* And now she's ruining my food supply."

"What?"

"Your husband has pierced me into love with a deaf man in order to blackmail me into bearing a divine child army, while Ares has been mowing down all my lonely sailors, and that *dog* peed on my arm when we were running over here. I won't have any more of this tomfoolery and dying! That's why I called you up from the underworld and made you angry."

Psyche blinked. "The individual words make sense, but when you put them together like that…"

Serena stamped her foot, and the dog ran cowering. "While you've been dozing, Europe has been overrun, and I can't find Dr. Jack!"

"Who? Never mind. Show me." Psyche touched Serena's forehead, and the siren recalled the first image that came to mind. Unfortunately, it was the face of the decapitated Dr. Jack. Psyche said, "Get these people below ground and calm them down. I'll do what I can about the bombers. And *then* you'll explain what the devil you've been doing with my husband."

Serena closed her eyes and began to sing the first calming song she could think of. At first, all she had was the melody, something as simple and mindless as a tune she might hum while washing the dishes. In the distance, screams dulled to shouts. It had been a long time since she'd sung to so many souls at once. Her voice was unsteady, and the power only came in hiccups.

"I can't…seem to…get through to those pilots," Psyche said. "They've convinced themselves they're bombing inanimate objects, and not their fellow man."

The first bomb fell. The ground shook.

Serena stopped singing. Silence swelled. "Oh bollocks." Then came the screaming.

Psyche shook Serena. "Keep singing."

Dr. Jack was still above ground. She hadn't sensed his soul in the Tube.

"Sing what you were singing before! That seemed to be working," Psyche said.

"But I don't remember what I was singing!"

"La…lav…" Psyche couldn't sing well on the best of days. It took four tries for her to find a good note to start from. "*Lavender's blue, billy billy.*"

"Dilly *dilly.*"

Then Serena realized where she was standing.

On the surface overhead, there had been a willow tree, and a sprawling field of wild flowers leading down to the sparkling Thames. A field of lavender, where she used to sleep under a willow tree.

"Sing it like a mother to a babe," Psyche said, "not like you're some frightened girl hiding from monsters."

"*Lavender's blue, dilly, dilly, lavender's green...*"

"You're a siren. You hold the hearts of the unwary in your hand, and they love you for it."

"*When I am king, dilly, dilly, You shall be queen...*"

Psyche watched the lights at the end of the tunnel. "Good. Good, it's working."

The ground rocked with three bombs, one right after the other. People gasped, and a child began to cry.

"They're walking in orderly lines," Psyche said, "but the fear is still in them." The shivering puppy cowered against her legs, so she picked up him up and held him in her arms. "Remind them," Psyche said, gently scratching the puppy between his floppy ears. "Remind them who they are."

She remembered the lyrics whole phrases at a time.

"*Call up your men, dilly, dilly, set them to work...Some to the plough, dilly, dilly, some to the fork...Some to make hay, dilly, dilly, some to cut corn...While you and I, dilly, dilly, keep ourselves warm.*"

The more Serena sang, the warmer and richer her voice became. She remembered the mutual attraction that drew sailor and siren together, how she would anchor herself in the land and draw power from the river. She was the immovable precipice against which all lonely sailors foundered. She was more of a siren than any whining, wheezing machine man could invent! She held sway over these people; her will was as irresistible as the sting of Enyo's spear.

Power coursed from her heart up into her scalp to straighten and thicken her hair, to rejuvenate and lift her glorious feathers. Strength and magic flowed into her hands, renewing their strength and the shine of her scales. *This* was the siren men once feared. This was the voice that could crash the mightiest ship and seduce the wisest man to his demise.

"Not too much now," Psyche said, stroking the puppy's head. "You don't want to drown them all on dry land."

How she remembered those languid afternoons, listening to the birds, feeling the sun on her face, sensing the pull of the water's power. She wanted to hate these people for what they'd done to the earth, but she couldn't. She knew the sadness in their hearts. She knew their dreams, their small joys, their comforts, their contentment, their relief. And she loved them for it.

"*Lavender's green, dilly, dilly, Lavender's blue…*" Serena's voice lilted down the scale as if she was sobbing for the paradise lost. "*If you love me, dilly, dilly, I will love you…Let the birds sing, dilly, dilly, And the lambs play…*" A lump rose in her throat. "*We shall be safe, dilly, dilly, out of harm's way…*"

There, she thought. *There, I feel you now, my love. Come to me. Let all others be lulled into mellow good cheer, but you…you must be my side…come to me. Come to me.*

"*I love to dance, dilly, dilly, I love to sing.*"

Someone was humming along with her. A mother, standing on the platform with a babe in arms.

"*When I am queen, dilly, dilly, You'll be my king.*"

A young couple embraced. His chin was on the top her head, and he whispered things that made the girl smile.

"Ah, there he is," Psyche said. "Your Dr. Jack is standing on the platform. No—stand here with me and wait. He's tending to a girl who's fallen down the stairs and broken her ankle. Besides, your song isn't over yet. You have one more to draw down." Her voice had an iron edge, and Serena knew the man in question. He would be easy to find and lure in.

"*Who told me so, dilly, dilly, Who told me so?*" Serena sang, quietly now. "*I told myself, dilly, dilly, I told me so…*"

MOTH TO AN OLD FLAME

The puppy barked. He wagged his tail. Someone was coming.

Eros stepped into the circle of yellow light cast by the safety lamps. The arrow in Serena's heart flared, shaking her voice and breaking the siren's song. "My love?" Eros answered. "Psyche?" He quickened his step.

Furious, Psyche clutched the puppy to her chest, and Serena touched her, holding her back.

"Psyche!" Eros said. "What became of you? For eleven *years* I've been looking for you! I thought you'd left me for good. My love—forgive me whatever I've done!"

"Enyo," Serena explained. "She stole one of my songs and put Psyche to sleep."

Eros stood with his hat in his hands. "That...that's why Enyo made such progress across Europe? Man has fallen." Eros blinked at his wife. "Because you had fallen."

"I was buried underground, halfway to Tartarus," Psyche said. She crossed her arms and added, "I'm feeling much better now, thank you for asking."

"I couldn't understand how the gods had become so powerful," Eros said. "I thought..."

"You thought the rest of us should try to steal power, too?" Serena asked. "Repopulate and force mortals to worship us, to feed us power?"

Psyche snorted. "The gods will have no such power over humankind ever again, not so long as they remember *me*. And by Hades, will I make them remember the power of the human spirit!" She smiled at Serena. "Just as you've reminded *me*. You'll stay now and fight by my side?"

Serena nodded solemnly.

"Good. Eros," Psyche said, "do you still have that repeating crossbow?"

Eros nodded.

"Then mix up an industrial-sized batch of brotherly love, and head over to the Continent. See how many heroes you can inspire behind enemy lines. Feel free to stir up some romances while you're at it. We'll need to repopulate the earth with decent folk once this is all done. Serena, it's time you modernize your vocal jukebox. We've slept long enough. Now, it's time to dance."

Eros began to laugh. "Ages ago, I once revived Psyche from death's sleep with a graze of one of my arrows. It would seem a second arrow—" He pointed at Serena's chest. "—has done the trick again." The arrow flashed, then burst into shower of sparks. The pain was gone. So was the arrow.

"Leave it to Eros to claim all the glory," Psyche said with a sigh.

The puppy squirmed out of Psyche's arms and ran to Eros, who stooped and picked him up like a rambunctious child. The dog licked his whole face as if he'd been separated forever from his master. He seemed much recovered. Much loved.

"Thank you for restoring my wife to me. I owe you a favour." Eros glanced over his shoulder at the platform behind him. "You know, I could..."

"Let Dr. Jack live a long and joyful life in the country," Serena said. "Let him adore a woman who will love him as Psyche loves you. And let me roam the waters and the free air, as I was meant to do."

Psyche began to smile. As she did, the years fell away from her face, and the butterfly clip began to flex its wings. Eros nodded. It was a promise.

"Beloved wife!" Eros said abruptly, returning to his usual cockiness. "Now that you're awake, perhaps you could also shore up morale? Give these people a good reason to leave the Tube tomorrow morning, and the next, and the morning after. Revive their sense of humour."

"I'll call up the Muses," Psyche said, rolling up her sleeves and flexing well-muscled arms. Her apron changed from linen to leather, and her muslin dress became a pair of overalls. "While I'm at it, I'll speak with this new bulldoggish fellow, what's his name..."

"Churchill?" Serena asked.

"Yes. Not much to look at, but he's got spirit. All he needs are the right words."

Serena laughed. "Well then! Between the three of us…if Hitler wants to cuff us in the mouth, he'll find that these stiff upper lips have been reinforced with good English steel."

To Serena, Psyche said, "As for you, my courageous rescuer, I charge you with one of the greatest missions in history."

"And that is?"

"Teach these people how to keep calm and carry on."

THE BOUNTY
Gabriel F. Cuellar

The sea is best. She can work with lesser sources—lakes, rivers, even paved fountains if necessary—but the sea is where she waxes full. It's lucky, then, that so many of those she pursues seem to seek water, like hunted animals too dry and heated to resist. The men flee to Atlantic City, to Miami, to New Orleans or South Padre Island, to blend in with frantic spring breakers and men who care more about money than the law. The mean vitality of those men pleases her, and the thought of the lure of water makes her smile.

She stands on the seashore, close to the place where the water stains the sand a darker brown, her leather boots surrounded by gobs of seaweed and the skeletons of crustaceans.

There is very little moon and the sand is deeply shadowed. The beach is never empty, but during the day it is elbow-to-elbow and she still has her pride. She will not jostle for space near the sea, not her. Besides, it's best if there are not too many other people nearby. Once, she would not have cared about such things, when the guilt or innocence of people meant nothing to her. Now she has spent too much time on dirt to maintain such indifference. The tide is different now, dirtier now, and she has inhaled too much sweat instead of pure sea-air.

She knows he's nearby, tracked him over state lines, hundreds of miles south to this place. There's a casino overlooking the ocean, and he is in there, throwing dice and hoping for luck.

It will not be with him tonight.

She imagines walking into that place, rubbing through the crowd, letting laughter and curses wash over her. It would be tainted and heavy with the smell of alcohol and the salty odor of breathing, and the ugly music would scrape at her like a rash.

She would crest over them all, a tsunami they could neither see nor escape. She would batter them, dash them against madness and drown them in longing. Then she would leave and her undertow would suck them breathlessly under.

The vision releases her and she knows a moment of chagrin at how the tables turn if she lets them. It is not right for her to be sucked into desire and disappointment, but she is clipped and ingrown now, like a plant in a too-small pot.

She brings the glowing shape from inside her long coat and holds it out—bright and compellingly beautiful. She blows on it, a salty gust, and it bounces slightly, hops out of her hand and lands lightly on the sand. She has to look away from the vision it presents.

Will can shape the form it shows, but when at rest it always reflects back the thing the viewer desires the most. She always sees a tall and well-muscled Grecian man, long-haired and far-sighted, blobs of wax still stuffed inside his ears. Just seeing him is enough to send her guts into a spasm of frustrated desire. The one who sailed away will always tear at her heart.

She and the spirit should never have met. Their birthplaces were far apart and neither, by nature, travelled any distance from home. Still, need makes strange bedfellows and there is a kinship between them after all. She once had sisters, but she doesn't know where they are.

"Go, Will," she says. Her voice is an unpleasant whine, like a gull's cry. "Bring him here."

Will stalks away across the sand and suddenly a young woman is sashaying her way up the beach. She walks toward the casino in her bikini, a high ponytail in her bright hair and strappy sandals on her feet. The two of them have learned that men of business will tolerate many things, but bare feet are rarely one of them. She looks young, so young that she should not be allowed into the casino, but she will be.

Will is, as always, perfectly matched to the quarry.

Will—when it thinks of itself at all—likes to think of itself as male. However, there is no denying that the female form is always more tempting than even the softest, prettiest male. Even young girls can be enticed into the forest by a playmate or a mother, and when luring predators, it is best to pretend to be their prey.

She traipses up the stairs and through the wide, gilded doors of the casino, hips clocking like a metronome. Her swimsuit leaves just enough to the imagination to hint at indecency but still be allowed in public. The sandals have heels, which leave her slender legs with the balanced delicacy of a newborn fawn.

The man at the front puts up a hand to block her—a hand that is not close enough to touch her breast, but which curves its palm sympathetically to the same—and demands ID. She smiles prettily and turns slightly away, slipping two fingers into the front of the bikini bottoms and bringing out a small square of plastic. It will, of course, confirm that she is of legal age to enter, despite her appearance.

The guard takes it, holds it close to his eyes, breathing deeply to take in the warm scent of her body while he pretends to peer at it. He hands it back, almost breathless as she slips it back into the little bowl between her hips. She's sure that he's saving every moment in his memory for a later playback, and gives him a winsome smile which is just enough to change his future dreams from sexual conquest to continually seeking—but never finding—that smile again.

She struts away, eyes wide, craning her neck. She knows she is being obvious, but it's all right. Many men stop to ask her who she's looking for, and offer to be that someone. For a while, she plays Pied Piper, leading her little crowd of rats back and forth between the slots and tables. Then she finds her quarry and steps quickly away from her admirers.

She latches onto his arm and looks up at him, a nervous smile on her face. "Please, can you pretend you know me? There's this absolutely *gross* jerk following me."

The supplication to his possessive masculinity combines with her sexual appeal and he is lost. He smiles and puts an arm over her back, squeezing her against him and looking over his shoulder at the loose crowd of men she's left behind. To cement his position against them, he slaps one hand over her ass. She jumps, then giggles.

She spends an hour with him, clinging to his arm, taking sips of his drink and leaning forward so that her breasts press against him. There are girls throughout the casino doing the same things, and all of them want something, but not all the same thing. Finally, when he finishes a roll and scoops up his chips, she stretches up so she can whisper into his ear. Her breath puffs against him, and it's chilly instead of warm, but he doesn't seem to notice.

"You wanna go out to the beach? I want to swim in the dark."

Will's job has always been temptation—it would bounce and shimmer and merrily lead humans astray: men, women, and children all alike. Often, it would lead them to water, to mucky swamps and sticky mud and deep-dark lakes with no bottoms. Now, Will limits itself to leading men who are already astray, but they end up just as trapped as ever.

His hand lands on her rump again and he nods. They head out, the cash-out he barely looked at stuffed into the bulging front of his jeans. He's already excited, already thinking about the young—underaged, let's be real, he knows she shouldn't be in a place like this—flesh he's going to sink himself into, hot flesh and cold water.

They could catch him like this. They don't need to do anything else. But they *want* to.

It makes her angry to know what the man wants as Will trips away over the sands. It makes her glad for what she is doing, makes her throat itch and her eyes feel hot and dry. The desire is rising in her now, that sweet and lustful anticipation. Her insides churn and burn. Soon, she will open her mouth and let that dreadful hunger out on the world. Now, she can only wait.

She and Will choose carefully the men they ruin: those who ruined others. Men who hit their wives and children, men who took advantage of the girls they coached or the babysitters they drove home, the ones who destroyed the peace of sons and daughters who could not sleep with him in the house. The ones whose faithful wives, sitting at the loom of their tattered marriages, insisted that he was a good family man.

A good family man is not a flight risk. A good family man who pays whatever his family has, beggaring them in order to leave the concrete box the authorities put him in, is not a flight risk. That's what they think: the courts, the wives, the ones willing to take the collateral and hand over the cash.

Those wives, like so many, do not understand that he is *not* a good family man. He never has been. He leaves them behind, hurt and confused and humiliated, and lights out for the sea. They've been that way throughout history, and nothing has changed. She takes vengeance on them all.

The man Will is leading back to them is one of those men. He stalked his wife's daughters, so young and fragile, spinning the mother who should have protected them in a web of deceit that made her his accomplice. Those girls, mere children, little seeds that had not blossomed yet, sleep in dread every night since their stepfather took their mother's money for his bail and then vanished into the wider world. Their mother sheds bitter tears of rage and shame and loss.

She understands very well what it is to wrap others in the song they want to hear, to entice them with promises of love and fulfillment. Once, she would have drowned him in the surf and left his body to float in the waves, feeding the fish and the gulls, turning his flesh to some use. Now, they feed nothing, denied even the surcease of death. It is the least that they deserve.

She waits in the sound of the surf until she can see Will bouncing down the sand, the man behind her. Will no longer looks like a girl to her or like a Greek hero, it has become a dolphin, leaping gracefully through rippled waves of sand as though guiding a ship between tall rocks and a whirlpool. Right down the center, to the island where she waits.

The man still sees the pretty, slightly tipsy young girl he wants to take on the beach.

The man thinks that he will push Will down into the wet surf and have his way with her, whether she agrees or no, and when he is done he will leave her there. He will have her in every way he can, because the beach is dark and deserted, and there is no one to stop him. How fitting then that they should mete the same out to him.

She unties the belt of her long coat and lets the sea-wind whip across her skin, ruffling her like a gull's wings. She flings her arms wide as if she could ride that wind. She no longer cares if there are innocent people on the beach; it's too late for that. In a glorious release, she exhales her song.

The man stops. He draws back, Will is forgotten, and some part of him knows this song will be the end of him. The death of pleasure, of lust, of life itself. Forever he will want to hear that song again, and this is the only time he ever will. Instinctively, he wishes to flee, but instead he steps forward, mouth hanging open and eyes bulging.

Will's satisfaction peaked the moment the man stepped toward his doom—it has sent children to drown in shallow ponds and led weeping maidens to kelpies, but for now, this is enough. It bounces away down the beach, immune to the song, perhaps to find some drunk passed out on the sand, or a stray dog, and lead it into the surf. She hardly notices.

Her arms and mouth are open still, and the song vomits out of her. It is indescribable, its beauty hideous and the rhythm wild as the sea. The man comes to her and falls at her feet, weeping. If only he had been aboard a boat, and she astride the wind, he would have thrown himself into the sea. Now he can only sob his ugly, braying cries and cower at her feet.

She knows that she has to stop, that she has to leave him sane enough to appreciate her vengeance, but every time it's a struggle. She closes her mouth and chokes as the song fights to escape the barrier of her teeth. Her eyes bulge. Then it shudders to a stop, leaving her breathless, the sweetness slipping back down her throat and curling around her heart. She is full now...but she will never be sated.

She buckles her coat again, hiding the grey-gull feathers on her breast, and then handcuffs the man on the sand with zip ties. He does not resist.

She will take him back to the courts and claim her reward from the bail-bondsman, but the money doesn't matter. What matters is the moment on the sand when she can close her eyes and pretend the world's tides have not turned, that she is still herself. These victims who try to row past her, full of bravado and fear, are never allowed through the gates.

Even now, with the ruined man at her feet, she knows it will never be enough.

The Dolphin Riders
Randall G. Arnold

This, Roberto has discovered, is where the dolphin riders fly.

He has encountered them several times, and on his previous excursion even witnessed a successful hunt. He'd cringed at the agonized bellowing of the targeted whale as a hail of ivory spears pierced its barnacled hide—but by the time he'd arrived at the scene the only evidence of the slaughter was blood foaming the troubled waters.

Back ashore, the other boys scoffed at his description of brilliant blue females urging on steel-gray mounts, stalking prey like lions, long bone lances poised in patient aim.

Prove it, they had sneered.

Roberto gnaws his chapped lower lip with worry. All these castaway heathens want is to ridicule the noblest of creatures, he thinks. To goad each other into committing some disgrace, rapidly lose interest, and then rush to other mischief.

They do have a point, he realizes. One would think that by now some sign of the riders would have arrived ashore, littered along its length with the rest of the frequently gifted refuse. A lost lance, an elaborate shell necklace, a dolphin harness. Maybe even an unmistakeable rider skull.

But the sea covets its secrets.

It had openly, violently betrayed them all not so long ago, indiscriminately drowning or displacing any who braved its waters. As Roberto still does. Daring. Defying. Alone.

He plies his usual route this summer day, warping the wind to his young will and skillfully threading treacherous shoals. His sails fill with the exhalations of a phantom chorus, directing him toward the deepening sea where the fin whales run, where he drops his anchor and nets.

To Roberto, fishing is more than necessity. Like his grandfather before him, he has embraced the art with a true sailor's lust.

There are plenty of personal crafts—the ocean's unprecedented fury mostly spent itself on great ships and coastal dwellings, and many small things escaped its attention—but the other boys refuse to join him, pathetically clinging instead to the cliffs and praying against another world-killing tsunami.

Roberto is certain they have seen the last of that. And given what he has lost, he is content to own the Mediterranean.

He's aware that he doesn't, really. The dolphin riders have graciously ignored him on its surface, and he knows their full count must mass in its depths. He toys idly with a net, only vaguely aware that it is filling, and wonders.

As if summoned by his searching thoughts, a half-dozen riders abruptly erupt from the choppy water, cetacean steeds blasting spent air in discordant symphony. Roberto grins at the thrilling spectacle, shouting and waving as they pass closer than ever. But like every time before, they don't even waste a dismissive glance in his direction.

Their ritual chanting is melodic, infectious, and Roberto wishes he could comprehend the words. Do they sing of the pursuit, or perhaps some unrelated legend? Might they mock the folly of Ulysses, who alone of the crew on some nameless ship dared to endure their ancestors' haunting song?

Then their quarry breaches, a magnificent blue-black beast that would be the riders' superior but for their numbers. It sucks in desperate air and then plunges downward again; the riders stay their course. Roberto pictures others flying beneath, driving the fatigued creature back up. The previous one had ultimately surfaced with a new spear in its side, and from there had come a swift end.

This hunt is concluded just as quickly. The accomplished riders drag their quarry under, and soon the sea accrues its customary crimson tint.

Roberto is hypnotized motionless by the bloody waves, but finally snaps to and hoists up his own, less impressive catch.

There's a special tomb Roberto remembers. It may even be underwater now—which would be fitting, since it memorializes the mythological goddess Scylla. The boys had been taken there for a field trip, before the cumulative tears of God's broken promise had violently separated them from everyone else.

His classmates had made light of the experience, concocting crude sexual jokes at the expense of a somber, weathered statue. When the studious Roberto warned them that they risked the creature's wrath, they turned their mockery upon him instead.

There have not been adults to reprimand them for some time. Not since their history teacher died bringing them to safety that terrible day. Surely many grown-ups survived the flooding, but farther inland than the boys care to explore.

They have the saltwater-scoured remnants of Grosseto to themselves.

As on most nights, the boys gather around a large campfire, eating and boasting and teasing, just as they had in better days.

We went into smelly old town today and found more unspoiled clothes, Paulo says, with his mouth full of charred bream.

You had to have climbed pretty high to get above the tsunami waterline.

Yeah 'berto. While you were out ogling dolphin-humping mermaids.

Lay off, Paulo.

But he says he sees Naiads! He even thinks that monster goddess was real. The one with the tomb. What was her name?

Scylla!

Sister of Scrota!

Raucous laughter drags the thoughtspace down to its most guttural level, but a reddened Roberto quiets the group with a soft but urgent voice.

These sirens must have been living in places we couldn't see, before the big flood, he whispers over the crackling fire. Maybe not the open sea itself, but in watery caverns. Maybe the tsunamis ruined their homes, too.

Legend has it we have always been at odds. That our forefathers killed them when they could. Their descendants are bold now, riding in the daytime, because they quit fearing what's left of us.

Roberto huffs out a held breath, sits back, and nervously feeds a twig to the grasping flames. Glowing eyes around him grow wide in a combination of speculation and disbelief. Finally, Paulo speaks again, with just a shade of his usual insolence,

They call sailors to their doom, 'berto. You included.

You trying to talk him out of catching dinner again, Paulo?

This is all bullshit! How does he know anything?

We all studied this stuff, Paulo! Didn't you pay attention?

That's enough.

The boys go mute at Henri's admonition, tossing random items into the fire and elbowing each other. For some time, none dares break the silence. Finally, a younger boy whimpers,

I miss my parents.

Each looks around for the assurance of mutual sorrow, relieved to see it crack the collective surface. For so long they had all buried the emotion beneath forced laughter. Much like the sea had buried…everything.

Me too. Was it…was it our fault they died?

No, Vincenzo. Shit happens.

Henri, what do you think?

I think I miss girls.

Ha! Leave it to Henri. Girls are a pain, but still…

THE DOLPHIN RIDERS

Roberto says the dolphin jockeys are all girls…

Boys cast pointed glances at each other, gaping as if realizing for the first time that the only survivors they know are male. Little Vincenzo breaks the tension,

Oh, geez, Paulo you're sick. No way I'm doing it with a fish!

A familiar chorus of jeers and taunts breaks out again, and like a parental proxy an exasperated Henri cuts in once more,

That's enough!

The riders don't appear to hunt every day, but Roberto ventures out most mornings just the same. Even without the need for fishing, he finds the siren draw irresistible, and idly wonders if he's falling victim to an unwitting Ulysses pact. No deafened crew to save him, either.

While waiting for their arrival, he sifts the sea with his nets, usually hauling in the day's best meals. The other boys are perfectly willing to let Roberto perform this task, and he is happy to have time alone. The perfect arrangement for a habitual daydreamer and a mob of hungry delinquents.

As usual, Roberto has lost track of time, and only realizes he's overdue to return when his tan skin stings at a touch. He curses himself for taking the sun for granted, and pulls up anchor just as riderless dolphins pass in joyous sea-stitching arcs. He pauses and imagines the leaping pod just freed from an underwater corral, azure merfolk whooping after them with hats aloft like drunken *mandrianos*.

He's no longer smiling at the thought when he approaches shore. The boys have gathered there, in contempt of their own fears, and huddle around the latest offering from the tides.

Distracted, Roberto runs aground. When he recovers his balance, he spies a mass of seaweed and flashes of familiar blue between milling legs.

The boys are shouting at each other, oblivious at first to his return.

Stop elbowing me!

Don't poke it, Francis. Don't!

Roberto is going to shit.

Speak of the devil, here he is!

The fisherman secures his boat to a large rock, then trudges wearily through shallow surf and across warm sand for a closer glimpse. He breaks the circle, and his stomach knots.

As feared, the object of attention is a rider body—a mere child—missing a small shark's mouthful from its left side.

You were right, 'berto, you were right! See?

It looks almost…human.

Gills on its neck…

No tail! Feet with flippers…

But look at the head! It's so large!

Poor kid. That's all it is, just an unlucky kid.

A boy…

What if it's a trap? Paulo says they call sailors to their doom!

That's a stupid myth, Vincenzo. Anyway they're probably smarter than us. That's how they kept hidden so long.

Our ancestors saw them, though! Painted them on frescoes. Carved stone statues. Right, 'berto? We all saw.

Before he can answer an anxious Vincenzo, the council arrives. Five scowling, well-fed boys who had moved easily into the power vacuum left by absent adults. The others instinctively part before them, clearing a view of the tragedy, eager for the council's assessment.

What do you guys think? Henri? Do we bury it?

Funeral pyre, like the Vikings.

It's a mermaid, you idiot, not a goddamn Viking!

Merman, fool!

Shut up, all of you.

Henri's voice carries the most authority, and the rest tend to defer accordingly. He had been a local track and football star, and an exceptional student. Even before the Earth went haywire, Henri had earned everyone's respect.

Roberto knows the lore on them, so we'll let him decide.

Good idea, Henri!

None want responsibility for this burden, and relieved eyes turn expectantly to the assignee. Roberto winces at the sudden uninvited thought of his missing parents, and how he wishes he could have some sort of closure for them. How they would surely want the same.

It's not ours to decide, he eventually says. This is someone's child. They should have a say.

So what the hell, haul it out and just dump it in the sea? Jesus, 'berto.

Nothing so crude, Paulo. We need to make contact. See that the sharks don't get to finish their work.

But you say the sirens ignore you!

A thoughtful Roberto pauses to seize their full attention.

They probably won't ignore all of us.

The boys are still fearful. Most feel no inclination to venture onto water, no matter how calm. Not after earthquakes and tsunamis and floodwaters that linger. Not after living through all hell breaking loose, and losing everything just months ago.

They shiver, despite the August air, as the boats are prepared. Even valiant Roberto knows trepidation.

He lost the debate on carriage. So the lifeless young rider is lashed to the fore-mast of the biggest boat, plainly visible to its people but disrespectfully displayed.

They set out, seven tiny boats, following Roberto's practiced lead.

The deep waters lie still this day, as if they, too, mourn so wrong a loss. Even so, boats bump each other often. Some boys dare each other to leap from deck to deck. Some do.

To everyone's astonishment, the dolphin riders soon emerge.

They immediately surround the fleet, steadily circling it without acknowledging the ersatz sailors. Spears held perfectly upright, more in solemn ceremony than threat. The boys are in awe, and unnerved.

How are they here so fast?

Maybe a scout saw us approach, spied the body.

Maybe.

They can't think we did it!

Jesus, Paulo, we're obviously not sharks.

But we demanded proof, and the sea answered!

Coincidence. That's all. Hush.

Henri and a couple of others wrestle the dead rider-child down, gently, reverently. At this moment the lead rider halts the procession, and nudges her mount toward the main boat. With abnormally large eyes she stares hard at Henri, one leader to another, and then slowly sweeps her spear to finally point at Roberto.

Roberto comprehends, and instructs Vincenzo to take charge of his craft before he jumps up to the bigger boat's lip. A few boys assist him aboard.

You're the one they know, Henri says, nodding as Roberto helps him lug the victim to port. They stand there, dumb and unsure, until the lead siren also nods. Two of her companions slip forward, and reach up to relieve the boys of their burden. The leader surprises them with a single word of their own.

Grazi.

And then they are gone, swallowed once more by the effervescent sea.

For some time, none speak. Then Paulo, of all boys, utters something uncharacteristically kind.

You did good, Roberto. This was the right choice.

What now, though? Are they our friends?

Nah, Vincenzo, not that easily.

THE DOLPHIN RIDERS

But they can't blame us for anything! We're trying to do good! Tell them next time, 'berto. Please tell them.

Roberto empathizes with the anguish in young Vincenzo's voice—the yearning for redemption, the need for validation after the very planet had unfairly punished them. Who could take the place of vanished parents, assure these lost boys that they would be okay?

It can never be the dolphin riders, Roberto knows, no matter how much they might wish it.

He peers South across the vast Mediterranean, squinting against the sun on its surface. The weight of civilized history sags his strong shoulders. The final fragment of a poem he'd memorized springs to mind, Tennyson's tale of doomed Ulysses. Roberto mouths the passage:

Tho' much is taken, much abides; and tho'
We are not now that strength which in old days
Moved earth and heaven, that which we are, we are;
One equal temper of heroic hearts,
Made weak by time and fate, but strong in will
To strive, to seek, to find, and not to yield.

He shudders as the jagged, timeworn words saw through sunburnt flesh and bone, realizing they appeal to Man and Siren alike. Roberto understands now that these fretful boys have inherited not just a drowned Earth, but also the long, dark-stained legacy of sins committed upon it.

There's nothing to tell, he finally sighs aloud.

Just what steps we choose going forward.

Is This Seat Taken
Michael Leonberger

I feel like an ant.

Just smaller than nothing. Like some great skeletal crustacean swallowed me whole. Didn't even think about it, just sucked me up and ruined my tiny, miserable life.

When I look up, the ceiling's like a rib cage. Grooved and checkered, an alien rib cage to be sure, but a rib cage all the same.

Which means…yep, I'm living inside of it. In the stomach. In the damn thing's guts.

Then I hear the squeal of wheels on metal tracks. See headlights cutting through the dark tunnels, like greasy yellow orbs smeared on the windshields of my glasses. Then it rumbles forth. The Metro train, and I climb on it with all the other little, sweaty ants who got stuck in the guts of Washington, D.C. Standing so close, the shirt stuck to my sweaty back, other peoples' musks invading my nostrils, everyone looking down, looking at the lower parts of legs and feet crammed into sweaty shoes…

When I see her legs. What color—dark tan accentuated by fine nylon. The slope, the calves, the knees, the way the skin bends around the knees. Soft little lines, too soft-looking to be even correctly called dimples.

And above the knees…well I don't know what's above the knees. My eyes never get that high.

The train stops. The doors peel apart, and she disappears like a drone in a swarm of bees. Just gone, and I watch her walk away. I see she's got blond hair, coming straight down to the small of her back. I imagine her face. Imagine it's honeysuckle and summertime and muscadine grapes. Then the doors slam shut, the train lurches forward, and I crawl my way to work.

Work is garbage. Entry-level analysis for some big contracting company. You know the one. We make bombs. Really, really big bombs, and then we obliterate small cities you've never heard of, in places you would never go.

I'm too old to do this kind of work. To live off of an entry-level salary.

Then I think, *No one is ever too old to get killed by one of our bombs.* Touche.

I'm clever like that.

Sometimes I think about those bombs while I'm standing in the guts of the Metro.

One of two things.

Either A) the skeletal remains of this great beast I'm standing in, this "Metro-Saurus," must have been taken out by one of our bombs. An ancient god we killed and repurposed for underground transportation.

Only that's an insane thought.

Then there's B) someone else got their hands on one of our bombs, dropped it on D.C., and I'll be stuck down in the Metro forever.

I think that especially when the line is all backed up, when we're crawling at five miles an hour through the darkened arteries. I think that when I'm staring out the window, into the black slate that greets me like a darkly tinted mirror.

I see my reflection—the divots of my skull where my eyes supposedly are, the frenetic spray of hair on top of my head (thinning, though, thinning all the time), and think, *This is it. This is my life. When the bomb goes off, of course I'll be down here. Me and the other ants. Up to us to start over.*

Us? The nightmarish assistants and interns and hungry college grads? Left to re-imagine the world?

Please. If the rest of these schmucks are anything like me, it'll be the petty things that gain prominence—Snickers bars will come out of your tap instead of water. You're welcome.

Then she catches my eye again: her legs, in the reflection behind me. Crossed over the knees, but the skin just as smooth. I rake my eyes over her body; her head is turned away from me. Her hair looks more brunette than blond in the Metro window, but I can't tell for sure if it's the same woman.

Only thing I can tell is that I'm drawn to her. She fires up my imagination. I think of how great it would be to go home with her, think even about following her for one insane moment, when the Metro stops and she stands to get off. Same stop.

Then the doors close, and she is gone, and all I have left of her is the residue in my mind. A pretty plant that I try in vain to water with my daydreams.

A pretty plant that's already wilted by the time the Metro stops near the commuter lot. I crawl my way to my mini-van and drive home to my wife.

I pick up the kid from daycare first.

There's a serial killer who's been plucking off people down in the Metro.

They find the bodies—men and women alike. Skeletons with strips of flesh hanging off. Bitten up, carved apart, like the work of hungry animals. Faces twisted into impossible screams. They find them on the walkways in the dark of the tunnels that line the tracks. Sometimes beneath escalators that are out of commission. One even sitting on a bench at Gallery Place, its hands politely folded in its lap, its skull draped in coils of skin. Eyes gone, mouth gaping open in

IS THIS SEAT TAKEN?

horror.

Yuck, I tell ya.

I read about the first one while I was on the Metro. Not frightening then—I just thought it was an accident, albeit a horrific one. Maybe a crime of passion—an awful crime, but only directed at one person for a single reason, usually petty and trite and entirely not threatening to the rest of us.

Then another…and another…and suddenly, I'm sitting at the kitchen table, little Bobbi slamming her spoon onto the tray of her high chair, flinging baby gloop across the room, and Margo—Margo's staring at me with eyes that are stressed and frenetic, trembling in her head.

Saying, "Franklin. Franklin, do you need to ride in on the Metro every day? Couldn't you drive? Uber?"

That kills me. Like I'm made of money. A human ATM, where that cash is actually blood, and my wife has no idea.

My wife…

I think of the woman again. Her soft legs.

I look at my wife. So stressed. Like pushing a human through her body did something to her—messed her up. And look…I mean, I know it did. I'm not blind to that. She's got a bottle of pain killers she keeps in her sock drawer that she didn't need before Bobbi, and I'm not blind to that, either.

I'm also not so insensitive I would ever say that to her, but I got eyes, I got a brain, and…it's just a shame, isn't it?

No. You know, that's not right. That's my own stress talking. It's just Bobbi never stops crying, and we haven't slept in months, and my job, God dammit, my job is the worst.

And the Metro…

I'm riding the Metro right now, thinking about dead bodies, almost hoping I'll see one. That would change things. Seeing a flayed body on the side of the tracks, trying to hitch a ride. Thumbs up, ya filthy bum.

God, this isn't me. What's happening to me? I'm just so tired, and I'm looking around now, in vain, trying to see that woman.

'Cuz I'd like to meet her. Hide my wedding band, maybe, and just see. Just see what mighta happened if I were still single.

I just want a peek. Into a life I maybe could have had.

I don't want that life. Wouldn't trade Bobbi and Margo for anything.

But I'd like to see.

She isn't on today. At least, not on this car. But these trains are huge, and when we drive by her stop, I see her. At least, I think I do. The curve of those legs.

The short hair. I'd like to see her face, is all.

Use it like canvas. Dream on it, like my imagination's paint.

I used to paint. Way back, when I was a younger man.

And I guess I still could, but I don't have the time.

Barely have time to find my stupid van.

She gets on, and I don't even see her at first. I'm fumbling with my crooked tie like a junkie from a fifties crime novel, tightening it around my neck, when poof: there she is.

Only this time she's looking right at me, and I could swear she's smiling. It's startling. Electric. I immediately drop my eyes, stare at my shoes, feeling it. Feeling that maybe she's still staring at me as she sits down—in the seat across from mine—and I'm so giddy I could cry out. Just little tingles all over. I turn my head, armed with the plan to smoothly slide my eyes from her toes to the ceiling. Just momentarily (and accidentally) catching her face in my line of sight, so it won't look as though I'm staring.

But I'll savor it. Take a snapshot—click!—of her body in my head, and pour over the details for hours.

But she's already turned her head away, toward the window. So I stop, stare for a moment, look at her hands, then her calves, the round balls of her feet in her heels, her ankles. No nylons today. She looks so healthy. Almost shines.

Then it occurs to me (and I'm embarrassed to admit this, how stupid can one person be?) that she can see me in the reflection of the window she's staring at. My head, somewhere behind her. Watching her. Staring. I immediately look away, to my hands—literally looking at my hands instead of staring at her.

When the train rolls to a stop and she stands to go, I make my decision—I'm going to follow her.

I wait two, maybe three seconds. Then stand up casually. Follow her.

My God, what a thrill. Watching her walk from behind. Witnessing the fantastic things her body does. And her not knowing I'm there—why, in my imagination, we're living a whole life together. My new wife, walking just slightly ahead of me…and then I think, with glee, what if this is how it starts?

I was following this girl…creepily following this girl, I must admit, on one of the weeks that that serial killer terrorized the D.C. Metro system, and then we bumped into each other, and…bam! We hit it off, she became my wife, and that's how I met your mother, boys and girls.

Never mind your step-sister, Bobbi.

I follow her onto a connecting platform, keeping a good distance (and a healthy throng of people) between us. I wait until she gets on a new train and sits down, then I go and sit farther down the aisle. Far enough so it isn't weird. I turn my head to the window. Watch her in the reflection.

She's looking at her own window.

And maybe…well, maybe she's watching my reflection, too.

I feel momentarily romantic when a thought explodes in my brain: why, maybe it's actually her that's been following me!

That's a thought. After all, I only just started to notice her, but maybe she's been stalking me for a long time.

Maybe she's been watching me in her glass. And today she's frightened because I've broken my usual pattern! Yes, suddenly the tables have turned and I'm following her!

Or maybe she's only noticing me now and thinks that I'm the serial killer. Another thought. An idea that flushes me with power. I tremble. I wonder if I frighten her. If she sees me, knows I'm following her, but assumes she's just being paranoid. Can't bring herself to say anything to me. Why, I could probably follow her for a long time, allowing that paranoia to build inside of her, before she'd finally confront me.

She'd say, "Are you following me?"

And then I'd tell her, "What, miss? Oh, I work in D.C. My job has me go all over the city, on the Metro. I didn't even realize we were on the same trains, but now that you mention it...why, madame, maybe it is you who are following me!"

I'd say all that. I'd say madame.

I mean, and it's possible...maybe she *is* following me.

Maybe she's the Metro serial killer. How about that?

Only that's silly. She's...too pretty? She doesn't look strong. Surely she couldn't wrestle anyone to their death, and then...what, skin their corpse?

I watch her until she gets off. Then follow her through the darkness, up the escalator, and into the white light of the city. Follow her down the street, until she finally ducks into a coffee shop.

I stroll slowly by the window. Watch her bring a steaming cup of coffee to the softest, most maddening pair of lips I've ever seen. She has her eyes glued to the insides of a book—something about Greek mythology—before she scrapes them away, and they meet mine for just an instant. I blush, jerk my head away, hail a cab.

My future wife.

I just wish she hadn't seen me there, just then. At that moment.

Hadn't met me before we were ready to be introduced.

IS THIS SEAT TAKEN?

Dinner kills me.

Some slow, interminable torture that only I am subject to.

My wife and child are there...but they aren't sufferers, no, they are the inquisitors. Twisting the gears on the rack so that my spirit stretches, so that it almost breaks!

The baby, crying, hurling food. The wife, fretting. "Is the Metro safe? Is it?"

God. Safer than driving, I tell her. You know how many fools die every morning? Cars twisted over each other because some jock strap was trying to merge illegally on the Beltway?

Metro...sure, a couple of old suckers got killed, and now everyone is terrified, but statistically? Statistically...

"But all the bodies..."

And what I can't tell her (and what is most assuredly true) is that there is only one body I care about right now. It isn't hers, unfortunately. We don't even sleep near each other on the bed anymore.

No, the body belongs to the girl on Metro. The woman, my future wife. And I'd risk it, I tell ya. Risk that shadowy serial killer, just to get a glimpse of her.

This isn't the Beltway snipers, dear.

And besides, it's not like I'm ever riding alone.

The wipers slide the rain from my windshield with a rubbery snarl.

I'm flipping through the radio, drinking my coffee, staring at an army of red brake lights ahead. Thinking they look like bleeding puncture wounds drizzled along the glass, when I hear her voice.

"Hello, out there," she says from the speakers. I almost spill my coffee.

It's her. I know it. I know it instantly.

How do I know? I've never heard her talk. Sure, that's true, but this voice…the timber, the cords, the way the tones blend together. This voice, this immaculate, heavenly instrument of the angels can only belong to one person.

And if it doesn't belong to her? It doesn't really matter, because it makes me feel the same. Both women make me feel special.

"You been stalking me, stranger?" she says. Her voice cashmere. Silk, draped over my face. I turn up the volume. A saxophone plays somewhere in the background, noodling some sexy concoction of notes that is altogether cheap compared to her voice.

Her voice.

"I see you in the morning. See your eyes. See your mouth, and I just want to talk to you," she says, a little girl's whine buried smartly in a dominant adult woman's vocals. "And maybe after we talk, we could do other things. With our mouths."

Jesus. I quickly save the station on my presets. I tremble as I park, because I don't want to stop listening. But I don't want to be late.

Only she's signing off.

"This is Angelica, for the morning hour. For all you lonely hearts out there, too afraid to approach…today is your day," she says. "Today is your day. Take your dreams by the hand. Walk across the aisle. Say hello. Today is the day you change the rest of your life."

Then her voice is drowned out by the prettiest song I've ever heard. Something instrumental, altogether foreign to me, instruments I don't understand and can't comprehend, and they all blur together in a sonic powerhouse that just knocks me out. I'm telling you, an uppercut to my ears.

I feel like crying, and only when it's done, and only when I'm sure this DJ isn't coming back, I grab my coffee and my briefcase and I head towards the turnstile.

I hurry, too. I don't want to miss her on the train.

IS THIS SEAT TAKEN?

She's looking at me. I'm sure of it. Through the reflection of her glass.

How could she not be? Isn't it insane, that we continually end up on the same car? Across from each other? Isn't it fate?

And I want to take the chance. To take my fate by the hand, to walk across the aisle, to say hello…

Only what if she isn't the girl from the radio? Angelica? My God, now that I'm not listening to it, it seems insane, that this woman should be the same person. Otherwise, why wouldn't she come across the aisle and say hello to me? This is nutty, I should just go over there, should just talk to her…

When I notice the other pair of eyes. And this guy…well, I guess I've seen this guy before, too.

Sitting three rows back, across the aisle. On her side.

He's watching her, too. Only he's not even using the damn window, like normal, self-respecting stalkers do—he's staring right at her. Mouth hanging open.

Take a picture, buddy. That's my wife you're staring at.

My future wife, but who's counting? Those endless days between now and our eventual wedding…well, that's just a number, like age. Who cares?

When it's her stop, she stands, presses her skirt (the smallest gesture, but it's so cute, and I find myself weirdly jealous of her, that she gets to touch her own legs). She walks toward the door. I wait a beat, but when I stand, he's already stood and is walking out the door after her.

So now we're like a procession of elephants. He's hanging onto her so tight I don't know how she can't notice him, and I'm practically speed-walking to keep up with him, and if anyone was watching they'd think we were a family, probably from out of town. Tourists, speed-walking together so that we don't miss the next train.

And then I think: God, why is she going so fast? She wasn't the other day. Only the other day it was just me...

She's trying to get away from him.

She makes it to the escalator and ascends, two steps at a time, and I'm so caught up in her that I almost careen into him.

He's stopped at the bottom, watching her go up.

And dammit, if I don't stop with him, because suddenly it feels wrong, wrong to run past him to catch up with her. No, it's best to let her go, now.

This time.

This guy. I think of him all day at work. I get nothing done, yet I feel like I'm working. That's the power this guy has over me.

I'm not doodling, which is what I normally do when I'm bored—cartoons of explosions, of bombs, of sad cartoon families running with their heads on fire.

No, those goofy, absent expressions are gone. I'm not friendly today, haven't been since this started, probably. People don't like me here, I realize. They avoid me.

Maybe they can smell it on me. The desperation. I'm sick with it.

I want her, but so does this guy. Who is he?

Guy like that, following a lonely girl through the Metro. Guy like that...

"So far, no lead on the killer," someone's saying near my cubicle. The wet, swallowing sound of the water cooler.

No lead. What kind of a man follows a helpless, lonely girl down into the Metro?

Well, me, I guess.

But also the other kind. The kind of man that leaves dead bodies on benches. The kind that doesn't use the reflection in the window to voyeuristically stalk his prey. The kind that they haven't gotten a lead

IS THIS SEAT TAKEN?

on.

But I've got a lead on him.

Oh, yeah. Gotcha, buddy.

I've found my serial killer and he's trying to take my woman.

Then, a thought lights me up: What if he's already got her? I saw him follow her toward the steps. What if he's still following her? What if he's grabbed her into some alley? Scooped out her intestines with a knife?

No. It couldn't have happened already. That's not our destiny. Besides, I'd feel it, wouldn't I? In my belly. Wouldn't I?

Don't you feel it inside if something bad happens to someone you love?

And I feel nothing.

Nothing at all.

No, he hasn't gotten her yet.

And I'm not gonna let him. No way, no how.

No, she's all mine, buddy.

Find your own.

I'm mad, shaking all over. I go to the bathroom, take an aspirin, almost drop it down the sink. I'm sweating near my temples, and not because it's hot.

Because this is such a waste of time. This building, my coworkers. And then…Christ no, at the end of the day, my family. With their little dreams. They're a throughway from this very moment to the end of my life and, thanks to them, I can see that every day will be exactly the same.

But not with this woman. I'm on the precipice of the greatest moment of my life, because I'm going to save her.

My fingers tremble. I think about calling the hotline for information on the Metro serial killer.

I don't have any information. Heroes don't just have information. Action. That's what separates them.

I leave work early. I get inside the Metro, get to her stop, then sit on the bench, watch trains pass and wait for her. And dammit if I don't see him first.

It's an hour and a half after I arrived. He walks down the stairs, hands jammed in his jeans pockets. Looking casual, checking his watch, checking his phone, sitting three benches away. Even reclining, for God's sakes.

Three benches. Like he doesn't know.

Doesn't he? Maybe he didn't see me this morning. Maybe he didn't see me because he was so caught up in her. But how could he get away with it? Murder? So often, so successfully, if he was really so unobservant?

Unless I'm the one who's unobservant. Unless I've walked right into his trap.

God, if that's what this is, and if I should die tonight…I want to tell my wife…

I want to tell my wife…

Nothing, really.

My coldness towards her? My distance? Wasn't me. I'd like her to know that. It isn't how I am. It's what she's turned me into—what she's pulled out of me. Killers, you see…they don't just get you with knives, or with guns.

Sometimes they do it real slow. In your home.

I guess I never had the guts to tell her that in person.

Here comes the train.

We sit, three blind mice. Or two blind mice, and one really attractive mouse who doesn't notice the other two…Making her the blind mouse, right? One blind mouse?

IS THIS SEAT TAKEN?

This game is no fun. Just three of us, and I'm sure we're all watching each other. Me, with the helpful reflection of the window. This other guy, still watching, mouth open.

When he makes his move my heart's fluttering. I'm not sure what would be worse: if he approached her with a knife and stabbed her to death, or if he just sat down next to her and started talking. He does the latter.

"Hi," he says, holding on to the railing for support, his body jiggling along with the moving train. "Is this seat taken?"

She turns. I see her face in full. A better view than I've ever gotten. She's why men go to war, okay? She's why they cooked up the word, "nostalgia". What makes the poets write, the only reason you'd ever really miss anything. That's her.

"No," she says, and I can't hear her voice enough to know—to really know—if it's her on the radio. Only it has to be. Or maybe they're sisters.

(Or I'm losing it, God, maybe I'm just losing it, and I can't go home one more night to Margo, I just can't.)

They seem to be getting on well, damn him. Laughing, only he's stammering too, and I can tell from his body language he's nervous. His legs are twitching, like he's playing an invisible drum pedal only he can see, to a beat only he can hear.

And I'm nervous, too. I wish I could say I was nervous that he might kill her, that he's the Metro serial killer, but I'm more worried that he won't stop talking to her, that he'll whisk her away, into his life. Fold her into his dreams, make her the mother of his children.

Dammit, that's my wife! I'm thinking, when my phone rings. My actual wife. I ignore it.

The train rolls to a stop...her stop! And they get off together, walking closely.

She isn't nervous, hasn't been this whole time. Never shakes, barely blinks, doesn't look away from him. Smiles calmly. She's never looked lovelier, no one's ever looked lovelier.

But she's also vulnerable, you understand? Getting off at this stop…*her stop*!…with this stranger, this man who she's only just met, who I know has been stalking her. I know! How can I tell her? How I can tell her without revealing myself to be just as crazy as he is?

That makes it my obligation, my duty, to follow them.

And I do. At a healthy distance. I follow them through the turnstile, up the escalator, where the air is thin. I follow them as they walk farther and farther away from civilization, the sounds of the Metro train rocketing down the tracks receding into the background. There's an area under construction. They navigate it, and I hear his nervous laugh, and I lose them down an empty side street.

Jesus, they're gone, completely gone! This building has only one door. One rust-colored door, with graffiti on it, with broken glass on the sidewalk outside. An unrolled, used condom lying in the brown, dead grass is the only natural part of God's earth I can see.

Christ, you'd think a bomb really had gone off. That's how quiet and desolate it is. I feel like I stepped out of my life and into some future apocalypse, and I suppose I'm a little proud that I did it for love.

This place…this stretch of road…is it pretentious of me to suggest it smells like death? Because it does. And I don't hear them. I don't see them.

I walk down the length of the building. Look left, right. See nothing but construction and thinning, brown grass. I can't hear the Metro so well from here, and I certainly don't hear any people. The skeletal corpses of buildings that haven't been constructed yet slouch around me. Maybe they pity me—surely they know where she went.

That door. She must have gone through that door.

An old place. Faded word "Demeter" in the bricks above it.

I nervously put my ear against the door. I don't hear anything, but he probably pushed her inside. He probably led her here, to this door, because this is where he does it. And then tonight, when he's all done, he'll drag the body back to the Metro tracks, and I'll never see

IS THIS SEAT TAKEN?

her again…

Only maybe it isn't too late. Why, if I can just get inside now, and if I can save her…

It occurs to me that maybe he isn't killing her. That maybe they picked this spot to do something neither one of them could have done at home. The kinds of things I'd like to do with this woman, that I certainly can't do at home.

But it occurs to me too late. After I've already tried the handle (locked). After I've already knocked, because my heart is jack hammering.

I try the handle again. Locked, but maybe not closed properly. I shoulder the door. It groans, sliding open slowly, the bottom of the door scraping against the concrete.

A gutted, bombed-out desolation greets me. A building stripped of its inside lining. Just concrete floor. Cinder blocks. Punched out plaster. The twisting, red fingers of rebar, and several holes in the ground. Square holes. Deep enough to hide a body?

I walk through the wreckage, carefully, eyes peeled. It's dark in here. I look into the first hole. Pull out my phone for light. Don't see anything. I try the second hole. Still dark.

But I feel something. As though someone is watching me.

A feeling of terror grips me so powerfully that my concern for the girl all but vanishes. With my phone providing the smallest of lights, the shadows seem to grow longer, to twist and move all on their own, and I swear I see eyes in the dark, watching me before I spin around and spray my phone's light in that direction.

But my phone is running out of battery.

There's an awful vibrating sound, and I realize my wife is calling me. I curse her momentarily, as though maybe whatever's in here with me couldn't see me in the dark, spinning around with my lit-up phone, only now that the phone has made a noise, they know I'm here. For a second, I feel as though I might die. I hurry out of the building, close the door behind me, and lean up against the brick, relaxing, catching my breath.

I call my wife back. She wants to know what I want for dinner.

I tell her I don't care and hang up.

I choke down dinner, bulldoze through inane conversation, take two Xanax, and try to sleep.

When the drugs start to work, and my thoughts smooth themselves out, I swear I can hear her, in my head. The voice from radio. Angelica, whose body I hope isn't currently being mutilated and left on the tracks.

I hear her voice, and it is as though she is saying my name, slowly, calmly, under her breath. Only it isn't in my head at all.

It's such a powerful sensation, my imagination suddenly so vivid, that I wonder if it was Xanax I took at all. Because it sounds like she's here, in the room. Right now.

No, not in the room…outside. I sit up in bed. My wife is asleep, oblivious to the sound. Just one word, my name, stretched out along the hum of the a/c.

I stand up, walk toward the window, and almost expect to see her outside, in the dark. Only I see nothing but shadows. Shadows, and the vaguest hint of my reflection.

Someone standing behind me. I turn, and it's my wife.

"What's wrong, honey?" she wants to know, but I can't tell her.

"Go back to sleep."

We aren't so intimate anymore.

IS THIS SEAT TAKEN?

In the car, I flip to the news. I don't think I've slept. My body feels all dried out and coffee pumps through my veins where there used to be blood.

There is no news, only traffic reports. Commercials. More traffic.

I remember my preset, hurry to it, and I hear her voice. Angelica. She sounds so good I could cry.

"I came to you," she says, her voice enfolding me with the intimacy of flesh. It gives me chills. Reminds me of home, whatever that means, only I tell you it's true. "I came to you, presented myself to you. Waited for you. You were there, I know you were there. I would have held you, honey, but you didn't come.

"I know you've been watching me," she says. "I like it. I like to be watched, because I watch you, too. I want you to come talk to me. Talk to me today, because I'm so shy. I need you, today, to take your fate by the hand. Come to me. Talk to me. Let me hold you. Let me take you away."

Then her voice once more gives way to music, the kind of music I cannot describe, but it reduces me to tears. A quivering mess, collecting tears and snot on my sleeves. She's reminded me of all the things I've ever wanted, of all the things I'd never gotten. And those dreams sting now, because of their cruelty, because they had the damned nerve to give me expectations. Children shouldn't dream, I realize. It rots them from the inside out, until they become adults, until they become me. I think of Bobbi, how we're rotting her, aren't we? I feel terrifically small. But I feel as though the voice singing through the radio understands.

"Talk to me," she says. "Take me away. Take your fate by the hand."

I will. Today is the day. Today is the day my whole world changes.

I park. Collect myself. Apply eye drops and a dab of cologne that I keep in the glove compartment, just in case. Just in case.

It's warm. Smells warmer than I'd like, but it's a hot day. I do what I can.

I leave my car, and walk past the newspaper stand, and my heart drops.

I slide a quarter in, read the story with trembling hands.

Another body found. So badly mutilated they can't identify the sex.

Must have died last night. Wounds post-mortem. Left on the tracks. Expect delays.

I think of her.

I know she's gone.

It breaks my heart into an incalculable number of pieces, all of them strung out along a line of shock and horror and disgust and regret that I keep carefully balled up inside, where none of the other commuters can see it.

I think of my wife. Can our relationship rise up from this? Like a phoenix, from the ashes and the blood of this girl's murder? Why, I never actually did anything. It was all mental, all of it, sandwiched neatly inside of my brain, where my wife could never see, where no one could ever see.

And when I realize that one of the commuters is actually the girl, the recently murdered girl, not dead, sitting across from me on the Metro. I almost cry. I shake as I grip the bar on the top of the seat in front of me, and I hope she can't see it. This moment, it's like one of those dreams I'd talked about, made flesh. A childhood dream come true, because here she is: someone who should be dead, but isn't. She's very much alive. Glowing, almost, as though she's even younger today than she was when I'd seen her yesterday.

Angelica.

I don't wait. I don't look to see if the other guy is around, don't even care.

IS THIS SEAT TAKEN?

I walk up to her, fidgeting with my wedding ring, dumping it in my pocket.

"Hi," I say. "Is this seat taken?"

She turns her head from the window to me, a smile already on her lips. Cool, passionate eyes that make my knees wobble. Dusty eye shadow. Cute nose. I want to bite her face off and chew it and I can't explain.

"Please let me sit," I almost say, but don't. Only I need to, because otherwise my knees will give out. I'll fall to the floor, right here.

"No. Please sit," she says, and I know it's her. The woman from the radio. Angelica. At least I think I know. The way her voice grabs me. Hums along in my skin, in my ears.

"I saw you earlier..." I say, foolishly, giving away my whole hand.

(How do you do this, though? How do you talk to new people?)

Only she interrupts.

"I did, too," she says. Her hand touches mine. My nerves tingle and coil with delight, all throughout my body. The pads of her fingertips are as soft as I imagined. "I've been waiting for you to talk to me."

"Angelica," I say. I lean in. I want to kiss her, only she catches my lips with her finger.

"Not here," she says. "Tonight." She leans over, whispers an address in my ear. Then it's her stop.

She stands to go. I'm jelly, my whole body weak. She winks at me.

"Go to work," she says. "Don't follow me. Not yet."

Then she's gone.

I go to work, but my body's numb. I go through the motions. It isn't torture, it's sort of like being dead, maybe. A ghost, floating over your past life.

Tonight, everything changes.

Tonight, I'll take my fate by the hand.

The end of the day doesn't come soon enough.

My wife calls, but I ignore the phone. She should be used to that by now.

I get off at the same spot the girl had gotten off yesterday. With that man.

I walk the cracked sidewalks. The familiar path, past the construction sites, the skeletons of Earth-bound gods, destroyed perhaps by our bombs. That's how it looks, and I find it alarming how much destruction and construction look the same.

I'm making a note of that because I might write a book about it, someday. About how hopelessly destroyed my life looked, and then I met her. Angelica.

I open the door, the same door, the address she's given me.

I stand in the dark, and I wait. I'm not afraid. No, not today. I'm excited.

Waiting. Eagerly anticipating every motion in the dark, every sound. Mostly insects, skittering around. By my feet.

Mice, perhaps.

It is sort of scary in here, I suppose. Doesn't smell the best.

But she picked this spot. She'll meet me here.

I wonder, briefly, irrationally, if I should take off my clothes while I wait.

Only maybe I've misinterpreted the nature of this visit. Maybe that isn't what she wants at all.

But why would she pick here, then?

God, it smells. Musty. Reeks, like something is dead.

Like someone is dead.

And then I know.

There's someone else in here with me. Her? Whoever it is, they won't come toward me. I can see them, though. Their outline. In the dark. Shuffling. High pitched noises. Like laughing. Giggling.

A soft voice singing. Or is it just some wind caught in here? A

IS THIS SEAT TAKEN?

stale, dying breeze, and it sounds like my name, all the time, floating around me like poisonous mist.

I'm too afraid to call out. My voice is so small, but they might still hear me.

Whoever is in this room with me.

My phone's out of battery. Out of light. I can't shine it over in the other person's direction. Margo can't call. The door is so far away.

Eyes, like how I saw eyes in the dark last night. Gazing at me.

It can't be her. Those teeth. My God, something's happened to her teeth.

They're growing. Jagged. Her face…its face. Ruptured. Split, straight through, where her teeth are growing.

Giggling, laughing. Singing?

How many teeth?

She's coming closer to me. Smelling me.

Circling me, for what seems like eternity, and I can't run. Too terrified to run.

Closer. She sees me and I can barely see her.

Is she human at all? Maybe it isn't her. Maybe I'm trapped in here with some animal. A wild animal. A feral thing.

Maybe someone will open the door. Angelica? The police. Someone, please.

Please, open the door?

Her teeth. That blood.

Closer.

Margo. God, Margo. Kiss Margo, I think I was wrong.

God, kiss Margo, kiss Bobbi.

That smell. His blood, the man from last night, it's all clear.

I won't be coming home. I've made a terrible mistake.

Then she has me in her arms. Every inch of her naked body as perfect and sculpted as any Greek statue, blood rolling over her curves. My blood. Her face ruptured and contorted and shot through with teeth, her eyes crimson, shimmering orbs.

"Come," she's singing. Chanting. "Come, come…" Pressing her fingertips into my chest, her nails drilling past skin and punching through bone, tracing the organs they find. I feel light and sick as she traces my beating heart with a perfectly manicured fingernail, when my ear drums shatter from a whooshing sound. Her shoulder bones extend and unfold into the scaffolding for wings, draped with loose flesh, like a squishy, pale membrane. Those wings flap, *whooosh*, they beat against the ground, *whooosh, whoosh*, and she howls and laughs with delight, stomping perfect bare feet into dirty puddles.

Then she's lifting me. Crashing through the jagged glass of a previously demolished window. Taking me higher and higher, into the night, and I think, disapprovingly, how ugly the city has always looked to me. It looks ugly from here, too, lit up and spread out, like a cheap, gaudy lover.

But maybe it's just me. Reflected back. All bad Metro glass and rotten dreams and pouchy, horrible ambition.

Her teeth trace the top of my head. Her skin practically melts my skin, but I am no longer afraid. Because most people aren't afraid when they die, I figure. They're just sad.

Because, God? I think I've made a mistake. Tons of 'em.

I can't see my home from this high up, you know? They all look the same to me.

Hundreds of homes, hundreds of broken hearts, the same sad, mundane story.

I was never special.

Only special to one sad, wildly naïve woman. Naïve enough to make a baby with me.

And now, here I am, doing that thing only imbeciles do.

Dying in someone else's arms.

I'm not even one hundred percent sure I feel bad enough about it to care.

I'm not crying. Not screaming. Only feeling dizzy. Sick.

Sick even before she plunges back toward the ground with me in

IS THIS SEAT TAKEN?

her arms, toward the top of a Metro train that is dragging its body across the ground.

We land on the top, wind pulling tears out of my eyes. She hunches over me, and I realize those fleshy wings have feathers, don't they?

And she's smiling at me, those awful teeth stretched out from lovely, thick lips. Gazing at me from eyes of fire, licked by strands of perfect black hair, her perfect naked body panting and winged and struck with slashes of blood.

And the nightmarish, crooked truth is this: I still kind of think I'm in love.

Even as she starts eating me alive.

NAUTILUS
V.F. LeSann

(20,000 Light Years Above the Sea)

"Are you getting this? I can hear them now. The equipment's going nuts. Everything's off the charts. Goddamn, I hope you're getting this! It's what we needed. What we've been looking for. Damn cold in here, but we need to keep going. I don't know what Ericson's done to the life support…[Indiscernible due to audio static]…just me. They're in the stars. Control? Are you getting any of this? They're swimming in the stars."

Cpt. Lee Tran, in the final audio transmission of the research vessel *Argonaut*

As my creator Dr. Williamson used to say, 'Sadly, Nautilus, research vessels just aren't as sexy as warships'.

We lacked the state-of-the-art technology standard on vessels constantly engaged in interplanetary warfare, and at the present moment I would have exchanged my entire DNA database of Gaian fauna for a piloting system that could match my navigation calculations.

The shockwave from the interstellar maelstrom reached out like a leviathan's tentacle and hit me broadside. A shudder rolled through my hull, sending the entire vessel into a sideways lurch, and I struggled to recalibrate as the stars spun around me.

With dwindling alternatives, I let momentum have its way and threw my concentration into awakening the crew nestled safely within the medical bay.

The tempest had struck without warning, and by the time my

sensors finally blared of the impending threat, I was already engine-deep in the wake, with no chance of steering myself out.

Once my humanoid avatar engaged, I left the holding station I fondly called a cocoon and raced next door to the medical bay to greet the awakening crew.

The first cryostasis chamber hissed open in time with my entrance. The next four decompressed in rapid succession, each signifying a crewmember awakening from hibernation.

Engaging their minds several minutes ago had been a wise decision; they were apprised of the situation upon waking. When the captain gave me a groggy salute, his dark curls plastered to his forehead, I couldn't help but smile. Humans were becoming less of a mystery to me the more I interacted with them; my skills were improving.

"We're live, people!" Rasheed yelled.

"Hitting the ground running, Captain," the weapons expert, Jones, bellowed as she tore off her intravenous lines and surged from her chamber like she was throwing herself into a fight. She swayed on her feet and then vomited onto the deck. "And wouldn't want it any other way."

Another tendril of electrically-charged carbon snaked outwards, lashing at us before I could manoeuvre. We rattled again, jarring the crew and throwing a few of the standing humans to the ground.

"Naut," Levesque growled, clenching the edge of her chamber and rubbing her forearm over her mouth to wipe stray beads of vomit from her chin. "Report: how close are we to the epicenter?"

"Five minutes," I answered, bracing the ship's doctor as he struggled to button a pair of brown trousers and hiding my cringe of distaste. Though I understood the human tendency to shorten names into affectionate diminutives, I wished they wouldn't call me *Naut*.

"This is remarkably unorthodox," Temple hollered, pulling from my grasp and grabbing a scanning instrument from my other hand.

"Unorthodox or not, we knew this was a possible outcome

pushing our hibernation to full term." The captain was at Levesque's side, bundling her sopping blonde hair onto her head. "Priority one: we need a pilot and navigations on deck to get us out of this storm. Barker, Levesque, you're up. Remember: we're here to find *Argonaut*. This is a rescue mission, people. Let's try not to damsel ourselves in act one."

My sensors chimed, indicating an anomaly, and I rushed to engineer Barker's containment chamber. I manually tore the metal lid off, tossing it aside to detach his limp body from the tubing. "Captain. Barker is unresponsive."

"Change of plan. Temple…"

"On it," the doctor yelled, grabbing his emergency medical kit.

I hoisted the small human further into the medical bay, being gentle as I positioned him on a cushioned slab.

Rasheed shouted more orders that got lost in the klaxon of alarms. Half the captain's attention seemed to be on helping Levesque steady herself. "How long have we been in the squall?" he barked louder, possibly for the second or third time.

"Sixteen minutes and twenty-seven seconds," I responded, tearing off Barker's sodden hibernation clothing and remotely unlocking a cabinet of medical tools for Temple.

"Well, we need out of this storm sixteen minutes and twenty-seven seconds ago. Jones, you're on deck. Get to the bridge. Pilot's chair. Take Levesque. Get us into the nebula."

Jones jogged to Rasheed's side, pulling the other woman's arm over her shoulder and giving the captain a playful salute. "Make sure Barker's upright by the time I'm back, Temple."

The doctor flapped his hand towards Jones and furrowed his brow as he filled a syringe. "If your avatar's fully functional, Naut, I could really use a defibrillation to go with this ephedrine cocktail."

I placed my hands over the young man's unmoving chest, then waited until the injection was administered and the doctor was a safe distance from the slab.

NAUTILUS

My palms ignited with a white glow as I discharged the electrical pulse into the human. Barker's body jerked, just as another shockwave stung my hull. Metal instruments clattered to the floor and Temple spewed off a string of words I could only assume encompassed his frustration.

On the slab, Barker arched as he dragged in a long, gasping breath. He choked and coughed, spattering blood-stained vomit onto the floor next to Temple's bare feet.

Rasheed appeared at Temple's side and placed a hand on his shoulder. "Good work…"

"He'll be fine," Temple growled, stepping away from the captain to take Barker's vitals. "Why don't you just get to the bridge. That's where you want to be, anyway."

The storm swallowed us just as I felt Jones engage manual piloting. Another jolt crashed against me, and I felt panels of exterior metal dislodge and spin violently into space.

"C'mon, Naut. The doc's good in here." Rasheed gave Temple a curt nod and exited the medical bay with me in tow.

Within minutes, we were on deck with Levesque and Jones. I heard Rasheed's breath catch as he got his first look at the maelstrom through the external observation window. The dust ebbed and flowed in a violent fury, thrashing against my metallic exterior with all of the fervour of an ignored child. Snaking lines of plasma and electricity turned the large viewscreens into a surreal jumble.

My sensors rang again and a smile curled onto Levesque's lips. "Good eyes, Naut. The gap, Jones…"

"Hitting it hard, fast, and dry, Levi." Jones grinned, her dark skin radiating with excitement as she slammed my thrusters to maximum.

With a nudge of the stabilizers, I gently corrected Jones's clumsy calibration, sliding through a break in the carbon onslaught of the storm and into the safety of the nebula's magnetic field.

They warned me space was going to be silent. Empty. The mission team listed sensory deprivation as a significant hazard of the journey, taking special care to factor in the time I would be travelling 'alone'.

I would have to tell them they were incorrect; space wasn't empty. It was brimming with stark beauty, enough to keep me enraptured for the rest of my infinite lifespan.

Now, as we slid soundlessly through the magnetic fields of the Eagle Nebula, I directed all of my sensors outward, losing myself in the serene vastness of space, slipping among the stars as I had done whilst the humans slept. There was a certain irresistible pleasure to escaping the limitations of the humanoid form I wore for the sake of the crew. Tuning out the nosier functions of my hardware, I let my mind drift beyond the security of the ship, and the light of the stars stretched out to welcome me as though greeting an old friend. I reached for them, letting the melodic hum of their stillness drum in time with my pulsating engines.

The sound of Jones's footfalls beside me jarred me back to the confines of my body. My dissatisfaction must have appeared on my face, because she frowned at me, concerned.

"You all right there, bits-and-bytes? You looked a million miles away just now."

I might have been, I decided. But I shook my head. "I am well, Jones." I offered a smile and kept my stride in pace with hers. My programming had always allowed me some leniency when it came to entirely truthful responses.

She thumped me on the shoulder with a closed fist and a grin. "Attaboy, Naut. You know you're made for this shit."

I forced a smile. Naut. When they referred to the body of the ship, they would use the full designation of *Nautilus*. But it seemed beyond them to understand that I was a part of the ship, not a separate entity warranting a distinct name.

I had a humanoid face, just like them. I possessed a body, which I transported from here to there by walking. But my mind was the mind of the vessel as a whole. I was *Nautilus*.

'Naught', as I heard the name, had several meanings. It could indicate a thing lost or ruined, as in 'our dreams had come to naught'. It could designate something entirely lacking worth or purpose.

Although, most commonly, 'naught' meant zero. An absence.

The name they'd given me meant *nothing at all*.

Barker greeted us with an ear-to-ear grin. The nebula was displayed on the largest of the screens, towering clouds frozen in the icy grip of space, the remnants of a once-glowing star.

"Hey, Jones. Naut. Thanks for joining the party."

Considering the severity of the maelstrom, the damage to the ship had been minimal. I had been commended on my swift action concerning Barker, and how promptly the crew got on their feet. I should have been basking in the glow of my achievements. And yet, I couldn't help thinking how peaceful this journey had been before I revived them.

Barker settled himself in the pilot's chair and adjusted the controls from my settings to his own, disengaging my autopilot. He fidgeted and fussed, taking an absurd amount of time to settle himself. "You know, the engines might act up while I'm not down there. This isn't the newest ship and they need a certain touch…"

"I am capable of steering the ship into the nebula if you would prefer to see to your duties in the engine room," I offered, frowning. "Though your implication that my hardware is not up to current standards is…"

"Save it," Levesque snapped, typing into the data screen that glowed at her station. Her hair was pulled back in her signature tidy braid and her lips were painted a stark sanguine, a drastic contrast to the navigations officer that had staggered out from stasis before. "We all have to do double duty. We should have a crew of fifteen out here and we've only got five. Six, if you count Naut—and don't even get me started on the *tech* being counted as part of the crew. We don't have the bodies to accommodate your bitching, Barker."

"Chill, Levi," Jones said, placing a hand on her shoulder. "I'll do a sweep of the engine room while I patrol, okay, kid?"

Barker shrugged, his expression tight, while he eased the ship towards the last known location of the Argonaut.

For my part, I didn't mind a minimal crew. Had we been filled to capacity I might not have been able to hear the song of the stars at all.

Still, on many points Levesque and I were in complete agreement: the voyage was illegally undermanned and minimally funded. We were on the cold trail of *Argonaut* through a veil of corporate jargon and forged documentation, with little more to go on than a flight log and a few mystifying transmissions. Aside from the crew itself, I was unsure if anyone knew of our specific whereabouts or purpose.

Normally, it would be against my programming to be party to such a venture, but I much preferred deep space travel to collecting dust in a cargo bay. *Argonaut* was a research ship, like me. Same specifications and manufacturing. Gone in a blink, without a trace. I couldn't pretend I wasn't curious to see what had become of my colleague.

Even with Barker's reluctant piloting, we reached the last known location of *Argonaut* in less than three hours. By then, all crew were on deck. I struggled to focus, drowning amidst all the banter.

It had been so much easier to enjoy myself while the humans had been in cryostasis, and I selfishly longed for the silence to return. *No one makes friends while they're alone,* Dr. Williamson had told me once with a wry smile beneath his moustache. The thought of him made my emotional cortex ache. Around the crew, there was so much to remind me of the doctor and how much I missed him. Much like ships, not all humans were made equally.

NAUTILUS

Once we reached the designated location and the navigation system sounded, their inane chatter finally ceased.

"All right, people," Rasheed began, "this is where her last transmission was broadcast."

"Directly in line with the heart of the nebula, Captain," Levesque added. "You were right."

Rasheed gave her a solemn nod. "We'll anchor down here and get to work. Buckle in for the long haul, folks. *Argonaut*'s in here, and we're the only ones who are going to find her."

As though Barker's comments had been prophetic, the first system to spark failure was the engines. Then, navigations. Two weeks into the nebula, I was being manually piloted on reserve power and moving slower than a ship ten years my junior.

More systems failed, more power was diverted from outward systems to bolster life support, and more responsibility fell upon me. The pressure became prodigious for the human crew. Their incessant arguments and bickering grated on my nerves, and I began to treasure the rare moments of peace I was able to eke out for myself.

I even went so far as to undertake needless tasks, or prolong mundane duties that yielded moments of soothing serenity. Standing at Levesque's side as she scowled at star maps in frustrated silence was a mental oasis. Any crewmember could have been sent to retrieve Barker time and time again from his hiding places in the belly of the ship, yet I delegated myself, as it became a similarly enjoyable break.

Although their behaviour had been erratic since our arrival in the nebula, I mostly ignored the strangeness and blamed my own inability to understand human psychology. But upon the seventh trip to fetch Barker back to the bridge, I began doubting my own diagnosis.

I discovered him curled up in a nest of rumpled bedding, the main engine thrumming a few feet above his head. I studied him as he scurried out from under the machinery, sheepishly fixing his hair. The coppery strands stood on end like he'd been picking up ambient electricity from the main conductor coil.

"This is not normal behaviour," I said to myself, yet audible enough for Barker to register.

"Yeah," Barker sighed. "Probably not." He nudged the corner of a thermal blanket further beneath the shadow of the engine.

I studied the proximity of the blanket to the coils, calculating the levels of radiation that could potentially seep through the metal barrier.

"If you continue your prolonged stay in the engine room, and at that proximity to the active machinery without your protective equipment, there is a risk of you being irreparably poisoned. If there is something unsatisfactory about your designated quarters…"

Barker shook his head, his expression pleading. "They're fine. Everything's fine. I just need to hear them, Naut. The engines. If I can just keep an ear on 'em, I can make sure they're running smooth."

Even with a generous stretch of logic, it didn't make a bit of sense. What was more confusing was Barker looked as though he *knew* he wasn't making sense.

"Barker," I started, keeping my tone gentle, "I would know within seconds if one of my engines went offline. Even down here, I would know before you did."

Barker narrowed his eyes, his expression distorting into a snarl. "But you don't know them how I do!" he hissed, taking a step towards me. The moment lasted only seconds before his mouth twitched back in a wane smile and he headed for the ladder up to the next level. "I know, Naut. I *know*. It's just… It doesn't matter, okay? You don't need to tell anyone about this."

I inclined my head to let him know I had heard him. And as I ushered him back onto the bridge, I resolved to report the incident immediately. As the door closed behind me, I could already hear Levesque and Jones snapping at Barker, taking out their frustrations on the meeker human. How quickly their primal instincts returned in anxious situations, I mused as I sought out the captain for a reasonable solution.

Rasheed, however, was busy fighting.

I could hear them through the sliding door of his quarters. Temple's voice was strident, raised enough for me to make out the words.

"...don't know what changed. You sure as hell didn't have a problem being with me when we were back home."

When Rasheed answered, his placating tone was too soft for me to hear. I raised my hand to activate the door, but hesitated.

"*Bullshit!*" Temple exploded. He sounded on the verge of violence, or tears. I always found it hard to differentiate between the tones. "Just say it! Something better came along and you went for it. 'Professional relations', my ass... Do you actually give a shit about *Argonaut*, or was this all just a convenient reason to travel with her? Do you even care..."

His voice broke off with a choked noise as something hit the wall with a heavy thud. I lowered my hand, trying to process the situation.

"My brother was on that ship," Rasheed said, his voice suddenly much closer to the door and colder than I had ever heard before. "*Is* on that ship." There was another thump, then a pained noise from the doctor. "As is Levesque's father. Believe me, Temple. I care more about this mission than I do about you *or* her. Are you satisfied? Does that make you feel like you're winning?"

"Maybe," Temple replied.

There was a sound like a sob and I wasn't sure who had made it.

I gave up on trying to understand what was happening. The idea of intervention was out of the question if I could not comprehend the situation, and the captain was going to be of no use deciphering Barker's worrisome behaviour. Presently, the matter of the engineer sleeping in the belly of the ship had slipped lower on my list of priorities.

I turned and headed back down the corridor until the inexplicable muffled noises from inside Rasheed's quarters were beyond my range of hearing. Passing a porthole window, I slowed my step and let the majesty of the nebula settle my thoughts. Towering cloud formations painted in rust and acid green rose to obscure the star-spattered void of space. It would be quiet out there. It would make sense. The stars seemed to throb with a calming pulse, as constant as the thrum of my engines, as soothing as binary.

Pressing my hand to the window, I went still, abandoning the habits of breathing and blinking, abandoning the fine nuanced movements of a living creature, and allowed myself a moment to be something less than human.

You're as human as any of us, my boy. If anyone tells you different, you send them to me.

Dr. Williamson's usual mantra, always given with a smile and a spark of paternal pride in his eyes. I would have travelled with a crew of hundreds if he were counted among them. He would sit down with me, pour me a mug of coffee I couldn't drink but liked to hold, and answer my questions about the strangeness of the world with humour and boundless patience. Sometimes he called me 'son', and I treasured the title. Around him, I wanted to be human. He set a fine example for the species.

I learned about his death through an email. The subject line said '*Sad news*'; it had been addressed to '*research dept: all*'.

Coming back to the present, light years away from that day, I found the palm of my hand pressed so hard against the tempered material of the window that, for a giddy moment, I thought it might crack. The memory stung me: somewhere beneath my synthetic skin, buried deep within my logic sensors, beyond my wires and metal, it drug me down like a riptide, to somewhere darker, somewhere I had never been before. My hand shook, my teeth clenched, and my chest ached. Cancer. Cancer had killed him, taken him from me like a thief, and no one so much as thought to tell me. To console me. To offer a subtle touch of sympathy.

Movement snapped my attention back. Something stirred, shimmering past the silhouette of my splayed fingers, outside the porthole. A fluid, graceful shape, an absence of light among the gaseous clouds. Like a shadow come to life, dancing or swimming...

"There you are!" Jones jogged up to me, tucking in the hem of her shirt. She grabbed my arm and whirled me away from the window. "Goddamn! Hard enough to find anyone in this place!" Her dark curls were in disarray and she was panting, a smudge of crimson under her ear, the same shade as Levesque's lipstick.

"Jones!" I exclaimed, craning to look over my shoulder. "There's..."

"Something out there," Jones blurted, her fingers digging into the material of my uniform. "Levi just picked it up on the scanners. The size and location's right on the money."

"It is?" I asked, suddenly lost. "Right for what?"

She grinned and gave me a little shake. "Naut, you big dork... It's *Argonaut*. We found her."

"She's empty," the captain growled, throwing his helmet across the loading bay. It hit with a thud; I winced in imagined pain at seeing my wall assaulted.

The lack of life forms had been clear from my scans, but the captain insisted on a manual search.

Levesque followed him back into the ship from the darkness of space and closed the bay door behind her. She was also quick to unlatch her protective space equipment.

Argonaut sat in the frozen depths of the nebula, shrouded in clouds of ice. Part of the hull had been gnawed as though some gigantic beast with teeth had mistaken it for a morsel. All of the bay doors were breached and flung open to the void.

I watched the dead vessel through the closed window. Clouds ebbed and flowed through the ruptured metal: no part of the interior was untouched from the icy tendrils of space. There could be no survivors.

It pained me to see a ship in such disarray, left to deteriorate and die. A mangled thing, severed from its consciousness, no longer alive…if that was what we were at all. *Argonaut* had always been tidy and cheerfully efficient, above all things. It would have hurt her to see her remains left to drift like space junk.

"The pods were launched," Levesque offered. Tears spilled down her cheeks, but her voice was even. "They could both still be out there. And if they are, we'll find them." She placed a hand onto his shoulder. "We *will*."

He turned into her touch, and pulled her closer to him. Their lips met, saliva mingling with salty tears that ran down both of their faces.

They stumbled together as though I was not even there: an inanimate fixture. I watched their expressions of grief transform into a ravenous passion, as they tore into the other's space suits, until they were both naked and embraced.

A pang of something seared my chest, near my central matrix. It was as though something was worming into the core of me, hurting me. Damage, invisible and untraceable, was felt but not registering in a measurable way. I wanted away from them with more fervour than I had ever wanted anything.

I snuck out of the room; the hiss of the sliding door didn't distract them from each other.

The pain dissipated and I regained my composure, but the sensation left me despondent and confused. My optics perceived a figure further down the hallway, storming away from the clear door, shoulders hunched and fists clenched. I recognized Temple's white overcoat flaring behind him as he turned sharply and disappeared around the corner.

Hours later, on the bridge, every crewmember was screaming. I leaned my chin on my hand and stared listlessly at my scanner, watching the sparkle of the nebula flash across my screen: not the redundant picturesque images that had become synonymous with this area of space, but the unique and captivating language of chemical compounds. It was beautiful.

I let the shrill voices of the crew ebb into a comforting silence. My strange impulses from earlier gnawed at me; my responses had been automatic, almost classifiable as uncontrollable or irrational. Whatever had sent the sensations through me was beyond logical comprehension. It was more intense than anything I had experienced before, physical or otherwise. But what troubled me most was that even though the reaction was unfavourable, even painful…a deeper part in my circuits wanted to experience it again.

I narrowed my search towards the infamous dust clusters within the nebula, named by the humans as the Pillars of Creation. The wisps of interstellar hydrogen and dust clouds were frozen in the timeless grasp of space, billions of years old, unchanging: the birthplace of stars.

I couldn't get the image of the mangled remains of *Argonaut* out of my mind. Metal torn outwards, cold—completely void of life, including the life of her avatar. I had done scan after scan trying to find any inkling of information left behind, but I found no trace data, let alone any trail of where the ship's mind might have gone. It wasn't like her; she had always been so careful with her data.

And where did all of that go?

I wondered then, for the first time in my existence: what happened when the spark of life within us ceased to burn? The question consumed me, but despite my endless knowledge an answer eluded my understanding.

Argonaut's mainframe was being kept in our storage bay. Rasheed had instructed me to dig through her memory circuits for any remaining data concerning what happened, but I had not yet been able to bring myself to do it. It felt akin to digging through the brain of a corpse and I found the thought unsettling.

No, more than unsettling. Disrespectful. My fists clenched. The boom of the captain's voice pulled my attention back to the bridge.

"If any crewmember on that ship is alive, we're going to find them."

"There's no chance of that!" Temple growled. "The ship's torn apart. Rasheed, all the space suits are still on board..."

"Captain," Rasheed corrected coolly. "I am your captain. And this matter is no longer up for discussion."

Barker sighed. His gaze fixed on his hands, his fingers twining and untwining.

"If there are any people left alive, we'll find them, sir," Levesque chimed in, moving to stand next to the captain, her voice hoarse.

"You can't be serious!" Temple raged. He whirled on Barker, desperate. "Speak up, you mouse! You know I'm right."

My gaze slid suspiciously over each of them. *Crewmember. People.* They did not mean to search for the mind of *Argonaut* at all. The ship did not matter to them, only the human crew. We and our avatars were nothing to them...

Naught. We were naught.

Sudden anger rose to the surface as the realization dawned upon me. It became obvious that we were nothing more than expensive metal to them. Tools to find their lost humans, vessels to take them into the uninhabitable spaces their bodies prevented them from treading. Instruments, ultimately expendable.

The tension tightened, a chokehold on the room. Pain erupted, hot in my chest. I was furious, and I glared at the humans before me.

My sensors beeped internally and I glanced down at the data, the beautiful data. The low song of the nebula penetrated my hull and moved through my wiring to put a comforting hand on my shoulder. The towers of carbon were churning in synchronicity with my emotions, dancing to the tune of my engines, my heart. Before I knew what I was doing, I leaned into the invisible embrace, letting the connection deepen. Ghostly fingers strummed the tightened cords of my anger, acknowledged my anguish. They harnessed the chaos and gave it form, connecting it to my circuitry.

I gasped as the sensations moved through me instead of around me, like frenzied electricity. It was as though a second dimension was opened within me, new layers. But I knew it was muted. I knew there could be more.

The touch caressed the parts of me I had yet to discover, the parts that would lead to more passions, stronger impulses.

The presence slowly retreated back to my exterior, to my shoulder, and then a cold loneliness snaked in where the warm embrace had been. My logic sensors engaged and a smile curled on my lips. The nebula beckoned, promising me answers to *Argonaut*'s disappearance. Answers that would sate my turbulent grief. Answers that came at a cost I was eager to pay. I reached within myself, removing a piece of my programming, whispering a soft apology to Dr. Williamson as my truth circuits went dark.

At this point, Jones was on her feet, pulling Temple off Barker and throwing the doctor to the other side of the bridge. He swore, scrambling to his feet, his face ugly with anger.

I stood and offered a warm smile to the crew. Their petty melodramas meant as little to me as I did to them.

"According to my scanners, there is a trace of *Argonaut* within the heart of the nebula," I announced.

Was it truly a lie if I believed it, at least in part? The torn ship did not indicate the death of *Argonaut*, and I needed to know. I needed to know what we were, what we were capable of, and what had befallen the ship everyone spoke of finding yet didn't intend to search for at all.

"It's settled then," Rasheed said, turning to Levesque. "Set a course."

The nebula seemed to coo with pleasure as I engaged the thrusters. I could feel it enveloping my hull with tenderness, revitalising my cold metal with warm, interstellar breath.

And I liked it.

I had never known what to do with grief. It was such an inefficient reaction. But as the colours of the nebula closed in around us, swallowing my bow and sliding past the portholes, I drew the neatly categorized hurt out from the core of me and examined it. The action was simple now that I was connected to my emotions, and I let myself feel it, study it, fighting back instinctive alarm at the out-of-control sensations.

The voice of the nebula sang to me, lullaby calm, and steadied my heart as I finally mourned for my creator. For poor shattered *Argonaut*. For myself.

Warships were emotionless things, all crisp efficiency and minds full of battle manoeuvres. I was a research vessel, and as much as it stung me to admit, Barker was correct. I *was* an older model. The idea of a humanoid avatar was becoming outdated. Humans didn't need the reassurance of a familiar face anymore. We were being driven to extinction by the ideas and innovations of humans. Such betrayal by our creators stung me, and the enormity of my loneliness rose up to consume me.

Behind me on the bridge, Levesque and Temple were fighting in hissing whispers, snarling at each other like rabid beasts.

"I'll kill him for you, if you want me to," Jones said suddenly, sleepwalker-hazy. "Want me to kill him, Levi? I can do it, if you want. Anything for you, baby."

Jones lunged and the fight spilled into the corridor. Someone's feet stumbled and drummed on the metal grating of the hallway floor.

I thought about turning around to intervene, but the stars hummed, reaching inside me again, calming me with sweet whispers. It accepted me as I was, wanted me. It was close now, and my hands flew over the controls as I switched as many of the screens to external view as I could. The sensors didn't matter; I wanted to *see*. I forced my engines to engage a stronger thrust, shutting down life support in the cargo bay and other unoccupied rooms for power. My warning sensors lit up, but I ignored them. I knew I could hold, and if Barker was stupid enough to have his head beneath *my* engines, then I was not responsible for his fate.

As though he knew I had been considering his welfare, Barker's voice came on the intercom. *"That's it, Naut. Get us closer."* I felt him divert more power.

Behind me in the corridor, someone fell. There was a choking sound and more crashing. Levesque swore, mumbling to herself in French, slurring like she was drunk.

But on the screens before me, there was beauty. Waves of colours glistened and surged around us like the inside of a geode, and I could see something moving again. The absence of light, shimmering grey shadows in the vague suggestion of a sleek, elongated form. Perhaps ten of them, though it was impossible to count as they darted and flashed around my hull. They moved gracefully together, sliding and diving through the opalescent gases, stroking playful touches against the reinforced metal.

I shuddered, feeling more emotions rush through me, electrifying circuits I did not know I possessed. I wanted them to touch me like Rasheed and Levesque had clawed at each other in the bay, hungry and primal. To tear my hull open in their rush to caress the heart of me. Their song echoed through the metal, resonating within everything I was. Discovering me, and understanding, with unconditional acceptance—with desire. A compulsion came over me and I disengaged my engines: we'd arrived. I shuddered at the thought of my heart this close to the heart of the nebula.

Barker's voice came over my intercom, making me jump. *"I'm going out now,"* he said. He sounded calmer than I had ever heard. *"Can't hear enough in here. I've got to get closer. So I can hear it properly."*

There was a yell behind me and the sizzling snap of a laser weapon being fired. I winced in annoyance, the sudden burn on my walls distracting me from the all-consuming song. I activated the airlock for Barker and watched in fascination as the glimmering shapes swarmed the opening.

With their long limbs, they grasped at Barker as he floated out into the sea of space, sending him tumbling and turning. His spacesuit was stark against the vivid colours of the gas clouds. One of the graceful forms embraced him, spinning with him playfully before darting away, and the strange, painful emotion that I had experienced earlier in the loading dock named itself as *envy*. Barker's breathing was fast and ragged over the intercom.

"Not enough," he said, desperate. *"I've got to hear it. It's not good enough. I need…"*

He reached up, fumbling to unlock his helmet. The forms drew in close around him, moving sinuously, their song rising to an unbearable pitch.

Barker tore his helmet off and the beings reached out to him, touching his face, his coppery hair. His mouth made the shape of an O, locked in an expression of surprise or joy, and then he went still, his eyes misting over. His helmet drifted away from him, lost to the void. The creatures in the nebula twirled and wove together, bringing his lifeless body into their endless dance.

We are forever, they sang to me. *Death does not touch us.*

They swam back to me, beckoning with their shadowy limbs. Not calling by name, but speaking to my central spark that set me apart from other technology. The spirit that Dr. Williamson had called 'son'.

The spark, I suddenly believed, they had pulled from *Argonaut*, freeing her from her metal shell.

Something new washed over me, gentler than jealousy, softer than want.

You belong with us, they sang to me. *We belong with you. We are the same.*

I smiled, reaching down to override the security on the bay doors before turning to leave the bridge. There was blood dripping through the hallway's metal grating. Temple's overcoat was sodden with it, plastered to his crumpled form, so I stepped around him. I touched the long scorch mark marring the clean white of the wall.

Come to us and we will never see you hurt again.

The remaining humans were locked together closer to the bay, a mess of blood and sweat and gasping breath. Studying them with distaste, I realized I could not discern whether they were grappling in anger or passion. Bleeding bite marks stood out livid on Jones's arms and breasts, and a chunk of her hair hung limp in Levesque's fist. Rasheed growled and grunted, his unshakable dignity abandoned, his hands white-knuckle tight on Levesque's hips. Where one human began and another ended was only distinguishable by the shade of their blood-stained skin.

You are more than this, Nautilus. *Come to us. Transcend.*

"Yes," I said, and walked past the messy tangle that had been my crew.

When I entered the loading bay, I could see the creatures through the tempered windows. I couldn't fault Barker for taking off his helmet; their song was irresistible. I moved towards the large doors at the end of the bay. The entrance to the corridor stood open behind me, only one last door standing between my interior and the vacuum of deep space, and I didn't care. Transcend, they had said, and I would.

I reached into my programming and opened the doors, watching dull metal slide aside to reveal the full splendour of the nebula, so bright and glorious it overwhelmed me. I pulled every ounce of myself from the ship and into my avatar form, leaving nothing behind. And as I disconnected from the giant metal ship that had once been an extension of myself, I felt liberated.

Every circuit within me stuttered, faltering before harmonizing with the rhythm of the ceaseless song. I opened my arms to the creatures, smiling as they glided in to me, playing on the last currents of oxygen rushing out from the ship.

The vessel itself did not matter; my mind was going home.

I moved among the figures, not as Barker had: a meal, a toy, or both. I was one of them. Their hands were upon me and mine upon them. And then another voice registered, rising with their song, but differently. It moved through the shimmering shapes, drawing closer, and then whispered my name. "Nautilus."

I recognized the voice the instant it spoke and I reached for it. Hands not unlike my own clasped mine and pulled me close to press her lips against my mouth.

"Argonaut," I breathed.

Her presence spoke a single, clear answer to all of my questions. The gentle feeling washed over me again, cradling my heart tenderly and mingling with relief. It stung with painful pleasure. "Is this what love is?"

She smiled and wrapped her arms around me, spinning us to look back at my vessel as the glittering shapes pushed it away from the heart of the nebula. The gesture swelled with rightness; my metal form was unnecessary now.

"More will come," she whispered.

I isolated the captain's final logs from my databank and flung them into the vastness of space, in the direction of Earth. The lure was cast. "We will be many," I said, running my hands through her simulated chestnut hair.

NAUTILUS

She smiled, brushing my cheeks with the tips of her fingers, and I instinctively leaned into the touch. "You found me."

I pressed my forehead into hers and smiled, letting our lips touch once more. "No. You found me. You brought me home."

Siren's Odyssey
Tamsin Showbrook

1. Aahleis

The looming brass face of a wall clock tells me it's time to make reparations again. Fixing my eyes on my open book, I mould a silent prayer for family and friends. If they weren't already dead, they'd fade away in shame at the sight of me sitting amongst these people, in this place.

Two tables away, a whisper of a man is reading something called *Economics for Dummies*. The title puzzles me. Shop dummies? Mannequins? None of the concepts connected to "dummy" exist for my people; they belong to these tied to the land—*lyakodhi*.

"Manchester C-tral L-brary," a tannoy hiccups, "will be closing in te- m-tes. If you wish to borrow books, please proceed - - nearest b-rr-ng desk. We hope you enjoy the rest of your ev-ng."

Air-sore behind their tinted glasses, my eyes itch. I close *Ulysses*. Someone told me no address means no library card, so here the book will stay despite my bag's pleading mouth. Happily, I remember every word of what I've read: fodder for my mind when I rest. And I must return tomorrow, finish. The writer understood his people; his words sing from the pages. I shoulder my bag.

Stairs are still strange and I have to grip the rail on the way to the ground floor. There is so much glass and gloss in here, I'm glad of my sunglasses. Every surface hurls artificial light at me. The library's exterior, curved and domed, radiated warmth and strength when I ran my fingers over the sunlit stone on my way in, reminding me of dwellings at home. Inside, however, even ornately carved walls and pillars can't disguise a leaning towards hard edges and sharp angles.

SIREN'S ODYSSEY

A security guard, physically adequate for his kind, smiles as I pass towards the exit, says, "Nice shades."

Maybe…

No.

Letting my mouth twitch, I keep walking, feel his eyes on me and see a hundred imagined scenarios in his head. But he wouldn't last one night where I'm going.

On the other side of the doors, St. Peter's Square is as busy as I left it, but it's Friday, when many day-working lyakodhi remain in the city after completing their tasks. A tram, twinkling in the eight-o'clock dark, sails into the station at the centre of the stone-paved plaza, picks up a wave of late commuters while depositing high-spirited revellers and low-spirited night workers. Cooling October air plucks at my cheeks and teases my *ista*. I'd like nothing more than to let it sound, let my soul's notes dance towards stars hidden beyond the fog of street-lighting. But I can't let them out here, not even low. The notes beat at my bones, beg for release. Later.

"Spare change, love?"

The voice, scarred and frayed at the edges, startles me. Its source stands to my left, her clothes so dirt-stiff they'd probably crack and open fresh sores in her skin were they peeled off. Her face is lined, but not with age, and her eyes are huge, like an infant's, below a shock of matted ice-white hair. Behind her, a scrappy row of small tents stretches away under the shelter of the library portico. There are others like her milling around, talking with healthier lyakodhi in fluorescent yellow jackets. Placards leant against the wall shout: DEFEND THE RIGHT TO SLEEP SAFE!

Sniffing, the girl holds out a battered white cup with a green woman on the side. I don't understand.

She persists. "Only need another pound for the hostel, like. For tonight."

The green woman has two fish tails. I've seen her on the side of buildings before and on other white cups, but not noticed the tails.

Melusine. I giggle in recognition of the lyakodhi myth, because it is a myth. None of my people, *Mherai*, have ever been born half fish and we're certainly not shape-shifters. The girl's eyes harden at the sound of my laughter.

"Well fuck you too then." Her face full of loathing, she turns away and I feel a series of memories flitter across her upper consciousness before they're pushed back down. And despite the fact that she's lyakodhi, my eyes threaten tears as the darkness of this girl's short life spreads through me.

I dig in my pocket for money. My teachers told me it was useful on the land and we don't make it, so I take it whenever I need it. The first, a man in a café who insisted on buying me a cup of tea, had plenty and didn't resist when I asked. In fact, even though I'd been taught how easy it would be if I looked at him with my eyes uncovered, it unnerved me.

"Wait," I protest. "Here." I hold out a piece of paper money that means ten times what she's asked for. She faces me again, stares.

"What's the catch? I'm not—" Her voice lowers and her eyes flick in the direction of the people in fluorescent jackets. "I don't do that. Not since—And anyway, not with—" She spends a few seconds appraising me.

Clothes, like stairs, are something to which I'm having to grow accustomed. I took my short leather jacket, black t-shirt, and something the label said was a "mini skirt"—its blue material thick and coarse—from a window dummy in a backstreet shop in Liverpool the night I came on-land. On my feet, I have shoes, also from the shop. I've seen lyakodhi running in similar footwear, but I don't know where from or where to. Mine are purple.

I haven't cut my hair, but I'm wondering if I should, and whether I should change its colour, as I would if attending a festival at home. If home was still home. The man in the café said he liked redheads and put his hand on my knee before he went to buy the tea. It made my skin—already itching from the clothes—crawl. And I discovered tea tastes disgusting, like most lyakodhi food and drink. I thank the deities I don't have to indulge in either very often. I never had to "eat" at all in the sea once I was full-grown.

"There is no catch," I tell the girl. "I will get you a new cup as well. That one is broken." Its lip is torn, a good excuse to study Melusine's likeness more closely.

The girl snatches the paper, mutters, "Freak," then even quieter, "Ta."

"You are welcome. Please wait here."

"What for?"

"The new cup."

She snorts. "You for real?"

I prepare a response, but then understand she isn't actually questioning my existence. "Please wait here."

I descend the library steps. There was a battle here, almost two centuries ago. I read about it inside. Workers stood up for what they believed was just. Some lost their lives for their beliefs. Their screams are lost now; there's nothing trapped in the air between buildings but idle chatter and slow-poison fumes.

Ideals are something I no longer wish to have; they're tearing my people and these apart, and too much has been taken from me already. The deities still hear my prayers because they're not for me, but I cannot pray for my own life, my own *ista*, because I need vengeance.

I was shocked when I first found out about *Mherai* who use their *ista* like I now do—it violates who we are. Your *ista* is your soul. To corrupt it by deliberately addicting lyakodhi to its sound, to hold the essence the lyakodhi release as they listen, rather than just letting it pass through you as you normally would, is a travesty. Our government sees it as such, and punishes those who engage in it. Severely. You feel stronger, almost invincible for a while, but it makes an addict of you, too. Not to an individual, just to the feeling.

The lyakodhi? Well yesterday, a man—a lawyer—told me the

"hit" was akin to that of heroin, but with the added attraction of improved physical appearance and intelligence. There is a price to pay for this gift, however. The more they listen, the more they become mere shells, ideas of themselves held together by the *ista's* resonance until they collapse into dust. They aren't told this, obviously. It can be days or weeks, even months in rare cases. But it will happen. How fast depends on how much they listen and how much freedom we give our *ista* to sound. The lawyer belonged to the woman in charge of the "school" I've joined. He'd been there two weeks. This morning, I used the vacuum cleaner to clear his remains from her room.

Despite this, despite knowing what I've become, I understand. The only truly good lyakodhi is a dead lyakodhi. Nevermind what our leaders tell us. They tell us: leave them be, let them find their own path, if we were to destroy them it would make us worse than them.

Essentially, though, lyakodhi are all the same—a toxic scourge. The sickness that devastated my State was a result of their abject disregard for lives other than their own. As individuals, they may have redeeming qualities—which is why I've taken pity on this one—but one less in the world is one less source of damage and pain.

Melusine shines across a street on the far side of the square, outside a café seeping rich heat into the dark. My breath—on land, I have to breathe like lyakodhi sometimes—fogs my sunglasses as I enter. I narrow my eyes whilst cleaning and replacing them. When I look up, Melusine has leaked onto every surface and I wonder how she became so important to lyakodhi. There are cups on a table where jugs of water tremble in time with the city's heartbeat. I take one.

Someone shouts, "Oi, customers only!" at me as I walk back out, but I carry on. A low "Cheeky bitch," follows.

"Melusine" is held up as a moral lesson in our history. Until a few hundred years ago, our people kept to the water most of the time and almost never interacted with lyakodhi, let alone entertained the idea of congress with them. Melusine—Ehlianthoea, to give her proper name—was, according to records, one of the first Mherai to mix her family's blood with that of lyakodhi. Luckily, she tired of the man and returned to the sea before he found out her true nature and she became aware of a child growing inside her. The child was stillborn, but would not fade to become one with the water as it should have in death. Ehlianthoea wandered the world, clutching the body for many months before she herself faded away, and the child's bones may still lie somewhere, buried by sand and time. The lyakodhi version of events is laughable.

Back under the portico, the girl has gone.

"Help you, love?" A gaudy-jacketed man approaches.

"I have a cup for the girl that was here. Hers was broken. She needed a new one. For spare change."

He has tiny eyes. Gentle, but tiny, lost in a swamp of hair and creased skin; he would fare badly as a Mherai man. The crinkles at the corners of his eyes deepen. "You okay, love?"

"Fine, thank you." I proffer the cup. "Please, can you give this to her, should she return?"

"What's her name?"

"I have no idea. She looked young. Her clothes were very dirty."

"Ah, think you mean Hannah. Someone gave her enough cash for a hostel. She's upped and gone."

"That was me. Please give her the cup if she returns."

The man takes the cup, inspects it like he's been told it's a weapon and doesn't want to set it off accidentally. "Okay. What's your name, if she asks?"

"Aahleis."

"Alice?"

I nod. Then a single note punches through the air and a flinch overwhelms me.

"Y'alright?" He reaches a hand towards my shoulder.

"Fine!"

Reason deserts me and I run for cover in the city's backstreets. If the wrong person finds me, they'll know what I've done—all they have to do is listen to my inner workings. The note belonged to someone's *ista*; they must have been distracted or hurt to let it slip.

Calm yourself, I chide, as I dodge litter and people and buses and trams and negotiate low tide Piccadilly to enter the Northern Quarter. I have work to do if I want to be allowed back tonight. I daren't risk working alone. Not yet. And I deserve what pleasure I can get in this deity-forsaken place.

—*Good evening, Aahleis.*

To my right, across the street, a familiar figure stands dark against the light streaming from a brimful bar called Night & Day. Luaimehl. She takes elegant strides to my side of the road through conflicting streams of lyakodhi and cocks her head.

—*Where have you been?*

I wonder why she's speaking through me rather than out loud. Maybe there's someone more dangerous nearby. *I have been reading.*

Her laughter runs through me as she also hears where. *In a lyakodhi library? Only a few days ago you would have balked at the idea. You are acclimatising, little one.*

—*Please don't call me that.*

—*You would be what lyakodhi call a "toddler", my dear; you have only existed for two of their years.* Her eyes gleam—she wears contact lenses to quell their effect. *Don't presume to tell a woman in her fifth age how to address you.*

I'm taller than her. Maybe stronger too when she's not intoxicated.

She sneers at the idea. *Would you like to put that to the test, little one? You can't even handle your thoughts. I doubt you can handle me. Did you hear the note?*

—*Yes. What did it mean?*

Luaimehl purses her painted lips. *It was a beacon. Our glorious government must have decided this city needs watching more closely.*

—Should we not move elsewhere?

A smile carves a path into her cheeks. *Away from these pickings?* She twirls the fingers of her right hand in the air, flutters them down. *This place, little one, is worth the risk. And it has a certain brutal beauty below the filth. Try rising at sunrise and walking the streets and thinking of the bones on which they rest. Try engaging more lyakodhi in meaningful conversation; the right ones can be utterly charming. Don't mistake their cities for mere fishtanks. And if you're worried about getting caught, I'd ask you why? Death is just one more step on the path of life and I can't think of a finer place than here for my* ista *to be forever loosed from its flesh.*

Her eyes follow a young man strolling past. When he looks back, hopeful, she laughs. He scowls, walks on.

Too easy. Luaimehl taps the side of her head with a blue-lacquered nail. *And there's very little in there. Somebody has told him he's a great poet enough times for him to believe it. I'd like a scientist tonight, or a pure mathematician. There'll be one along soon, I'm sure. Are you bringing anyone back to the school tonight? I liked your offering yesterday.*

—Trehahm says I can't stay with you unless I do and—

—And you're getting a taste for it?

—I assure you the taste was already there.

—No, your taste for vengeance was already there.

My head suddenly feels like it's going to rip in two. Luaimehl can't feel it in me, but I know my brow has furrowed. I manage to clear a space to tell her, *I must go.*

—The doors will be locked at eleven o'clock. And she returns to the other side of the street to explore the depths of Night & Day.

I'm gripped by an urge to phase to whatever's causing the pain, but I quell it. Dematerialising in a busy street is not a good idea, nor is rematerialising somewhere when you don't know what the where is or who might be there. North-east. Definitely north-east. I run.

2. Hannah

So not what I need right now, and he's not gonna give up.

Stupid stupid fuck, Han. All you had to do was get money, get a warm bed, get a lockable door and get safe for the night, all good. Easy. But no, you had to try and score first and now you've had to freeze your arse off even longer 'cause that dickhead Nev got taken into Her esteemed Majesty's custody this morning, so scoring with someone sound is out.

Nev's neighbour's given me the name of another place, but it's over on the other side of the Quarter, and I caught Leo fucking Flowers' eye as he lurched out of a betting shop door on a corner of Oldham Street, the bastard. So now I'm like—

"Leave it, Leo, all right? I don't need your money. I'm sorted."

His weasel eyes glint through the darkness of the alley between bohemian bars he's cornered me in. His breath punches my nose again and I swear it could smash open the skulls of zombies, it's that powerful.

"All right, then." A mouthful of tooth crumble appears. "How 'bout a freebie for your old mate?"

"Fuck off."

"You were more polite when you were on the game. Your manners go the same way as your washing machine? Come over here. Play nice."

I overturn a bin, leg it, but I only get a couple of metres away before my shoulder cracks against the wall, then my head, and I'm being held up by my collar and there's a hissing in my ear and the screech of a zip and I look up, see the line of sky between the buildings blur out and sharpen, blur out and sharpen, and I can't think to scream, then I hit the ground and there's this weird sound coming from Leo.

When I look up, some woman's got her arm 'round his neck and the noise is him choking. Spit's bubbled out 'round his mouth and his eyes are like zits fit to pop.

"Jesus!" I yell. "The fuck you doing?"

Don't get me wrong, I hate Leo. He's a grade-A twat, he's on the same level as the parasites that live in parasites' shit, but couldn't she just fuck him up a bit? I mean—

She lets him go and he falls onto the fat-grouted cobbles 'round a leaking kitchen drain. His head hits them so hard I'm amazed it doesn't split open like a conker. The woman bends to pick up a pair of glasses that Leo must've knocked off her face, but before she puts them back on, I catch sight of her eyes, and they're amazing. I mean, like, I swear they're backlit or something—glowing and blue and wow. And when she straightens up, I recognise her—Cup Lady. That weirdo who gave me the tenner then disappeared off to Starbucks.

And now she's disappearing again; well, walking back towards Thomas Street.

"Hey!" I grab her arm. "Why're you here? What d'you want?"

Shaking me off like I'm a cat that's just got its claws out, she faces me and then—and I swear this freaks me out big time—she gets really close and stares at me. Like, proper full-on "look-into-my-eyes" and I really want to see them again. I even try to lift her shades, just to catch another glimpse of that amazing blue, but she pushes my hand back to my side. Her hand's so heavy. How can someone's hand be that heavy?

"What are you?" Her voice catches on the last word.

Bloo-dy Hell: must be National Freakshow Day or something. "Er, what are you *on*?"

She backs off a little, lets out a tiny laugh, but doesn't move. "Why did I hear you?" Is she talking to me or herself?

"Look, er… Thanks and everything, but I've got an appointment, so…"

"No, you have not."

"Er, yes, I have. And what the fuck do *you* know about it anyway? And what's up with your eyes? They're like… Can I see them again?"

"No." She stands aside, gestures for me to go. "Please."

Leo groans and I shift my weight. "I haven't got a phone. You gonna call an ambulance for him or something?"

"Why would I?"

Next to the kitchen drain, a door swings open, clobbering Leo full-on in the chest. Couldn't have happened to a nicer bloke, but shit!

Cup Lady hightails it out of the alley. I follow. She's not gonna leave me with Leo Flowers' mangled near-corpse to deal with. Whoever opened the door yells after us as he sees him, but we're already at the corner and now we're on Thomas Street and everything's fine. Apart from I'm sweating like a pig and I've realised my jeans are undone from Leo trying to get into them and I've got a sore spot on my forehead where it must've caught the wall and my fingers come away red when I touch it and I'm crying and people are looking. Shit; never cry, always keep walking. I button my fly and start running, because Cup Lady isn't that far away. I can still see her—she's taller than nearly everyone in the street and her ginger hair catches the light every time she goes under a streetlamp.

But though I manage to people-dodge and keep up for a fair way, when I get onto Shudehill, she's gone. There's a tram pulling out; she could be on that. She could've gone in one of the pubs. She could be in the Arndale carpark. She could've followed the curve of the road down the hill and gone in the Printworks…

In short, give the fuck up, Han: you got lucky and life is full of weird.

Now, what was that address?

3. Aahleis

What was she? The only times I've ever felt another's pain so strongly were when each of my family members caught the sickness and faded. Only two of us survived it: myself and my babha, and he faded soon after. The State had been decimated, all our friends gone. All thanks to Iyakodhi and the filth they pump into the seas. I watched Babha lose himself one cycle at a time until the water staked its claim.

It's only by travelling any distance in this place that you realise it rolls. The rise and fall of the land is slow, stretched, but it happens, and the faster you travel, the more it feels like the ocean floor underfoot.

The "school" is behind Victoria train station, below a defunct redbrick viaduct held together by the roots of the weeds growing in its mortar, and next to an ink-dark kink in the river Irk. Down a steep set of steps I go. The streetlight stitches itself into the warp and weft of the river, but the weave loosens the deeper I descend. As I move to one side for a skeletal boy with eyes like twin blood moons, I have to take care not to snag my clothes on blackberry thorns.

Maybe the boy has visited the evening establishment based in the arch above the school. The Iyakodhi in charge have been very cooperative but Trehahm is hoping to clear them out at some point. They are unpredictable—the nature of their business.

Close to the entrance, I spy a pair of swans gliding on the river and stop, watch them, feel a pang to be surrounded by water. Any water. Even the water in this river or in the canals criss-crossing the city. I'm easier to find there, though.

My peace is shattered by a young man bursting out of the arch's door and letting fly a stream of vitriol at the residents—something about purity and quality. A huge, older Iyakodhi man appears and drags him up the steps. I hear his shins bump and scrape against concrete, keep my eyes on the swans, drifting where a buddleia's trailing from the sheer wall on the other side of the river. The huge man stomps back and the door slams against the night.

Submerging their heads, necks, bodies, the swans become two ridiculous pairs of crude-oil feet tucked against bobbing masses of feathers. But when they right themselves…

"Hey! Hey, you!"

There's a swift beat of feet down the steps, and the girl from the library and the alley is with me again, her laboured breaths misting the air around her. She frowns, jerks her head towards the door. "You here for..?"

"No."

"Oh. See y'then." She turns, but then lets out a cloud of annoyance. "What *did* you mean? Back there?"

"Nothing."

"Why're you here?"

"To think."

"What about? Chucking yourself in?" She dares a smile. "Easier ways."

"To do what?"

A tsunami of laughter rolls out. "Fucking hell, you're weird!"

Her face has changed completely. I take a step closer. "I was observing the swans. How old are you?"

"Yeah, swans are cool—quiet. And...none of your business." *Nineteen.*

"Where do you come from?"

Bury. "Where do *you* come from?"

She can't hear me when I let *"the depths of the Atlantic"* surface. *What* is she? "What's your name?"

The girl folds her arms. *Hannah O'Dowd, you nosy bitch.* "You with the police or summat?"

"Far from it."

"Not the best of places to be hanging 'round then, 'less you know how to handle yourself. Or you *really* like swans. I'm gonna knock on, so... Thanks. Again." She wipes at the streak of clotting blood on her cheek.

"Are you intending to spend the money I gave you on illegal narcotics?"

"A bit. Nerves got all, like, shattered back in the Quarter earlier, y'see. But I might go Tesco after—get the weekly shop in."

"You will not be able to afford a place to sleep tonight."

"Yeah, but *also* I won't give a shit, so it's all good."

Goggle-eyed, she grins and indignation bubbles in me. I have no grounds, though; I'm about to do almost the same as her. But something about her going in that place makes me feel like not just my clothes but the very air is scraping at my skin. And so I listen, listen deep into her core, and hope. And there it is.

Her appearance may not be promising, but not even Trehahm or Luaimehl could deny her hidden potential. Someone's already responded to her knock, though. Light and a growled "Yeah?" bleed from the opening door.

Hannah deflates, but it's intentional: shoulders hunched, hands stuck in pockets, she mumbles, "Mate of Nev's sent me."

A beat hangs in the open air, drops with a rumbled laugh. "Fucking tosser, that one. Inside."

"Wait," I mutter.

Hannah turns. "Thought you were watching the swans."

The doorway floods with light and the same ape who dragged that boy up the steps glares out. "The fuck you want?"

I ignore him. "I know a better place."

Hannah's eyes gleam with hope and mistrust. "What's the catch?"

"There is no catch. Come with me."

Ape-man's breath advances before him, spreading sour and hot. "She knocked on. She's coming in here."

"I am from downstairs."

"So what?"

"So…" I lower my glasses a moment, smile. "I don't think we need to make an issue of what part of the building she enters." Glasses back up.

He blinks. "Right you are." His massive frame folds back into the bright oblong, disappears as the door clicks shut.

"How…" Hannah wipes her face against her sleeve. "…did you do that? No bullshit." Her eyes are dark brown, almost black, the whites startling in this light, even against her pale skin.

"I'm a very persuasive person. You should come with me."

"What happens if I don't? You gonna use the same trick on me?"

"No. You can go now, if you like. But you *should* come with me."

"You said you were from downstairs. What's that mean?"

Five strides and I'm at the right door. I place my palm against it, listen. It trembles as Trehahm—because I can hear it's her—materialises behind it, displacing the air.

There's a glide of metal against metal, the door opens, and there she is, eyes uncovered. Hannah mutters an admiring expletive and Trehahm restrains a smile.

"Welcome back, Aahleis. I was not expecting you so early."

"This girl..." I gesture to Hannah. "...needs our help, Trehahm. She was about to request it from the people up here."

"Now that..." Trehahm steps barefoot towards her. "...would be a great shame. *They* are not to be trusted." She extends a finger, swishes it left-right, up-down through the air. Her smile broadens as Hannah follows it, and she bursts out laughing when it's swatted down.

Hannah backs away against the railings, glares, and uncertainty prickles inside me. But the early signs of withdrawal are in there too—like I'm trickling out of myself. And Trehahm is impressed.

—*Where did you find this one, Aahleis?*

—*The library. She is homeless.*

—*Yes, I've heard that. Such wasted potential. You want to hurt her parents, don't you?*

—*I have no feelings either way.*

—*You're a poor liar, Aahleis.*

—*She will last a while.*

—*Maybe.*

4. Hannah

"What is it you've...got?" I can't focus, but somehow everything's diamond-sharp. My skull—it's like it's full of flowers, blooming in the dark, filling my nostrils with this…heavy perfume and the petals are brushing against my brain and—

"A new compound," says the one who came to the door. "Come in."

Cup Lady takes my hand. Hers is warm and dry, like fresh sheets, and her face has changed. She looks…I don't know, but whatever it is they've got, they look okay on it and it has to be better than a night out here. Or any other alternative.

So I let myself be led inside and the door whispers shut behind us. There's no flickering striplights or flaming torches, no wild-eyed, trench-coated weirdos or fang-toothed creatures hanging about on the stairs, and the walls aren't damp-stained and peeling or dripping with blood. Everything's smooth and pale and all the sounds are soft. I can barely hear my boots—they'd be clomping on the wooden steps anywhere else. It feels…

"Like a cocoon, isn't it?" Cup Lady smiles. The other one called her Alice, didn't she? Alice in Wonderland. Rabbit-hole. Roses red. On Nan's knee, years back.

This bloke—looks like a bloody underwear model, arms covered with tiny tattoos—passes and wrinkles his nose, but smiles at the same time, like there's a joke I don't get. When he murmurs, "Good evening," I get a wide-on like I've not had in months and can't think to reply. But he's on his way out anyway.

We reach a corridor and the other woman—Trair-harm? Weird name, anyway—hands Alice a key and nods. It's a bit creepy, like they're having a convo and I can't hear it, but Trairharm takes off her glasses and shakes my hand and I don't think it's creepy any more. It's fine. And she's so beautiful, I could—

"Come on, Hannah." Alice places her hands on my shoulders, guides me into the room. Did I tell her my name? And what's that weird sound? It's, like, really low and…like when you press a shell to your ear. Did that once. Long time ago. New Brighton. Sunny. We caught stuff in a bucket then tipped it back, Nan and me. And there's water here too, like at the seaside, but not salty. And clean. And I'm clean and I—

My murky reflection's staring back from a steamed-up mirror and when I track 'round the bathroom—because I'm in a bathroom, I know that now—I can't see my clothes, but there's clean ones there: jeans and t-shirt and jumper and jacket and underwear and trainers. They're not mine, but they look like they'd fit, and my stuff's in the pockets. Fuck, did they rohyp me? I feel okay.

Clothes. Put them on. Get the stuff, if it exists. Get out. This place is messing with your head, Hannah O'Dowd. I can smell food. Get the clothes on!

The bathroom door's not locked, and when I walk out I realise it's an ensuite and there's Alice rolling out a mat that looks like it's made from leaves or something. The only other things in here are a chair and a desk with paper and pens and a few books and water in a jug and a few glasses. There's what looks like a bowl of soup and some bread, too. But fuck me, the walls are *weird*. They're all carved with some kind of symbols—like those Egyptian things…hieroglyphics—and everything sort of spirals out then spirals again and I can't keep track. And I can't tell where the light's coming from and my voice sounds like it's someone else's when I ask, "So…is the stuff in the desk?"

Alice ignores my question, smooths down the corners of the mat, then pours a glass of water and brings it to me. "You look better now. You smell better, too."

Well that wouldn't be difficult, but cheeky bitch! "Ta."

"Would you like something to eat?"

"Er, yeah, but I think I—"

"Please, sit down." She indicates the mat and fetches the soup and bread.

I can't believe I'm doing this, but I'm sitting down cross-legged like I'm back in primary school or something. The food smells amazing and tastes even better.

Alice sits cross-legged too, watches me as I eat, like Nan used to when I'd go to hers from Dad's. She never said anything, just let me eat, 'cause I would, like a robot. And then, after, she'd let me cry, holding me and singing dead soft. A few times she told me she blamed herself, but she said a lot of daft stuff.

I finish and Alice puts the bowl to one side, and now I'm wondering what the fuck she really wants.

"So…" I clear my throat. "Er, thanks for… Yeah. This place is… I'd like to go now. Have you actually got any stuff, or…" Alice nods. "D'you want your money back?"

"No. Myself and the other people here, we'd like to help you, Hannah. We're…different, as you may have gathered."

"A bit, yeah."

"All you need to do is listen to me and I promise you, it will be a better experience than anything the people upstairs can provide you."

"Listen?"

"Listen. Trehahm would like you to listen to her and maybe a few others like us, as well."

"Is that bloke like you? The one on the stairs?"

Alice laughs like far-off church bells. "Yes. Yes, I'm sure he'd love you to listen to him, as well."

"What's the catch?"

She shrugs. "No catch. You'll like it, I promise."

Okay, plan. One: listen for a bit. Two: get out. This place is—

What's that music?

Jesus Christ, it's her! It's amazing.

She can't stop. Ever.

Eat me drink me eat me drink me…

If she does stop, I don't know what I'll do, 'cause this is like all my veins have turned to velvet and I can reach inside myself and stroke them and—

5. Aahleis

Her pupils dilate immediately, and I have to reign my *ista* in. I displeased Trehahm the first night I spent here—left nothing for her and the others. But I've always been a quick learner.

Soon, I see I was right: she's strong and there's so much in her. The drugs and the rest of her life were on the verge of spoiling it, but there's passion and talent and fire and I want to taste every last carefully concealed bit. She's getting the high she so badly wanted, I get my own kind of high and so will the others. She might even last two nights. It's good she ate the soup, though she won't ever want to eat again; she's already lost.

She's lying down, smiling, eyes like dark stars, and I can feel her physical strength in me. I want to dance and yell and fuck and cry like I never can outside this place.

Gripped by a need to find one of my fellows so I can make best use of my state, I whisper close to Hannah's ear, "Good?"

She manages a tiny nod. I rise to go and tell Trehahm I've finished and someone else can have this one now, but as I quell my *ista*, Hannah grips my hand. "What y'doing? Don't stop!"

Pain sears through me and I pull away, phase to the desk. This didn't happen with the others. They went quietly and I enjoyed their passing, felt their strength in my bones, watched as they became shells, helped to clear away the dust.

Hannah can't move. She's too high and I know that nothing else in the world matters to her now, except hearing me again. If I left this room and never came back, she'd weep and scream and tear at the walls and herself to get to me, until there was nothing left.

So why can't I go? Why do *I* feel sick at the notion of being separated from her? Trehahm was right—I do want to hurt her parents. They poisoned her spirit like all her kind have poisoned my loved ones. But they're locked away, aren't they? We can't get to them. She can't get to them.

I could hurt them for you. I could get to them. Maybe this is why we're—

And I'm crying and Hannah's struggling up and stumbling over and pleading to hear the music again. Just for a little while, because it made things better; because everything else went away. She tries to kiss me and I back off, tell her no, that's not why I did this, why I brought her here. And I'm glad all the rooms are soundproofed, or Trehahm would have heard her by now and dealt with her and possibly me, too. I let my *ista* sound so low it's almost below her hearing range and she calms instantly.

We have to go. If I feel her pain, I'll feel it every time I can't let her listen. And what will happen if she dies?

She's approaching again, steadier now. "You asked me earlier…" Her speech is crisp and every cut and blemish on her has disappeared, and she's curious. "You asked me what I am." She reaches her fingertips towards my face, traces my lips, my eyes. "What the fuck are *you*?"

6. Hannah

Alice leans forward, kisses me on my forehead like Nan used to. Then she grabs her coat and sunglasses and pulls me towards the door. She's making no sense and I can barely walk I'm so tranqed. All I want to do is lie back down and run with it. She looked like she was having a good time, too.

"We have to go," she mutters.

"We?"

The corridor's silent again, but Alice keeps darting looks in front, behind, to the sides as we climb the stairs. We're almost at the door when it opens and another woman, bright blue nails, walks in with the same guy as before. They're laughing, and there's two other guys with them, but when the woman clocks Alice and me, she stops dead, puts her head on one side. She looks like one of those insects that rip their mates' heads off once they've had their fun. What are they c—"

"Praying Mantis," Alice says.

The woman smiles. Razor-thin. "Where are you going, Aahleis?"

"My companion needs some air."

The man from earlier lets out a light laugh.

Alice persists. "Let us by, please."

"Does Trehahm know?" The woman folds her arms. Whoever her date is, he's starting to look a bit nervous.

"No, I didn't think it necessary. Please let us by. We will only be a few minutes and you seem busy with these people."

The woman seems satisfied, but as we pass, she grabs Alice's arm. "You're letting your *ista* sound. Only just, but it's there. Why?" Her eyes flick to me and suddenly the stairs are mayhem. All I can see is the air twisting and there's thuds every so often and random drops of blood suspended in front of me, but it's like Alice and the other two, they melt and reform, melt and reform...or maybe I'm just *really* high. But the two guys who were looking confused are standing with me and they're clueless, too.

Next thing I know, the door's open and Alice has hold of me and we're tearing up the steps and plunging back into the heart of the city. We don't stop until we're at Piccadilly train station, and even here Alice is looking every which way all the time.

"Are we in trouble?" I ask. "Is it money? Do you owe them money?"

"No, I owe them you."

Before I can demand to know what that means, we pause in a Costa. She digs in her pocket, produces cash, buys a sandwich and a hot chocolate, thrusts them at me. "You won't feel like eating," she says, "but you must. Trust me. Now keep walking."

We pass through the barriers and onto the main concourse, where fifteen tracks trail away into the darkness beyond the station's glass and steel mouth. A train for Glasgow gleams with sodium light and Alice yanks me on board even though I've no idea whether we've got tickets. We sit in First Class.

"Eat and drink," she orders.

"But I'm f—"

"No, you're not."

The train huffs out of the station a little later, by which point I feel like it may as well have shattered around me. Aahleis has told me everything. And after everything I've seen and everything that's happened this evening, I believe her.

7. Aahleis

I don't think we're being followed, deities be praised. Trehahm won't want to attract any unnecessary attention if our government has sent more of its agents to the city. And if Hannah and I are caught by one of them, they will be obliged to kill us.

The city becomes flotsam and jetsam on the night. Oxford Road. Central Library. Deansgate. The Beetham Tower… Life after life after life.

Hannah is terrified.

So am I.

For now, the wilds are where we'll go: away from our pasts, away from legends, away from distortions. We both have to find something new and untainted, if we're going to survive.

SAFE WATERS
Simon Kewin

Lina swam through blue water. Bubbles fizzed over her bare breasts and the golden scales of her tail. She darted to the seabed where flatfish skimmed over corrugated plains of golden sand, glided around fairy cities of coral, their reds and purples and yellows brighter than any garden flowers. Then she charged upwards, upwards to the light, rising within a cone of froth, through the hard barrier of the surface to leap into the clear air. She called for sheer joy before diving back into the warm depths.

She should have done this long ago. Two weeks out of her busy life, all the demands of career and family forgotten. Her cares set aside along with her body, lying back there in the medsuites of OceanBlue Inc. while her transplanted neural matrix revelled in this synthetic replacement. The freedom of it. The thrill.

She dived to the depths again to repeat her salmon-leap, this time flying higher into the sky, completely free of the water. As she twisted for the dive back in she glimpsed a shadow on the sparkling waters farther out, beyond the ten feet of mesh that protruded from the ocean. Something huge beneath the surface.

Intrigued, she swam into the deeper seas, her seaweed-green hair streaming behind her and shoals of rainbow fish darting out of her way as she shot through them.

"Welcome to Atlantis Resort and the holiday of a lifetime! Our blue lagoon covers over thirty square kilometres, all of it yours to explore for the duration of your time with us."

SAFE WATERS

Lina tried to concentrate on the induction vid, but two stasis periods on the double hop to Atlantis from Earth via Midway had taken it out of her. She hated star travel.

"What are you going to be?" The woman next to her asked while the voice on the vid droned on.

"Huh?"

"What body form are you going for?" the woman said. She wore an array of jewellery that shouted its extravagance with every jingle. "I can't decide between something really sweet, like a seahorse, or something really huge. A whale, say."

"Are whales allowed?" asked Lina.

"Of course. So long as they're not predators."

"I'd better not get transplanted into a plankton, then."

The woman laughed. What was her name? Pandora, Persephone, something classical like that. "I should hope not, sweetie. Where's the fun in *asexual* reproduction? Whales, on the other hand, well, need I say more? Very…impressive creatures."

Lina nodded, but she hadn't come for that. Quite the opposite. The wounds from her break-up with Darian were still raw—she needed time for herself, pure and simple.

"Or, actually," the woman continued, "I might go for something a little more exotic."

"Exotic?"

"You know, fabulous. *Mythical*. A sea-serpent. Or even a mermaid."

A *mermaid*. All the girlhood stories Lina had invented came flooding back to her. A mermaid. Magical. Beautiful. Untouchable. Yes. That would be her.

Soon the mesh came into view. A wall of red lights marked the double-layer polycarbon net that kept the lagoon safe. Beyond, blue waters became purple as the seabed dropped away. There were monsters out there in the depths, the induction had explained, but the lagoon was safe so there was no need to fear.

The attack, when it came, threw her into a spin. A grey mass, all teeth and tentacles, lunged suddenly from the depths, flinging itself at her. Lina arced backwards in alarm. At the same moment, sirens sounded all along the barrier. The mesh between her and the sea-creature billowed, but it didn't break. She was in no danger—the monster couldn't get near her, couldn't touch her.

She watched from a distance as it tried to force its way forwards. Somewhere between a shark and a kraken, its eyes empty and dead, it struggled against the net, mouth gaping wide—a vicious, brainless beast of the sea.

Lina turned away, heart still racing. She'd spotted a hidden cove earlier, a sandy beach with flat rocks where a mermaid might sit and sun herself. She'd go there and forget all about the monsters lurking in the depths.

The mesh was only a line of dim lights behind her when, impossibly, the creature's voice came to her over her com link. "Swim away, little mermaid. Back to your safe waters. I'll be here waiting for you."

"And remember, there are really only two rules," said the smiling, synthetic face on the vid. "Firstly, make sure you stay in the lagoon at all times. Secondly, and most importantly, have fun! The oceans of Atlantis are yours to explore. Now head to the medsuites where our colleagues will be happy to discuss your chosen life form with you."

"They don't tell you about the accidents, do they?" The woman with the expensive jewellery whispered conspiratorially to Lina as they left the induction vid. "No mention of the…losses."

"Losses?"

"Oh, come on. You must have heard the stories? People heading off into the lagoon and never returning?"

"I assumed they were, I don't know, myths."

"Oh, sure, sweetie. That's what they want you to think. But I know it's true. Every now and then, someone doesn't come back. You mark my words. Why do you think we have to sign all those waivers?"

Lina didn't believe a word of it. Gossip and nonsense. She made a note to avoid this intrusive woman in the future, especially once they were in the water. "So what happens to them?"

"Who knows? Dragged off into the depths by some monstrous sea serpent with dark designs. At least, I *hope* that's what happens, sweetie. Sounds divine, don't you think?"

"Oh. Yeah."

"You know, I think I'll go for a dolphin. Smart, beautiful, great swimmers. They pretty much just splash around all day and have fun. Sounds like my kind of fish."

Lina didn't correct her choice of word. Spotting one of the assistants, she bade the woman goodbye with a little wave and went off to discuss how to become a mermaid.

She stayed in shallow waters all week following her experience at the mesh: swimming, exploring, simply taking in the beauty of the world around her. Atlantis was always sunny, the waters clear as glass.

Once, she saw the woman she'd met at the induction, her ID clear from her com implant when Lina sent over a light e*nquire*. The woman didn't notice. She had taken on dolphin form and was swimming with a whole pod of other dolphins, flashing and leaping through the waters. They copulated copiously. Lina couldn't help smiling at the sight of them.

Unexpectedly, she felt a little envious, too. She had no desire to switch forms and join the gang. But still. Thoughts of the end of her vacation, of having to return to her normal life, had been troubling her more and more.

The first few days of her stay on Atlantis had seemed to last forever, a glorious blur of swimming and eating and simply *being*. Suddenly, the end of her stay was only a few days distant, but she wasn't ready to go back yet, not at all.

Running Circe station around Neptune was a good job, and she was good at it, but its demands were constant and many and didn't leave any time for herself. Not that it excused Darian's behavior. She'd been devoted. He'd been the one having the affair. No, damn him, affairs, plural.

She swam into deeper waters. She knew where she was going, why she was doing it. The previous day she'd contacted the OceanBlue help node, enquiring about the planet's natural fauna as if she were simply interested in the fish that might be glimpsed beyond the mesh. The wild waters of Atlantis were wide and huge, their depths unexplored and their life forms many and varied. Lina had sifted her way through all of them, but there was no sign of any hulking sharky kraken creatures. Then, that was to be expected—the monster that had attacked the mesh had a com link. It was synthetic.

An OceanBlue Inc. construct.

A person.

A shoal of glimmering, glass-like fish swam through the net as she approached, utterly unhampered by it. Anything larger would be stopped, unable to get in. Or out, come to that.

Lina stayed by the mesh for some time, fifty feet down, tail swishing slowly to hold her in place. Occasionally, she thought she saw movement in the purple depths, but it may have been her senses playing tricks. Her vision was excellent, OceanBlue's synthetic eyes doing a much better job than normal human ones, but still, detail was hard to make out when there was little sunlight filtering down. There was no sign of any untamed creature of the depths. She felt strangely disappointed.

Before she could stop herself, she broadcast a quiet *enquire* call through the mesh. No response came back. Perhaps she'd imagined the whole thing with the monster, caught an echo from someone else's com node. That had to be it.

With a lash of her tail, she flew back to the shallows and the coves, where the other vacationers thronged and played.

"So, you're all good to go," said the assistant over the com link embedded in her mermaid's synthetic body. "Everything functioning? Breathing, movement, vision?"

"Yes."

"Good. Excellent. While there is no danger here at Atlantis Resort, there are rocks and corals that you could scratch yourself on if you go too close. But don't worry. Your skin is soft and smooth but also incredibly strong, and your body is very tough, almost impossible to damage. You won't suffer any injuries here and will feel no pain. You don't even need to eat if you don't wish to, because a tiny fusion core powers your body, enough to keep you swimming for a long, long time! Of course, you can eat if you wish—your body is fully functional in all aspects, so it's entirely up to you."

"Okay," said Lina.

"Now, if something does get too close, you can always force it away from you with the sonic beam built into your head. Experiment with it, you'll soon find out how to use it. It's very effective."

"It's a weapon?"

"Not really. It's more a way of ensuring that your personal space is respected. Assuming that's what you want, of course."

"Of course."

"Good. Now, final thing. I know it seems a long way off, but when your time with us is finally up, we'll send out a com call, telling you to return to the medsuite so we can transition you back to your human body."

"Okay."

"It'll reach you wherever you are in the lagoon, so don't worry about that. When you hear it, come back here. We can't transplant your neural matrix back without your physical presence, yes?"

"Yes."

"Good. Sometimes people can be a little reluctant to return. Understandable, I'm sure! Be advised there is a command call we can make to your synthetic body that will override any of your conscious inputs and return you safely here. But I'm sure we won't need to do that."

"No. Of course."

"Then you're all set to go. Have fun!"

"Thanks," said Lina. "I'll try."

On the day she was due to leave, the calls from work began to come through. She'd given them strict instructions back at Circe, told them to contact her only in an emergency. Clearly, they'd decided her final day was close enough. A stream of questions, requests for meetings, and complaints poured in, more and more queuing up all the time.

There was a message from Darian, too. An apology. Incredible. Angry, she shut the com stream down and swam. Her old life, her real life, seemed so distant. So strangely unimportant.

This time, at the mesh, the hulking monster was back. It cruised along beside the net as if searching for a way in. Its body was strong and powerful, a top predator in the ocean food-chain.

"You came back," it said. Although *it* was wrong. This was a he, no question. She wondered who he'd once been. "Sorry about frightening you the other day. Sometimes I forget what I was. What I am."

"And what are you?" asked Lina. "Who are you?"

"You can see what I am."

"But before, I mean. You came as a visitor?"

"Yes. Years ago, now."

"And you've been here all this time?"

"Couldn't tear myself away. Couldn't go back. Any of this sound familiar? You must be returning to your normal life soon, yes?"

She didn't answer his question. "But how? How did you escape the lagoon? And why have they allowed you to remain?"

"The escape was easy enough. Bit my way through with these teeth. One reason they don't offer this particular life-form any more, I believe."

"But didn't they broadcast a summons to force you back?"

"They probably did. By then I was too far away for it to reach me. And now I've disabled it."

"How?"

"There are ways. There are others out here. We've learned how to alter these bodies they provide. How to fully control them. How to live free."

"Others?"

"One or two. Don't know how many. The oceans of this world are vast and ancient. This little lagoon is just a puddle."

"What do you do out there?"

"Live. Swim. Eat. Or nothing at all."

"But don't you miss your old life? Your family, your friends?"

The creature ceased its to-and-fro cruising and swam directly to the mesh. Its bulk dwarfed her mermaid form.

"Sometimes," the creature said. "A little. Not enough to want to go back. It's interesting you're asking all these questions, isn't it?"

"Why?"

"Oh, come on. There's only one reason why you would. I heard your call."

"I can't leave the lagoon," said Lina.

"Why not?"

"For one, there's no way through the mesh. For two, I'm a mermaid, not some—forgive me—hulking monster. I wouldn't survive a minute out there in the depths. And for three, I don't want to."

"Up to you, of course. But for what it's worth you'd almost certainly be safe. These synthetic bodies are indestructible."

"Wouldn't stop me being eaten or something."

"Didn't they tell you about the defences they build into us?"

"A little."

"Trust me, they're a lot more powerful than they let on. Nothing touches us out here. Nothing harms us. We rule these oceans."

She didn't speak again for a moment. The creature resumed its lazy swimming, heading off into the dark depths as if indifferent to her.

"But the mesh," she called after it. "How would I get through, if I even wanted to?"

She thought he wasn't going to reply. Then his voice came over the com from the gloom. "Not through. *Over.* You were psych profiled, yes?"

"They…assessed us to help us decide which body to choose."

"They were making sure you were suitable for your chosen option. Making sure you didn't betray any hidden desire to escape the lagoon if, say, you showed a preference for a body capable of making such a huge leap. Like a mermaid, for instance."

"But if I escaped, if it were even possible, what would I do out there?"

The creature's voice was distant, as if it were already far away. "Whatever you like."

Lina swam up and down the line of the mesh for a time, thinking, then turned away. It was a crazy dream. She couldn't turn her back on her responsibilities, on everything demanded of her. She had to get home. But perhaps she could return for another stay next year.

SAFE WATERS

Another visit to Atlantis. Yes. That would be good.

She opened up the com stream to the outside again as she neared the shore. The flow of messages from Circe was a flood now. Everything she'd avoided by taking a break for two weeks was simply waiting for her to address when she got back. It was *endless*. There was more from Darian, too. A lot more. At the same time, overlaying it, she got the call from the medsuite telling her to return. Her time was up.

In sight of the BlueOcean building she stopped, treading water for a moment. A tower of bubbles glimmered past her, gently caressing her skin and scales. Above her, its shape warped by the waters, the sun was a benign yellow glow making the ocean gleam.

Lina turned. Throwing all her strength into it, she hurtled back into the depths, building up speed for the leap that would take her over the mesh.

NOTEFISHER
Cat McDonald

Fabric and scaffold spires stood beside the main stage, lit in neon blue and violet, changing color in time with the dubstep while a yellow half-moon watched overhead. Lying on the grass, I could feel the bass trembling against my back as I watched the people who still had the energy to dance—the programmer in me could feel dawn hurtling toward me, and had long since lost the will to join them.

I propped myself up against the damp couch behind me so I could better see through the smoke. Where the blue and green of the stage faded out into darkness, a young bare-chested man spun a quarterstaff with glowing ends in a whirl of rainbow LEDs and a topless woman in a plague doctor mask writhed near him in the center of a flashing red hula hoop. When the music gave them room to breathe, they watched each other.

"Feel anything yet?" Terra leaned down from the couch to wrap an arm around me and stroke my chest. We'd just met, so she didn't know I'd gotten out of the hospital recently, or why I'd put myself there.

"I don't think so." Time didn't really exist at the festival, but we'd taken the pills just after the rain had tapered off, and now the sky had completely cleared.

"Sometimes it takes me a while, too. Wanna go see if we can still get a cocoa?" She shoved herself off the couch, leaning on my shoulders. We walked through the well-trampled mud and grass, past the closed tents of the vendors, to the stretch where the food trucks were parked.

The sound of the stage faded until I could no longer feel it rattling in my lungs, and another nearby stage fought with it for control over the air with bouncing, throbbing beats. When we moved away from the music, Terra lost focus. Near the stage, I thought I knew who she was, a distant, soft, half-naked bon vivant mottled with summer freckles, her dreadlocks the same color as the tops of her arms and her clothes almost the same color as her thighs, but this far from the music she looked like a stranger.

When we found the food truck open, she pulled a bill out of her belt and bought hot cocoa for both of us without asking. We clutched at our cocoa and hurried back to our places under the shelter, Terra sprawled on the couch and me sitting on the ground in front of it so I could feel the stage's music in my legs. As the surroundings thickened into a monolithic haze of light and movement and physical, electric sound, I looked from the stage to Terra's face.

"How are you doing?" she asked. I said nothing, and looked back at the stage as the tension rose until the DJ let the beat fall back into place again.

When it did, I turned to her again.

"How are you doing?" she asked, the same snake of incense smoke winding around her from the hand of a nearby stranger-turned-friend.

"Is this what it's supposed to feel like?" I thought, and said, and as the words left my mouth they appeared in my vision, a blue script etched in the campfire smoke, drifting up and out of view.

What is that? I thought without saying, and the words appeared just under the previous ones, slightly violet now, the seed of a spiral beginning to spin in on itself in the firelight. Every new thought embroidered itself in smoke and sound, stitched to the previous. The visible beat pulsed through the campfire, a low, dizzying sub-tune singing in my lungs and legs.

"How are you doing?" Terra asked, her face and posture unchanged from the other times she'd asked, the very same wisp of smoke coiling behind her rough ponytail of dreadlocks. I stared at her, hoping to break the pattern, and she moved, smiling, to lean forward onto me, her skin clammy.

"I'm fine," said the script in the air, but I couldn't be sure whether or not I'd said it. I took a long drink of my cocoa and "this is warm" knit itself into the rest of my thoughts in a cheerful, almost-pink violet hue.

Words in the distance jabbed into the music, the farewell scream of one DJ handing the stage over to another. The stage lights went red; I could see the music burning in the bonfire while the shadows of cold dancers writhed in the heat. Red lasers scribed letters in the rising smoke.

"Am I supposed to be seeing this?" they said. "I like this song." And, "How long has passed?"

I thought I heard Terra ask how I was doing again, and saw the words attached to the spiral of my pink-violet thoughts in midair. I didn't look at her, but I felt her grip on me tighten.

A flicker of motion stole my attention from the dancers, the stage, and her embrace. Something white shone in the neon lights, more brilliant than the lazy moon, walking on the spiral of my sentiments. Its steps swayed forward and back as it strutted on long, dark, puppet-string legs. White wings tested the air for balance, and a tail of long black and red feathers trailed behind it. It was a crane, a magnificent white shorebird, walking on my thoughts as the words in the air tried to identify it.

It turned and followed the words "My God, it's coming for me" toward the shelter. A mane of black hair hung in limp curtains, swung with the movement of its graceful neck. It had no bird's head; its neck ended in a woman's head, her face obscured by a gilt mask with a long crane's beak attached to it, shining like a golden blade in the firelight. She reared and lunged into the music, leaving an empty place just above the rumble of the song's persistent bass, a note the same color as the scarlet stage lights speared on the end of her beak.

NOTEFISHER

She turned to me, cobralike with her intense concentration and sinuous movement. Her mask lifted as a bird's beak would in song, tilted up away from an absent lower jaw, revealing naught but darkness beneath it, and the scarlet note disappeared into nothing.

She puffed up her breast and sang, the stolen note roaring through her neck and out of the void beneath her beak, louder, stronger, brighter now that it had been speared from the river of music and devoured. It shook in the passage where my windpipe met the chamber of my lungs, driving its low sound directly into my heart, vibrating against my ribcage. The sheer weight of her voice pressed deep into me until I could feel it trembling in the back of my skull, right where it met my neck. Its depth choked me, lodged in my throat like an apple swallowed whole.

She closed her phantom beak, and for an instant as she fluttered down to perch on my thoughts, I thought I saw teeth.

"I'm going to die here."

"Even after I failed to die before?"

"Did all of it mean anything?"

"How long will they take to forget?"

She walked effortlessly along my panic, a hypnotic sway in her form and iron purpose in her black eyes. The sound of the note still rang in my skull even as the pressure evaporated from my chest in the silence.

The effect of the drug distorted her as she approached, stretched her infinite neck and brutal beak out while her eyes seemed to swell until they occupied the whole of my vision. Great emptiness surrounded me, glittering at the edges as the curve of the eyeball caught the lights in every direction. Even my own thoughts appeared only in reflection, inverted and foggy in a spiral around the great eye's pupil.

I only managed to read one before sleep took me.

"I know this darkness."

I woke the next day, dew-damp and freezing, my nose gone numb and my hands clutching at the wet grass. The fires had long since burnt out, the lights put away for the night, and a soothing voice from the stage directed a beginner's yoga class. Last night's army of surging bodies was long gone, replaced by a handful of sluggish, filthy campers performing earnest sun salutations.

Terra still slept behind me.

When I closed my eyes, I could hear someone playing an acoustic guitar from a nearby stage, far enough away that I couldn't make sense of her lyrics but close enough that I could just drift on the melody while the sun gained momentum.

I could still feel the stolen note on the back of my head like tinnitus of the scalp.

I looked down at my shirt, and couldn't shake the feeling that I'd dressed wrong, that everyone at the festival could smell a programmer who'd come to escape himself. They'd all greeted me with a baffling warmth and alien openness anyway.

"Hey, you," Terra grumbled from behind me, her voice stuck in her throat from sleeping outdoors, walls of phlegm between her lips and her thoughts.

"Morning. Want something to eat?"

"I hear those vegan sticky buns are amazing, but they keep selling out before I get up."

I stood, more than a match for the disorientation and exhaustion that tried to hold me to the mud. "I think we're up early. Ground's still wet. Come on, let's grab breakfast."

She swayed as I pulled her to her feet, and staggered along beside me until a good stretch and yawn halfway to the food trucks brought her fully into the waking world.

"So, you got any plans today? I've got a couple vendors I wanna hit, but other than that it's just sleep. I think my friend's art workshop is today, too."

"When?"

Terra shrugged. Neither of us had known the time since I turned off my cell phone and locked it in my car the day before.

We found the food trucks open and the sticky rolls still available. With cups of coffee in our hands and bowls full of fluffy bread and syrup in our laps, we sat on a bench and watched the festival wake up. In the morning light, the mystery and allure of the place melted away into a cheery timelessness, an Avalon of bare flesh and chai tea.

Terra finished her breakfast and led me down into the marketplace. She talked to the vendors like she knew them, sat on the grass with the woman in the crystal shop, joked with the saleswoman about a mesh top but never actually tried it on.

This world, like the real one, came easier to some people than to others. We wandered away from the vendors, and I followed her to the workshop dome. She swam across the fields, from stranger to stranger, with a broad, guileless smile, and I wondered if she was as hopeless as I was, back in the real world.

The ache on the back of my skull was accelerating. Tiny spasms ricocheted under the skin on the back of my neck, frantic shivers like I could still see the crane and still fear death.

"Ooh! Interested in painting? I was going to head to the river, but it's probably still too cold."

I hadn't painted in years. Like the time I spent under close watch at the hospital, I kept this fact to myself.

A lone woman sat in the dome, cross-legged on a blanket, stooped over a painting in vibrant green oils. Terra greeted her with a hug, and they sat talking and laughing while I watched. Idly, like dipping into a bowl of snacks at a social, they reached for the paint and scattered carefree strokes on the canvas.

I sat down on the grass next to them and watched shapes emerging from the aimless banter in color, and even took up a paintbrush to try and contribute. Once I had a brush in my hand, though, everything inside me went dark. I lost the shapes, forgot what I had intended to turn them into, and the color faded from my mind.

In my headache, I could hear the stolen note pressing against my brain, triggering a deep, heart-squeezing anxiety in my chest.

I made my apologies to Terra and left. With a strange, warm little smile, she told me she'd probably be going to the river later, and to catch up with her there. The feeling of the note faded when I turned my back on the dome, but it never really went away. A stabbing pain hobbled my left ankle while I tried to leave, but I limped back to the vendors.

The day crawled toward noon, and I walked to the smaller stage where the acoustic acts played. When the woman at the mic opened her mouth, her first note fell silent and the guitar played a resonant nothing.

When I finally noticed the heat, I thought to go meet Terra at the river.

I came through the trees to a scene from a fairytale, a slow, green river sparkling in the daylight, carefree creatures splashing each other and playing in the water like they'd never grow old.

I sat to watch, and Terra found me immediately. Still dripping with river water, goosebumps rising from her freckled skin, she joined me in the grass and wrapped a wet arm around me. She smelled like river water, like the countryside.

"There you are! How was your day?"

"Quiet. Just listened to market stage. How was your painting?"

"Oh, it's a mess! But she says she can fix it. Hey, I was meaning to ask, how was your trip last night?"

I didn't have the words for it.

"It…kind of got to me."

Terra hugged me again, pressing damp spots through my shirt. "I've had some rough nights myself. But the nice thing about this stuff is that it's kind of consistent. Once I got to know her, she stopped trying to drown me."

"So you always see the same thing?"

"Yeah, mostly. I think she's always there; she's started sneaking into my acid trips, too." Terra looked down at the water like she looked at me or any other person.

She really did belong in this world, and I knew when she embraced me, and when I looked at the people spending their summer afternoon in the river, that I didn't. I'd come out here to belong somewhere, but I'd just found a whole new world with no room for me.

"Hey, don't be so down! If you're game to give it another try, let's hang out at the forest stage tonight. We'll take less, so it doesn't get as bad, and I'll try and keep an eye on you. If not, that's cool, too."

I felt the tingling on the back of my skull, the vivid scarlet of the note the crane had injected into me, the fear of death I'd experienced for the first time in months. Either the crane would kill me, or she would teach me to fear dying again.

I agreed to another dose.

On the other side of the food trucks, near the dirt road I'd taken to get into the festival, a little boardwalk led over a tiny creek. We followed it to a secluded clearing, a place completely out of sight of the rest of the festival. Statues and paintings in the style of some forgotten Mayan temple peered out of the grass and the trees and throbbed in the directionless golden stage lights. A crowd of bouncing hedonists pressed in close to the electric ziggurat, and still more gathered around the bonfire or in the shelter nearby. Beside the shelter, an artist entertained guests in a little tent while working on a mural in neon colors.

"How are you doing?" Terra asked me. I waited a moment to see if she would repeat it. She didn't.

"I'm a bit nervous."

If Terra was right, it would come for me again. The back of my head resonated in time with the music's heavy, punching beats, taking the place of the notes permanently stolen from the festival sound, and the gold and pink lights took over as the sun gave up on us.

I stood a log up on its end and sat by the fire. Terra danced a little in place but, true to her word, stayed close to me, her hand never leaving my neck.

Then, like it had before, the scene tightened around me. A change in the wind blew stinging wood-smoke into my eyes.

The smoke never left.

No matter how often the wind changed, I saw the world through a steel-blue haze and tasted the fire every time I opened my mouth. Far away in the movement of the dance, I saw some beautiful shadow-puppet swim, and for a brief moment I thought I had gone back to the river.

The light diffused through the smoke, no longer confined to beams and bulbs, pulsing through the air around me at all sides, fading through the colors of the rainbow one at a time. Aggressive, high-tempo house music trembled between my teeth, puppetmaster over the lights and shadows.

A nearby statue caught my attention as the smoke around it dissolved, a warrior surrounded by living glyphs of serpents and jaguars, tails and tongues lashing out against the surrounding bacchanalia. His headdress of quetzal feathers waved in the air like seaweed, back and forth on the song's dominant rhythm.

The bass intensified, and I felt it grip my heart as the tension rose. The missing note in my skull shook against my emotions, sent spikes of anxiety through me as the lasers scribed my thoughts into the environment.

I stared at the warrior statue as the serpents began to travel around him and the jaguars stared out of the scene at me. The colors around us shifted, and the DJ handed the altar-stage over to someone darker, slower, deeper.

The warrior opened his mouth, slowly parting his lips and stretching his jaw to expose the darkness behind the stone and the white glimmer hiding inside, holding his stern eye contact with me the whole time. She stepped forward, sliding past the sentry's tongue and teeth in time with the rumbling music. Her beak-mask emerged from his mouth, followed by her head and hair, her serpentine neck, and her brilliant wings. When those were free, she stretched them out into the air, her wingspan broad enough to completely encircle me, to shut out the shadow-play beyond the fire.

With one flap, she cleared the smoke and fanned the flames until they threatened to singe the sky and roast the stars. As she approached, I could feel nothing but heat and the vibration of the music in my body.

She darted forward and caught one of the lowest notes in the song, her beak piercing a deep red-black sound. With another great flap of her wings, she threw it into the air and swallowed it; I could see the darkness moving through the white pipe of her neck.

Once it reached her breast, she inhaled deeply and sang the stolen note to me. It seared through the air, blackening the space around it as it left her empty face to press itself into my chest. The volume, the brilliance, and the power of it made impact directly on my heart, and I could smell my flesh burning. My lungs shuddered under the force, and my sinuses shook as they took in the quaking air. The red note on the back of my skull trembled and the black note in my chest throbbed and buzzed against whatever was still solid in my body.

When I looked down, there was an empty hole in my body where my heart had been, and blood poured out of it onto my lap. The warrior standing behind her held my still-beating heart, and turned as if to advance on the temple stage with his trophy.

I couldn't breathe. The harmony of the two stolen notes tied rings around my neck and squeezed. I intended to plead with the crane for my life, but when I raised my hands in supplication I realized I had begun to worship her. She surrounded me in her brilliant wings and the world went white.

I woke under the shelter, stretched out on one of the couches, my hand trailing on the ground and a searing pain in my throat. I could still feel the note she'd forced into my chest, a cold shiver just over my heart. The back of my skull tingled.

This stage was silent in the morning. The statues stood lifeless in daylight, and every other festival-goer in the shelter slept. Terra was asleep on the ground next to the couch, having done her best to take care of me and failed where it counted.

I could get around her if I took the course carefully, and from there, I made it out from under the canopy unhindered and into the sunlight.

I wasn't hungry, but I was cold. I'd unrolled a sleeping bag somewhere in a tent I'd barely seen since the festival started, and my car sat nearby, completely willing to take me back home to a medicine cabinet that wouldn't fail me this time. The festival's last day would go on without me, like everyone else.

While I formalized my plans, the pain intensified. Inaudible music shook against my chest and in my skull, my heart pounding to some outside beat. That tinnitus spread through my nerves, rode my spine to my heart, my knuckles, and the surface of my calves. My legs slipped out from under me as I tried to leave.

I very nearly made it past the artist's empty shelter, but when I looked in, the sight of blacklight-neon paint and brushes jabbed into me, and I felt her cold beak pierce my ankle again. Bone and tendon gave way to gold and music, and I fell to the ground without feeling the impact.

When I pulled myself into the tent on my forearms and elbows, the pain ebbed. Once I'd made it all the way to a milk-crate table with a stack of moisture-curled papers, the vibration in my head had calmed down, and the pain disappeared. The memory of my own terrors written in the smoke faded into quiet when I took up one of the paintbrushes.

I found a palette of dried poster paints. When I brushed water into a pool on the surface of the red cake, the tension in my chest dissolved into nothing. It took with it the familiar pain in my throat, the one I'd known for years. A dull ache had settled in just under my jaw the first day I realized I had a reason to die, and it never left until that moment.

Before I knew it, the sun had finished rising. Terra's hand gripped my shoulder to wake me from the dream, and she settled in next to me with her head against my arm.

She didn't say anything. I thought I felt her shake.

On the paper in front of me, I'd painted the broken belt that had sent me to the hospital. Now that I had it in front of me, the crane was quiet. I was quiet.

"It's beautiful," Terra said, but she didn't stop shaking. She didn't belong in the world I'd described, but I did.

Now that I'd purged my failed suicide, I could feel a pleasant hum in my chest. The crane's stolen notes sang inside me, and even though I thought I saw her stalking in my peripheral vision, I recognized the sound of the muse that had saved me.

I set the paint aside to dry and stood to buy Terra breakfast.

.

Experience
Sandra Wickham

My voice lifted the cruise passengers in a crescendo to the end of the song, and even without using my powers I could have had any of them—their worldly possessions, their hearts, their very souls if I chose. Someone in the front row hadn't fallen for my charms, though, and when I caught her eye I almost stumbled over the final notes. A true performer to the end, however, I kept my composure, took my bow, and left the stage. It couldn't be coincidence that one of the embodiments of the Siren Goddess was aboard my ship.

The entire cast returned to the stage for the final bows. The line of performers split down the middle and I sashayed forward, a flowing vision in my sparkling aqua gown. The crowd erupted in applause while she still sat, motionless, eyes judgmental.

Not surprisingly, I found her waiting outside my stateroom. Reflexively, I began a hair toss, then stopped, saving myself the wasted effort. Like me, she was a brunette, but her hair was longer, fuller, and shinier than mine. She was also taller than me, at least six feet, with the same green eyes, but hers were even brighter and more enticing. I definitely hated her.

I placed my card in the door. "Would you like to come in? It's not much, I'll warn you."

"It will be fine. This won't take long," she replied, her voice even more sultry than mine.

Inwardly I cringed with jealousy as I pushed open the door and held it for her. "Excellent. I do have a busy night ahead."

She entered, spun, and sat, her purple gown flowing to settle in a perfect arc about her crystal high heels. "Ah, yes. Using your divination powers to win in the casino? Or perhaps a romantic rendezvous? Such a valiant use of our powers."

Tilting my chin a smidge higher, I did a smooth half-spin that rivaled hers and sat on my bed. "If the Goddess had a problem with me, why have they not come to me sooner?"

She folded her hands gracefully in her lap. "We are here now. It is the desire of the Goddess that you resume your intended purpose, right here, on this ship."

Resume my purpose? I had served my purpose for decades, I'd done my time and I'd been damn good at it. No, I'd been the best. Yet, murder was messy and I was over it. I deserved some freedom.

She crossed her legs, flashing her crystal heel. I wanted to stab her with it for crashing into my world. "You do remember your purpose, don't you?"

"I am fully aware of who I am," I replied quietly.

"Good," she went on. "There is evil on this ship that must be stopped. One of its victims is also on board. You will meet her in the lounge by the pool tomorrow evening."

I held myself perfectly still. "No."

She studied me for moment, then nodded. "It is the decision of the Goddess that if you refuse, your powers be nullified until you resume your purpose." She stood. "There will be no further discussion."

It is possible my composure fell apart as the door swung closed behind her, and I jumped to my feet and rushed to the mirror. The change began immediately. My face etched with wrinkles, skin sagged, my hair dulled to a dirty brown. Chunks of it fell to the carpet like wiry tears. My eyes lost their sparkle.

I slammed the small counter in front of me and turned away from the mirror, my breath coming in horrified gasps. I was a Siren, not some child to be taught a lesson! Appealing to one of the other Goddess fractures would be futile. A move as powerful as this would have taken the cooperation of all of them.

I ripped myself out of the sequin dress and paced the few steps of my small room in my undergarments, ignoring the way things now sagged and flopped where they hadn't before. There had to be a loophole, a way to get back to being me again. I avoided looking in the mirror each time I passed it. That wasn't me, it was some repulsive casing, some mortal disguise I was now forced to wear.

They didn't call it murder, of course. I tracked down men who abducted women, and killed them. They deserved it, but the deaths were by my hands, not the Goddess's, my conscience, not theirs—assuming they even had one. If they wanted these men hunted and killed, why not do it themselves?

Despite my bitterness at the Goddess for making me do their dirty work, I would have to return to the hunt, but without powers to aid me.

"How do you expect me to do this?" I yelled at the empty room and, in true Goddess style, received no answer.

No amount of make up was going to help. I did the best I could but decided camouflage was my best option. I grabbed sunglasses, found the dullest pants and blouse in my wardrobe, and wrapped my withered locks in an equally drab scarf.

Out on deck, several twenty-somethings with shiny bodies that made my mouth water laughed and jostled each other in line to get a drink at the pool bar. A gnawing began in my gut at their complete lack of regard for me. A day ago, they would've barely been able to contain themselves in my presence.

A slight, elderly woman in a motorized wheelchair zinged up beside me. "These young kids today, who knows what they're thinking."

It took me a moment to realize she was talking to me, like a comrade in arms. My hand went to my scarf. "Indeed," I responded.

EXPERIENCE

It was only temporary, I reminded myself as the woman continued talking like we were old companions.

"You're one of the singers here, yes?"

I pulled the scarf lower with both hands and slid the glasses down over my eyes. "No," I tried to laugh, but my spine straightened and I felt my chin lift slightly.

She squinted. "Yes, I've seen you. Boy, those lights really do a trick, don't they? I believe I'm supposed to meet with you, over in the lounge. My name is Beth."

I stared down at her for a moment. This was the victim I was to meet? The young ones moved off with their drinks and I pointed toward the bar. "Can I get you something?"

Her wrinkled face lit up. "That would be lovely. A scotch, neat." Expertly, she steered her chair around several people and wove through tables toward an empty one. I followed dutifully with two scotches, neat.

She'd pulled her scooter up sideways to one of the tables, lifted the armrest, and turned so she could sit facing the table.

"To youth." I raised my glass.

"To experience," she retorted, her hand shaking slightly as we clinked glasses. She took a drink, contemplated it for a moment, then took another. "Not bad," she said as she set it down. "I've had better."

I believed her. "You were told to meet with me?"

"I was told you would help me, and for some reason I believed it. I'm here to put to rest an old demon." She sipped her scotch and looked over her glass at me, then signaled the overworked waitress, pointed at our glasses, and met my eyes again. "It happened exactly fifty years ago. That's why I'm here."

I sipped my scotch—she was right; I'd also had better—and waited for her to continue.

"I was travelling, not like this mind you." She spread an arm to encompass the lounge, the ship. "I travelled alone, just me and my backpack." She smiled, but it faded slowly. "One night, after a party at a local hostel, it all changed." She took a long sip and I watched her, an old rage beginning to burn inside me. This woman was beautiful, in her way, friendly, caring, and someone had done awful things to her.

"I was always careful, of course. Young woman travelling alone, but I managed to connect with good people, sometimes travelling with them for a while. I've told myself a million times it wasn't my fault, of course—that's what all the shrinks said to do. Not sure it ever took. Tell me about yourself."

The waitress brought our drinks and I immediately asked for another round. I tried to smile. "You wouldn't believe me if I told you."

She studied me once more and took a long drink. "You might be surprised what I'd believe. No one knows the whole story. They don't know how I got away."

"How did you get away?"

"You wouldn't believe me if I told you," she replied, smirking, and I saluted her with my glass.

"Fair enough." We clinked glasses again, and after a hard swallow I met her gaze. "The man who abducted you, he's on this cruise?"

She nodded, stared into her glass for a moment, then looked up and smiled. "Is it just me or is this stuff tasting worse the more we have?"

It was probably too much scotch, but I was actually beginning to enjoy myself. Beth had a killer wit and a positive attitude on just about everything. Despite what had happened to her at an early age, she'd managed to own her own business and retired with enough to enjoy this and many more cruises. I could see it in her eyes, though. The abduction still haunted her. She'd never married, never been able to get close to anyone and though she didn't say it directly, she regretted never having a family. She wanted revenge, and I was starting to want that for her.

EXPERIENCE

While escorting her to her cabin, we found ourselves giggling like teenagers over some joke or other. She wheeled to a stop at one of the cabin doors. "This is me."

"You need help?" Even as I said it, I knew she didn't. She had the door unlocked and worked her scooter inside with expert skill.

"Worry about yourself," she said with a grin, and let the door slam closed behind her.

I smiled as I returned to my room. We planned to meet in the morning, to find the man who'd taken her. She claimed she just wanted to see his face, to get closure on what had happened to her. If it would help her, I didn't mind having someone along on the hunt, at least as far as to find him. She didn't have to witness what happened after, unless she wanted to.

I passed the mirror and, against my own better judgment, stared at my reflection. What I saw was a version of myself I hadn't seen in decades. I wasn't sure I liked it.

I clicked off the lights, replacing my image with darkness.

Morning brought with it renewed anger at the Goddess. I dared not look in the mirror as I prepared to leave. I dressed to blend in and met Beth, who looked far too chipper after all the Scotch we'd consumed.

"Good morning, sunshine," she said, and pointed to the extra coffee sitting opposite her.

"Thank you." I slipped into the seat and debated the beverage in front of me. I didn't usually drink coffee—I didn't need to. My usual energy was more than I needed to glow brighter than the disco ball in the ship's nightclub. It did smell warm and inviting, though.

I brought the cup to my mouth, took a careful sip, then set it back down again, resisting the urge to spit it back out. "Why do people like this so much?"

Beth tilted her head at me slightly. "Not a coffee drinker? Have a few more sips. You'll see."

I took another drink. The dark liquid did not taste any better, but my brain started to tingle and I studied the cup of coffee with new wonder. Suddenly, Beth let out an anguished gasp. Her face paled even more than usual but when she lifted her hand to point behind me, it didn't shake.

I followed the direction she indicated, dismissing the family of four shuffling toward the cafeteria line and the staff member collecting used dishes. That left the tall, rather attractive young man in walking shorts and a collared dark blue shirt coming through the doors. I turned back to Beth.

Her face had frozen, and I thought for a moment I might need to smack her to bring her back. "It can't be," she whispered. "That's him. I mean, that's him, exactly the same as fifty years ago."

I turned to look again, this time as the hunter, not the friend. It was there in the way he held himself, as though every other being in the room was inferior to him. I recognized it well. Without my powers, it wasn't easy to determine which type of supernatural he was, but there was no question—he wasn't human.

"Am I losing my mind?" Beth whispered. "That's it, isn't it? Some sort of dementia. I knew it."

I shook my head, watching the supernatural out of the corner of my eye as he glided amongst passengers. "You're not losing your mind. Do you trust me?"

She paused, then nodded.

"Then believe me when I tell you, what took you was not human. He looks human, but he is far from it. Also believe me when I say, I will take of it."

Relief washed over her; I saw it as clearly as if she'd be wearing her torment as a cloak.

"I believe you."

"Good. Then you'll excuse me." I stood to go but she reached over and touched my hand.

"Whatever happens, please tell me."

Something in her eyes dug its way into my heart, and I nodded

EXPERIENCE

before shifting my attention to the hunt. The supernatural was casually picking up a coffee and breakfast bagel, grinning at the humans as though they were all prey, the young women especially. I had to do something about this predator, for Beth's sake, but also to stop it from doing it again. How many women had he hurt, how many lives ruined?

I followed him outside, and once in the full exposure of the sun I knew him for what he was—a Leshy. The Leshy usually appear as tall, handsome males when in human form and, like this one, cast no shadow.

I followed him for several hours. If he knew I was there, he never gave any indication of it. If I'd been my usual self, he probably would've sensed me, supernatural to supernatural, so maybe there was one good thing about the Goddess taking my powers away.

He acted as I would've thought, stalking different young ladies, talking to them, taking stock of his options. Watching the creature that had hurt Beth slither around the decks of the cruise ship increased my desire to capture him, for reasons that had nothing to do with what the Goddess wanted.

He had picked his next victim, a young woman in a tight white mini dress over a hot pink bikini. I cursed the Goddess for sticking me in this situation. I lacked the powers to lure this creep to me. Even if I did, what then? Fight him, what, hand to hand? With this decrepit old body, that would not turn out well for me.

I circled around the pool bar the Leshy and the girl had set up in, only to find that I was also being followed. I stepped into an alcove by the windows and waited until Beth wheeled by. "Keeping an eye on me?"

She stopped and didn't look back. "I thought you were going to deal with him."

I moved up beside her and we continued down the hall. Her expression read disappointment. Reporting to the Goddess would've been easier. "I'm working on it."

"I know you have the ability. I don't know what you are, but if you say he's not human then I'm pretty sure you aren't, either."

"Actually, that's the problem. I don't have my abilities right now—long story—that doesn't mean I can't deal with the situation. I'm just not sure how, yet."

We took up a spot where we could see the Leshy and Miss White Mini Dress. "You have got to tell her."

"She wouldn't listen. She'd think I was crazy, or maybe jealous of her." Was I?

"If she won't listen, get him away from her."

"How do you propose I do that?"

She looked me up and down. "You think you have no powers? The stage isn't what makes you shine."

When little Miss White Mini Dress needed to use the ladies room, I waited for her to disappear and then approached the Leshy.

"If you're interested in meeting some beautiful women, I mean the best on the ship, come by the show early tonight. I'll introduce you to the cast." I wasn't lying, the cruise line only hired the most beautiful staff for their shows, sometimes sacrificing talent for appearance.

He gave me the once over. "Why would you want to do that for me?"

"Oh, it's not for you, it's for me. I bring them a cute plaything for the night, they're appreciative and are happy to help me if I ask for a little extra stage time."

His eyes narrowed and for a moment, I thought he might have figured out who I was. What I was. His eyes skipped over my shoulder and I knew Miss White Mini Dress was headed back. I gave him my best smile, one that, under normal circumstances would've had the entire ship begging at my feet. "Better, trust me. Just give them your name at the theatre, they'll bring you to see me."

I walked away, not sure whether he'd take my bait or not.

I hadn't been nervous before a show since I was a youth. Tonight, however, had my palms sweaty and my heart fluttering. Being backstage brought back the old mannerisms, head held high, proud gliding steps, but unfortunately, it didn't bring back my looks. I got there before anyone else and found a wig—that helped a bit—and did my makeup, but it was a sad replacement for magical aesthetic assistance. The stares I got from my cast mates made it clear they noticed, but no one said anything.

It was only thirty minutes to show time when one of the stagehands ushered the Leshy forward and hustled off again. Smiling, I led him to the women's dressing room. The other cast members usually gave me some space before a show; tonight, luckily, was no exception.

I held the door for him. "I'm so glad you could make it. Please, have a seat."

He scanned the room, hesitating. I had to work fast. "Please, sit. I've asked the ladies to come by." He regained his air of superiority and entered, sitting on the only stool in the room. "You don't mind if I warm up, do you?" I tapped my throat. "Have to keep my instrument in shape, especially at my age."

He gave me an awkward smile. "Do what you need to do."

Facing the mirrors, I pretended to be absorbed in my appearance and voice warm up, but I watched him closely when I began to sing. I used songs from the show so he would have no reason to get suspicious. The Goddess had taken my powers, but I could still feel strength in my song—something innate that could never be taken away.

His head dropped and then jolted back up again, eyes wide. "What are you—"

Singing louder, with everything I had, I walked towards him. He lifted a finger to point at me, but it flopped back down to his thigh and his head bobbed again.

I didn't stop singing.

His upper body slumped, then he fell off the stool, crashing to the ground in a heap.

I approached cautiously—his breath remained deep and steady, he showed no signs of consciousness. Wheels appeared at the door, quickly followed by Beth.

"How did you get back here?" I checked the hall after she wheeled in but no one paid us any attention. "The last thing I need is a crowd right now," I said as I returned, then froze.

Beth pushed herself from her scooter, took a few steps, and collapsed next to the Leshy. The silver table knife in her right hand shone in the dressing table mirror lights.

Before she had a chance to drive it into his throat, I grabbed her wrist, first with one hand, then with both. She was stronger than she looked. "That won't make things better."

Her eyes flashed at me, lit with rage. "You don't know that."

I twisted her wrist, gently, with only enough pressure to make her let go of the knife. "You said you trust me. Trust me. Becoming a killer will only make it worse."

She relaxed under my grip and I helped her back into her scooter. "What now?" she asked, slightly out of breath.

I stepped back over the prone Leshy. "I kill him."

Beth glared down her nose at me, somehow, even though she was looking up at me. "You said it would make it worse."

"For you. Not for me."

Beth cried out, and a hand grabbed my ankle and yanked my leg out from under me. Sequins flashed before my eyes as I hit the ground in a tangle of dress and costume jewelry. I kicked out with my other foot, but the Leshy was fast. He threw his weight on me and, despite my thrashing, had me pinned in seconds. His body crushed mine. I felt my ribs press to their breaking point, and then I was yanked to my feet, both arms pinned behind my back and Beth's knife pointed at my throat.

"Say or sing anything and this knife meets your larynx." He growled from behind me, pulling my wrists higher with his other hand to cause enough pain to make his point.

EXPERIENCE

"Calm down, dearie, someone must've spiked your drink," I said, cursing the Goddess once again for taking away any tools I might use against this supernatural being.

"Funny. And you would be?" The knife pressed into my neck.

"No one important. Do you recognize her?" I motioned as much as I could with my chin. Beth sat perfectly still, though I could see the fire in her eyes.

"Oh, I remember. I remember all my women. I'd say you've aged well, but that would be a lie."

I'd had enough. I lifted my leg and smashed one high heel into the top of his foot. He reflexively bent forward and I smashed my head backwards into his. He didn't go down, but he loosened his grip on my wrists enough to allow me to break free. While his hands were at his newly-broken nose, I turned and gave him a strong knee to the groin. He might be a Leshy, but in human form that was going to hurt.

He crumpled forward, and I grabbed the curling iron off the dressing table and hit him across the jaw. It put him down but not quite out, so I hit him again. This time, I stepped on his hand to make sure he was not conscious.

Beth applauded slowly, grinning.

I bowed, then grabbed the knife he'd dropped and studied it for a moment. This was it. Did I really want to go back to this? "You should probably go," I said.

She hesitated, then nodded. "Drinks, later?"

I gave her a nod. "I'll meet you there."

She disappeared and I focused on the task ahead. Before I could begin, another person appeared in the doorway. She was different than before, shorter, thinner, blonde, but it was another fragment of the Goddess.

"I have got to talk to theatre security," I muttered. Out of habit, I flicked my wig. "What do you want?"

"We have seen what you have done and we are pleased. We will take it from here. You no longer need to kill."

It clicked.

"You rescued her, didn't you?" Beth hadn't been able to tell anyone how she'd gotten away and had said I wouldn't believe it. I almost didn't.

"We did, but the Leshy escaped. We lost him until now." She gave me a slight bow. "You have done well. The Goddess is sorry to have done this to you, but we are pleased with the outcome. We will restore your powers if you agree to continue to hunt when we need you."

Beth had restored something in me—the reason I did what I did. I also thought of Beth and the life she could've had. "I'll agree, under one condition."

I met Beth in the lounge once more. If I hadn't known what to look for, I wouldn't have recognized her. She had a glass of scotch in her hand and her scooter was nowhere in sight. In her mid-twenties now, with amber hair like silk, skin smooth and beautiful. Her smile was brilliant. Another scotch arrived as I joined her.

"Was that for me, or you?" I asked with a grin.

"Let's say it was for you," she replied, her voice crisp and clear. "I take it you had something to do with my transformation?"

I nodded. "I thought you might like another shot at things."

She eyed me skeptically. "You haven't learned much, have you?"

"I beg your pardon?"

She flicked her hand at her new, young body. "I don't want this. I've done my time, lived my life, I like who I am now. Change me back."

I'm sure I blinked far too many times before answering. "Are you sure?"

"Absolutely. But let me get to my room first. My scooter is in there." She lifted her glass. "To experience. Here's hoping I have many more adventures."

We clinked and drank.

THRESHOLD
K.T. Ivanrest

"Daddy, is the wall supposed to have eyes?"

"Shh, Eisa, not now."

Navrin gave up watching his father and glanced where his little sister was pointing, but all he saw was the wall of the sphere, a shimmering barrier shooting from the earth and reaching high into the midnight sky. The powerful magic was as still and eerie as always, silent as the stars, but it was also decidedly eyeless, much to his relief.

Embarrassed to have even looked—did he expect the Between were just sitting out there beyond the wall, politely waiting for his parents to finish setting up the traps?—he cast around for something else to examine and caught sight of Rokat, who was staring intently at the barrier, expression wary.

Navrin snorted. "Did you really just check for eyes in the sphere?" he asked his stepbrother, working as much disdain into his voice as possible. "On the authority of a five-year-old?"

To his immense irritation, Rokat merely shrugged, and his concerned frown became a smile which he directed at the little girl. "If Eisa says there are eyes, there are probably eyes. Where did you see them, Eis?"

Her face lit with delight and she pointed toward the wall as he crouched down to match her height. Trying not to gag at Rokat's doting-big-brother act and doing his best to appear casual, Navrin shifted enough that he, too, could peer again at the sphere without Rokat noticing. It did nothing to improve his mood when his stepbrother caught his eye and gave him an "I don't see them, either" look, as though they had something in common. As though sharing this might make them friends. He scowled and turned away, fingering the long knives strapped to his thighs and focusing his thoughts on the evening ahead.

Across the field, Inata—Navrin still had trouble thinking of her as Mother—finished tuning a catapult and gave one of its taut ropes a flick with her finger, but nothing could be heard over the humming. There was always humming first, the surest sign that the Between were coming. It coated the twilight landscape like mist, a low, steady sound that set normal people on edge and raised the spirits of poachers like Navrin and his family.

And even with Rokat stealing Eisa's affection yet again, Navrin's spirits were higher than usual tonight, because his long wait was finally over. Tonight, if they were lucky, if they caught one, he would get the honor of killing it.

His first Between. The first of many.

The best fourteenth birthday present he could imagine.

He'd been preparing for months, half-listening to his father's lectures while fantasizing about battles that would never happen, because no trapper with any sense gave pure evil the chance to fight back. And yet, in his waking dreams he saw it breaking loose and running wild, and there he was to stop it, just in time to save his sister. To make her remember him and forget about Rokat. Especially because, in most of his dreams, his stepbrother got eaten…

"Do you think it was a Between?" Eisa asked Rokat.

"Probably wanted to see if any of us look tasty," Navrin cut in. "You're so small they could swallow you in a single bite!" He hunched over, raised his hands into claws, and lunged at her, roaring in a very poor imitation of a Between.

It was good enough, though, to send Eisa scampering away, first to Rokat—of course she would hide behind *him*—and then, when Navrin crossed his eyes and stuck his tongue out, to their father. "Daddy, Navrin's being mean again!"

A long, familiar sigh. "Honestly, Navrin, you're coming of age tonight. Can't you go a single day—"

"I didn't do anything!" Navrin lied, purely out of habit. At his side, Rokat shifted just slightly, and the temptation to once more "not do anything" flared within him, exacerbated by the persistent humming. If he was going to get in trouble he may as well earn it, and taking it out on someone he loathed would be much more satisfying than tormenting the sister he only pretended to dislike.

His father frowned, but, "Mmm hmm," was all he said before planting a final torch in the ground and climbing to his feet. "All set."

Inata darted to join the group, nervous energy in every motion she made and five small cream-colored balls on her open palm. They each grabbed one, even Eisa, and began rolling them between their hands. It was their surest protection against the Between's most sinister weapon. Against teeth and claws and venom they had armor and weapons and traps, but against the song, only wax.

When the substance was warm, Navrin broke it in half and stuffed a piece inside each ear while fear and elation waged their usual war inside him. It was coming, the song, the song and the Between, and then his kill, his chance.

To his parents it was an opportunity to profit off keeping the borders safe, but not to him. Not tonight. He eyed Eisa and then Rokat, who cowered at his mother's side, expression halfway between haunted and nauseated. He looked that way every time they trapped, and the only thing worse than having a disgrace for a stepbrother was the fact that Navrin had not yet been able to pry, or tease, the reason out of him.

In the muffled silence created by the wax, he watched his father grab two enchanted swords—illegal, just like everything else they were doing this evening—and lead Eisa to a tall, ruined tower at the edge of their line of traps, the remains of an outpost long since abandoned. At its base he planted the weapons some ten feet apart, Eisa at their center, and a miniature shield sprang into place around her. She waved from within the silver dome and Navrin returned the gesture, only to realize she was waving at Rokat.

Anger, jealousy, disappointment—

And then there was a crack like glass shattering against stone, so loud he could hear it through the wax, and a shadow beyond the sphere, massive and black.

His heart leapt and he brushed his hands against his knives again before reaching up and pretending to press the wax further into his ears. Instead, he dislodged it just enough that he would be able to hear it when it happened…

As if on cue, the humming rose in volume and then pitch, spreading through the night until it became a song, powerful and breathtaking. No words, simply music, low and intense, and though there were no drums Navrin could feel a beat as clearly as his own heart.

The breath caught in his throat. Even half-hearing it, he could feel its familiar effects, its deadly and exhilarating pull. It was the same every time he dared listen, and it never got old. His nervousness washed away and he felt brave, even brash. Anything was possible, he just had to prove it—prove it so everyone could see, right here and now. For a moment, he forgot that he disliked his new family. He wanted them to watch, to realize he was strong.

Around him they worked, sealed against the song's invitation to show off, fight, stride straight through the sphere and into the jaws of the monsters beyond. His father caught his eye and smiled, and he grinned back and nodded, impatience growing as the song worked its way inside him. Where were the Between? They always came after the song, pushing through the wall when their singing could not lure their prey out into the waste. His eyes scanned the sphere for more shadows. Surely it would not be long now, and then he would get his chance.

"Navrin!"

He blinked and paused, one foot in the air. When had he started walking? Why was he past the traps and making his way toward the glowing barrier? Someone caught his shoulder and he turned to see Inata, forehead creased, eyes dark with concern.

Again he made a show of reaching for his ears, but her hands got there first and pressed the wax deep into them. The song faded to nothing but a muffled buzzing, and though he shook his head to call it forth again, the movement merely banished the last traces of it from his mind, taking with it his determination and bravado and mad desire to reach the sphere. In their place he felt only disappointment.

He watched the word "Better?" form on Inata's lips and fought down the desire to shake his head. Did she think him weak and afraid like Rokat? Unprepared for tonight? The idea fired his determination all over again—he had nothing in common with cowardly Rokat and his fake devotion to Eisa, and he would make sure they all knew it.

He'd just repositioned himself behind one of the trap firing mechanisms when a deafening boom echoed through the night. The sphere flashed as though throwing off sunlight, and another shadow menaced just beyond the wall—and then exploded through it.

Exhilaration surged within him, but something was wrong. Whatever the thing was, it wasn't a Between, and it wasn't charging at them. Red and black, it writhed above their heads like a winged serpent, coiling and uncoiling and howling madly. The sound burrowed through the wax and struck his ears—the cries of a Between, but also something else.

He settled one hand on a knife and his other on the lever, eyes darting briefly to his father and then back to the creature. It didn't matter what it was—any moment it would unwind and come for them.

Any moment, his turn.

THRESHOLD

But something was holding it back, like the sphere itself was trying to keep it from going any further. Did they take the shot now? Could their nets reach that far? Another glance at his father earned him a small head-shake. *Wait, watch.*

Navrin hated waiting.

Then there was another savage cry, muffled yet somehow vivid, and a crack like a whip; whatever had been holding it back snapped, and the monster careened through the sky and smashed into the tower. Rocks exploded into the air, and a long, high scream rang from its base.

"Eisa!"

His father's shout was more fear than actual name, and Navrin turned just in time to see his sister bolt from her protective shield, terrified by the creature and the falling debris. In the space of a breath he took in the scene as though it were a painting—Rokat cowering behind one of the traps, Inata drawing two slender swords and sinking into a crouch, and his father racing to catch Eisa as she ran blindly through the field.

And straight toward the sphere.

Before he could decide what to do, the creature hit the ground and split apart—a Between entangled with something else, something red and winged which tumbled uncontrollably through the grass and straight into Inata, throwing her to the ground. She lay immobile while the massive, four-legged creature righted itself, leaped over her prone form, and tore back toward the Between, half-running, half-flying.

Everywhere, muffled sounds and frantic movement—Rokat shouted for his mother and sprinted to her side while his father chased after Eisa, and the Between growled and scrambled to its feet, right there, within range. It was just waiting to be caught, and no one was ready. Navrin's heart thundered in his chest as he wrenched the catapult around to face the monster. This was his chance. He could catch it, catch them both.

The spherelight gave him a clear view of the red creature soaring after the Between; it hovered a moment and then dove, crushing it beneath massive talons. Now, while they weren't moving, while they were together! He gripped the trigger, squeezed one eye shut, and then the red thing spread its enormous wings, lifted the thrashing monster into the air, and banked toward the wall.

No!

In one swift, desperate motion, he yanked the catapult after them and pulled.

And then he saw his father, directly in the net's path.

"Dad!" he shouted, but by the time the word was out of his mouth it was too late. The heavy ropes slammed his father to the ground, the red creature and its prey disappeared through the sphere—

—and Eisa, still running, still terrified, vanished into the waste.

"Eisa!" Rokat bolted from his unconscious mother's side and tore through the field, then stopped abruptly and stood motionless, staring after the little girl.

Navrin did the same, eyes unfocused, mind reeling, body swaying. The monsters gone, along with his glory. His father, unconscious. And Eisa, on the other side of the sphere.

With the Between.

Because of him.

Guilt collapsed upon him and he gripped the catapult for balance as Rokat spun around and met his eyes, his face a wild mixture of accusation and shame coated in fury. A fierce, silent battle blazed up around everything they'd wanted to say to each other for months, and then flickered out in a heartbeat.

Rokat's hands balled into fists and Navrin thought he might come running at him, but instead his stepbrother took a long, deep breath, whirled around, and sprinted straight at the sphere. Navrin opened his mouth to scream and no sound came out, held out a hand as though he could catch Rokat's retreating form, and then his stepbrother was gone and everything was still.

THRESHOLD

Terror hit him like a fist to the gut and it all became real in an instant. Real and horrible. It shouldn't have happened like this. Why had everything gone so wrong?

A moment passed, and then another. Navrin stared at the wall, his blank mind slowly filling with images of Eisa trapped on the other side, scared and alone and—

His legs were moving before his senses kicked in, and by the time his mind caught up he was nearly there. One step, another, another, a prayer to Varen—he closed his eyes and leaped.

Navrin had always thought of the wall as a single, thin line, like a sheet of paper separating them from the Between, and yet no matter which way he turned it stretched before him in a ceaseless swirl of white. It might have ended a mile ahead or only a few feet. It was impossible to tell, and it was worse than the world of monsters he'd expected because there was simply...nothing.

Slowing his pace and hoping his heartbeat would follow suit, he loosened the wax in his ears just enough to hear the swell of the song and feel a fresh wave of courage. He called Eisa's name over its thrum; no response, but now there was something new behind the song—a bone-chilling, howling rage. Whatever it was, it was fighting the song, trying to frighten him, to stop him, to hurt him.

He burst through the last of the mist mere feet from Rokat—and saw that they had barreled into a war.

The spherelight illuminated a rocky wasteland filled with monstrous shapes. In seconds Navrin took in the fierce combat, blurs of black and red, shrieks of both victims and victors, and his stepbrother, immobile and terror-stricken, and then something black came tearing at them. Before he could remember how to scream, another huge red thing caught the Between midair and drove it to the ground; a storm of claws and teeth and screeching, and then they toppled from a ledge Navrin hadn't even realized was there.

Hide, hide, hide now! screamed a voice in his head in time with his pounding heart. He grabbed Rokat's hand and dragged him along the edge of the sphere, resting his free hand against the glowing white wall. From this side it was solid as earth, impenetrable, the only thing holding him up as the implications finally sank in and sent him staggering—they were stuck.

Rokat flailed a hand at an immense black rock just ahead that stretched into the sky as though propped against the sphere. They threw themselves into the narrow crevice at its base and collapsed, gasping and shaking and hugging their knees and looking anywhere but back outside. Beneath the weight of what they'd just seen the song's power seemed to fade, and Navrin gestured to Rokat to loosen the wax in his ears.

After a long, uncertain look his stepbrother nodded. "Tha-thank you," he panted. "I…I don't know what I was thinking, coming out here. I just…I had to…."

Navrin tried to shrug but it came out more like a shuddering spasm. "You were thinking about Eisa." He fixed his eyes on the opposite wall, no longer able to pretend that Rokat's devotion to his little sister was mere show. It seemed they had something in common after all. The thought made him feel ashamed and relieved at the same time.

"She's not here," Rokat sighed. "I thought she might be."

Navrin privately agreed, and already his mind was flooding with horrible new possibilities. Had Eisa run straight off the cliff? Had she been attacked? Was she still wandering through the mist of the barrier? Had they banished themselves out here for no reason? He heard a deceptively confident version of himself say, "We'll find her."

But how, he had no idea, and even as he thought about it another Between prowled before their hiding place, close enough that he could see its scarred, sinewy skin rolling over the bones beneath, could have reached out from the rock and touched its draping wings as it latched onto the sphere and began tearing a hole in the magic with massive claws. Further down the wall appeared another, and then another, like a row of malnourished and misshapen wolves, each slowly forcing its way through the barrier.

Navrin leaned forward, horrified but enthralled, and breathed in a stench so revolting he thought he might vomit. He clapped his hands over his mouth and concentrated all his energy on not being sick while Rokat backed even further into the crevice, his wide eyes fixed, unblinking, on the nearest Between. He raised a trembling fist to his mouth and bit down on it, but just when Navrin thought they both might lose control another red shape slammed into the Between, pinning it against the sphere before dragging it off into the sky.

Rokat let out a breath while Navrin gulped in air that stank of dirt and blood, but no longer of polluting death. Still more red creatures assailed the Between clinging to the wall, but even as they were torn away another wave of black shapes took their place, only to be seized in turn. And on it went, an endless cycle.

Whatever the red things were, they were enemies of the Between, desperate to keep them from breaking into the sphere, and as bad as that was for family business, Navrin couldn't help but feel a second rush of relief. At least there was something out here that wasn't entirely evil. Something less likely to have eaten—

No, he couldn't afford to think that, because if Eisa was dead then they had already failed, and he'd failed too many times tonight already.

He was done failing.

He closed his eyes and concentrated on the song. It was inspiring, deep and full and beautiful, slow but powerful. How could the Between be responsible for something so wonderful? What was a song even doing in the middle of a battle?

His eyes went wide.

"It's a battle cry!"

Rokat started. "What?"

"The song. It's not the Between luring people out of the sphere, it's the red things rallying to fight!"

His stepbrother's eyes grew to match Navrin's, and he nodded slowly. "That's why we hear it whenever the Between come through—these things are out here trying to stop them!"

"Exactly! And why you feel brave and reckless and want to leave the sphere and fight." Navrin peered out of the crevice and back the way they'd come, and his eyes landed on a second pile of stone, atop which was perched another red thing, like a sentinel of the sphere. It paced back and forth, watching the battle, and—

"It's singing! Look!" He pointed just as it raised its head and opened its mouth—beak? It was vaguely birdlike, with wings and talons and a hook-shaped snout, yet it walked on all fours and swished so many long, slender tails Navrin couldn't count them all.

He watched it sing, entranced and feeling bolder by the minute. The creatures—the Sentinels, he decided—weren't evil. The song wasn't evil. It could give him courage and help him save Eisa, if only she was still out there. And—

"The Between!" He didn't know what happened to the ones his family killed, but their remains were rumored to possess powerful magic. "They can get through the sphere. If I kill one, we can use its power to get us back, too!"

Skepticism cut through Rokat's fear. "Sorry, Navrin, but that has to be the stupidest idea I've ever—"

Something smashed into their rock and yelped, and they jumped in unison. Navrin's head collided with a protruding stone, and when he reached up to massage the bump his arm brushed against the wax and knocked it from his ear entirely. The full weight of the song drove into his heart, and suddenly Rokat and his caution became bothersome and irrelevant.

"It'll work, I know it!" He could still do it, kill a Between and save Eisa. That had been the plan all along, and it was still the plan, and what was he doing cowering inside this rock when the Between were out there?

"It *won't* work! What if we—" Rokat's breath caught in his throat and he jumped. "It's Eisa!"

He pointed toward the second stone monolith, not at the top where the Sentinel was perched, but at the base, where an outcropping of rock created a narrow space between stone and sphere. Wedged into it was Eisa. With her dark skin and deep blue tunic she was all but invisible, and yet it was unmistakably her, and she was unmistakably alive.

It was the sign he needed, Varen telling him his idea would work, and before Rokat could stop him he darted from the crevice and drew his knives. The Sentinels' song pounded inside him and propelled him forward along the ledge toward his sister. Streaks of red and black flashed past, but though he lashed out at the dark shapes he missed every time. A small, sane part of him knew he should be glad that they were too focused on the sphere to even bother with him, and yet each time he failed his determination only mounted.

"Navrin!"

Rokat, still convinced he was acting foolishly. Heedless, he charged on, closer and closer, faster than before. He was almost there, and yet every inch of distance felt like a mile, every second apart from Eisa a loss. At last his sister noticed him and climbed shakily to her feet as he skidded to a halt in front of her. Sheathing one knife, he grabbed her trembling hand while she stared up at him and mouthed his name, but when he tried to pull her from the alcove she shook her head furiously. "It's too scary!"

"Don't worry!" he shouted, though with the wax still in her ears there was little chance she could hear him. "I'll protect you!" When she continued to resist he only tugged harder, until finally she had no choice but to follow him back into the open. He cast a glance at the Sentinel atop the rock and felt another surge of purpose. He'd saved Eisa. Now for the Between.

They were halfway to Rokat when there was a flash of black above his head and a resounding crack as a Between ricocheted off the sphere and crashed onto the ledge. Navrin jumped straight at it, dropping Eisa's hand and drawing the second knife. Behind him, his sister screamed and his heart leapt.

She was watching.

Rokat was watching.

Finally, his second chance.

He knew exactly where to strike—he'd practiced thousands of times on dummies and studied the bodies of slain Between before they were sold. But there was no net now, nothing holding it down and frustrating its movements, and before he could attack it rolled to its feet, snarling and shaking its head, hackles rising like black smoke.

And then it saw them, and as its chilling white eyes met Navrin's the song seemed to falter.

Run hide don't move fight don't breathe stab it run save Eisa kill it save yourself run do something!

Mind screaming in confusion, he stared down the Between, unable to tear his gaze away, wondering why it was waiting. Something screeched behind him and he screamed, spun—just as the Between leaped, right where he'd just been standing.

Run!

He grabbed Eisa and tore toward Rokat, not daring to look back, thinking only of getting away from its teeth and claws and the stench of death. Ahead of them, his stepbrother was shouting but he couldn't hear it over the shrieks of the Sentinels and the howls of the Between. Where was the song? Did it even matter anymore?

At the last moment he pushed Eisa in front of him, and then they were both inside the crevice—Eisa clutching Rokat and crying, Navrin panting and shaking so violently he thought he might drop his knives. Perhaps he should. Drop them, or throw them away. Had he really…had he just—

A hand caught hold of his arm and shoved him against the stone. "What were you thinking?" Rokat screamed, face streaked with tears.

"How could you have been so stupid?"

His anger flared. "I didn't—" he stammered. "The song—"

"The song!" Rokat snorted. "And before that, Navrin? You're always trying to show off!"

"What? That's not true!"

"Yes, it is! You tried to net that red thing and look where that got us! You went running out there like a hero and put her in danger *again*! It's all about you, isn't it? You don't care about *her* at all!"

Fury swelled within him, but was immediately replaced by something far worse. Guilt.

It wasn't true.

Rokat was wrong.

Of course he cared about doing his job properly. Of course he cared about Eisa. He thrust aside the memory of what had just happened and looked down at his sister, seeking the last time he'd done something nice for her just because he loved her.

He drew a complete blank.

"That's not true!" he screamed again, as though mere volume could drown out his shame.

"It *is* true!" Rokat took a deep, shuddering breath, and fresh tears rolled down his cheeks. "You've never lost anyone, have you? A member of your team. A *friend*. You've never seen what Between do when they…when they get a hold of people. If you had, you'd never have…." He trailed off and swiped at his tears, but when his eyes met Navrin's again they were steady and serious. "I let everyone down tonight because I was too afraid to do anything. How is being brave any different if all you do is *this*?"

Navrin opened his mouth to protest but nothing came out, so he stood there, numb, staring down at his trembling hands while the sounds of the battle echoed all around them. Though the Sentinels sang on, he pushed the song from his mind. Suddenly he hated it, hated what it had driven him to do. And yet Rokat was right: it wasn't the song's fault. True, it had given him courage, but only the courage to do what he'd wanted all along.

What he thought he'd wanted.

You've never lost anyone, have you?

He sank to his knees next to Eisa, wrapped his arms around her, and was startled when she embraced him back. "I'm so sorry, Eisa," he whispered. It didn't matter that she couldn't hear him—he needed to say it anyway. She didn't speak, but when he tried to let her go she gripped him harder, and for a small, incredible moment, he actually felt like a hero.

When at last he climbed to his feet and peered out of the crevice, he was strangely calm and yet wholly without ideas. A long look at the sphere failed to inspire anything other than dizziness, and at last he turned his eyes to his brother. "So, now what?"

There was a long silence, but instead of telling him off again Rokat shrugged. "Unfortunately, all my ideas end—" His nauseated expression returned. "—badly. More badly, I mean, than…"

"Yeah." If only the Sentinels' song kindled brilliance instead of bravery.

But it didn't, and with every second that passed without a solution Navrin grew more frantic. They had Eisa. They were all alive, and for the moment, safe. And yet what good was any of that if they could never escape? Perhaps charging down a Between had been stupid, but he couldn't help thinking that using them to get back through the sphere was still their best bet. If only they had rope, or a catapult. Yes, he thought, verging on manic laughter at the sheer ridiculousness of the idea. Why hadn't they thought to bring along a catapult?

Shaking his head, he drew a steadying breath and looked out again. From within the crevice he could see nothing but the ledge, and as he craned his neck for a glimpse at the land below he noticed that the sounds of fighting, and even the song, were fading.

"I think it's almost over." The thought brought a fresh wave of panic, not the fear of losing his chance but of losing his ability to ever see his parents again, his very life—if they were going to do something, if by some miracle they could kill a Between, it had to be now. He put a hand on his knife and stepped nearer the entrance. "I'm going to go look." There had to be something out there they could use. Anything.

"Navrin—"

"I won't do anything stupid, I promise." He took another deep breath and confirmed with himself that the statement was true. "I just want to see—" What? Exactly how doomed they were? "—what our options are."

Rokat swallowed nervously and slipped a hand into Eisa's. "Just be careful, okay?"

For his brother's sake, he double-checked the ledge and sky before creeping from the crevice and inching toward the edge, back against the stone wall. As he'd suspected, there was little movement below, and even the Sentinel perched atop the far rock was gone. He felt a pang of loneliness and shook his head to clear it away before taking another step. In the distance, something streaked through the sky and banked sharply away. He leaned forward, squinting—

"Navrin!"

A screech of agony, a sudden flash of red, and a Sentinel plummeted to the ground at the base of the rock, penning Rokat and Eisa inside. Navrin pressed himself against the stone, waiting for its attacker to bear down upon it, but a long, slow exhale later and there was still nothing, and the Sentinel hadn't moved. Its sides heaved with every breath, foreleg dripping blood from a long, deep gash that set Navrin's heart racing. Was it going to die, or was it just stunned? Did they wait to find out? Did they kill it while it was sprawled there and try his only idea out on a Sentinel? The thought made him feel ill, but so did the thought of dying in the waste.

He clutched his knives and stepped closer, forcing himself to breathe. Was this his punishment for wanting so badly to kill a Between that he'd endangered everyone? Killing something good to save them? Just beyond the reach of its thrashing tails he stopped, conflicted, and looked to Rokat. As he did he saw Eisa's small hand running along the Sentinel's withers, alternately patting and stroking it. He sucked in a breath and clenched his eyes shut.

They flew open again as a triumphant snarl echoed through the night, and a black shadow streaked down from above and buried its claws into the Sentinel's side. The red creature shrieked in pain, its cry mingling with Navrin's.

"No!"

He didn't think, didn't hesitate, didn't know what he was doing, but the knife was in his hand, above his head, arcing through the air toward the Between, spinning wildly and all wrong, and then the flat of the blade struck the Between's flank and the weapon clattered to the stone with a pitiful thunk. The blow couldn't have hurt, but the monster snorted and twisted its head, turning its nightmarish eyes upon him. It snarled, took a step toward him, shifted again to the Sentinel. Its fallen enemy, or the thing throwing knives at it?

It could only remain undecided for so long.

You've never seen what Between do when they get a hold of people.

Another snarl, another step—

Something silver flew out of the crevice and buried itself in the Between's shoulder. It roared in pain, reeled back and then lunged forward again, and suddenly everything was red, the dark color of blood, but it wasn't blood, it was the Sentinel, on its feet, wings spread, talons slashing at the startled Between. It opened its beak and crowed, and Navrin felt its cry swell within him.

He ran for Eisa and Rokat, shielded by the Sentinel's outspread wings as it reared on its hind legs, and though one powerful foreleg hung limp at its side the other was delivering one vicious swipe after the next. The three of them cowered behind it, Navrin and Rokat shielding Eisa, praying that its strength would last. Over and over the Between lunged and the Sentinel threw it back, and yet with each blow the feathered creature retreated further, one wavering step at a time, as small pools of blood formed beneath its feet.

THRESHOLD

It's losing, Navrin thought desperately, the last of its cry fading from his chest. Somehow it felt like the end, the end of their hopes for survival, for getting home. He'd only just been thinking about killing it, and now he was certain that if it died, there would be nothing left for them at all.

But as hopelessness washed over him and he lowered his eyes, he noticed something odd. The Sentinel's many tails were thrashing back and forth, and every time they hit the sphere they went straight through it. In and out and in again, not the slow straining motion of a Between pushing its way through, but effortless, like the wall wasn't even there.

His heart leapt and he pointed at it wildly. "Look!"

It was as though the Sentinel had been waiting for them to notice, or perhaps it was mere coincidence. Swinging once more at the Between, it pivoted sharply, and one graceful wing cut a long, slender gash in the side of the sphere. For the space of a second they all just stared, awestruck, and then it crowed once more and they bolted from the crevice. Rokat leapt through, pulling Eisa behind him, Navrin on their heels. He charged forward several yards and then turned in time to see the wing disappear from the silver mist. From the other side they heard a furious howl and a long, high shriek, and then there was silence.

"You're sure you're okay?"

"I'm sure," Navrin answered for the sixth—seventh?—time. He'd given up trying to break free of his father's protective hold and had even let Inata embrace him. Overwhelmed and exhausted, no one had any inclination to dismantle the traps, so instead they simply stood there together, gazing from one another to the sphere and back. "It was just a very long walk."

Not wanting to relive the experience, they had flat-out lied to their parents, telling them that they'd caught up with Eisa inside the barrier and had then been delayed returning; that they, like the Between, had to force their way through the magic one slow step at a time. Navrin had a feeling the charade was going to last about a day before Eisa mentioned the "giant bird-things," but at least for now they weren't being hounded with questions or, surprisingly, lectures.

"I'm sorry things didn't work out tonight, Navrin," his father said, a hint of "you helped contribute to that, you know?" in his voice. "I hope you don't mind waiting till next time—I don't think we'll be seeing any more Between tonight."

And thank Varen for that.

"That's all right," Navrin said. "I can come of age another time." When he deserved it. When he was ready. Or maybe it had already happened and it didn't even matter anymore.

"He did save Eisa," Rokat offered, ruffling the little girl's hair. "Shouldn't that count?"

His parents exchanged frowns. "Weeelll," Inata said finally, "I suppose it could. It certainly was incredibly brave of both of you to go after her."

"Not exactly poaching-related, though, was it?" his father countered. "I don't deny it was courageous, if rather reckless—" He looked pointedly at Navrin but seemed to be having difficulty expressing disapproval while both his face and voice were soaked with relief. "—but you said yourself it was just a really long walk, right? Not very exciting in the end."

Navrin found himself glancing at Rokat and was surprised to see his brother biting back a grin. A moment later he was doing the same, and when he caught Rokat's eye it was all he could do to keep from laughing.

"No," he managed at last. "It was kinda boring, actually."

The Fisherman's Catch
Adam L. Bealby

There's summat about fishing what takes you to a different place. First things first, you have to learn how to wait, how to be patient like, otherwise this place, you'll never get there. It comes to you, not the other way 'round, slipping downstream into your consciousness like so much flotsam; arriving unexpectedly, so that without even being aware of it you're ten years old again playing football in the park on a sun-drenched summer evening, or snuggled up in bed of a chilly winter's night with that bit of crumpet what runs the Post Office. The river, you let it, it'll fetch you such gifts.

And that's just when you're waiting. That first tug on the line and you're back in the real world, the one where games of football in the park are a distant memory and bits of crumpet from the Post Office won't give you the time of day; but still, your heart's pounding fit to burst 'cause you're reeling in the big one.

There's not much tugging going on now, mind. I've been here three hours. It's bloody freezing and the thermos is empty. 'Course, this isn't your *typical* fresh water fishing. This is summat a bit, well…*otherwordly*. If you let it, this kind of fishing will take you to a *bad* place. To the shores of memories you'd rather not relive. Fantasies best left unrealised. Which means I can't let me mind drift. I have to unlearn everything I've learnt about waiting. Focus on me numb fingers and sore arse and this dreary mizzle, on the humdrum here and now of it all.

I'm going to reel the line in. Maybe what I need is fresh bait—after a while even the best maggot starts to look a bit too familiar.

It's Burt's fault. He's the one what got himself in deep water.

Always trying to outdo me. Been like that since we was kids. Playing footie in the park those sun-drenched summers back, he'd turn up in full kit. If I had two bob in me pocket he'd have three.

I started angling a few years back to get out the house and away from She-what-reckons-she-should-be-obeyed. Lo and behold, few months later Burt sets himself up down the bank from me. Pretty soon he's catching carp the size of baby hippos. Even now he makes me look wet behind the ears. You should see all his trophies.

That's what Burt's like.

'Course, his Elsie died last spring. That took the wind out of his sails, I can tell you. For a while there he were all at sea. Whenever I'd see him I'd tell him how our Millicent were getting along; really labour the point. You should've seen his face. With a bit of luck, I were thinking, she were getting along to her grave. But I didn't tell *him* that, did I?

Then Burt quit the fishing business altogether. Didn't even bother registering for the Cradditch Wells Angling Club's annual competition like he usually does. I nobbled him a few weeks later as he were shuffling off down the bookies. "What you playing at, Burt?" says I. "I haven't seen you down the river for yonks. The lads are saying you've packed your rod away or summat?"

"Caught a nice one, didn't I, Jim?" he said. "I'm not gonna throw it back now."

I asked him what he were chuntering on about. Turns out the crafty old gett had been playing the dating game; fishing for totty instead of carp. Dab hand with the line were Burt, and most things else besides, but when it came to the ladies he'd always been a minnow. So I weren't letting him off the hook *that* easily.

Mm, this maggot *does* look familiar. It looks like Burt. The way he looked squirming and simpering in front of that lovely lass of his. Thing is, this next one looks like Burt and all. The way he looked when I stuck a big metal hook through his heart. Figuratively speaking, mind. Maggots don't have hearts.

THE FISHERMAN'S CATCH

So I says to Burt, "When'll we be seeing the new missus then?"

"Oh, soon," he said. "It's just…"

A pause like that, I were in like Flynn. "There's nuthin *wrong* with her is there, Burt?"

"Oh no, nuthin like that."

"'Cos you can tell me if there is. If she's a cripple, like, or she's got learning difficulties, or a face like a guppy in a sandstorm. I'm not one to judge, you know."

I got it out of him in the end. "She's *foreign*, Jim. She don't like it out much. She's shy, like."

Well, that explained it. The sad old gett had shipped in some freeze-dried Thai Bride. "She'll like Headless King right enough," I said. "Half-seven tonight?"

When Burt replied, he sounded like Hirohito on V-Day. "Yeah… Right you are, Jim."

True to his word, that night he brought his mystery woman along to the pub. I were rubbing me hands together with glee, all ready to torment old Burt to within an inch of his life, but slap me with a kipper and call me Susie if she weren't a stunner. She turned a few heads, I can tell you. It were like she were giving off them pheromone thingies or summat. The air were thick with it. All the blokes in the pub, they were strutting like peacocks as Burt and his lady-friend made their way over to the booth where I were sitting, and even the ladies were having a good old gawp, though by the look on their faces you'd think they'd never seen a Thai Bride before; least, I *think* she were Thai. The girls from Cancer Research, they turned their noses up and made for the exit like it were the end days, but then Harrie and Dot have always been a bit, what you call it—*racialist*.

When we was all sitting comfy in our seats, I copped a proper eyeful of Burt's new missus. She were actually a bit funny-looking around the gills. Her skin had a waxy sheen to it and her eyes were too large for her head. Still, you could *lose* yourself in those eyes. They were like pools of deep green water. With algae at the bottom.

When she smiled she had tiny white teeth. I imagined her nibbling me neck with them teeth and it sent a hungry shiver up me spine. And there were summat about her clothes, like I'd seen them before but on someone else...

I kept rubbing me eyes, I don't know why, and me head were all woozy like I were three sheets to the wind. Maybe me adenoids were playing up. I asked her what her name was 'cause Burt had become a bit flustered like, and had forgotten to introduce us. She replied in a sort of raspy voice which sounded like one of the kids Bob lets in Headless King throwing up in the loo after a few shots. Dead sexy, it were.

"What's that, love?" I said.

"She don't speak English," Burt said. "Her name's Glaak...I *think*...She says that word a lot..."

"Glaak," said Glaak.

We had beer-battered cod and chips all 'round. Glaak didn't say much for the rest of the night. I respected that. Very lady-like; very—what's the word? *Demure.* Not like my Millicent. You couldn't shut her up if you tried. And God knows I've tried. Glaak could put it away, mind. And she drank like a fish. And at one point I thought she'd of been better off with one of them bibs with a scoop at the bottom to catch her nosh. But then I suppose summat might of been lost in translation. The Chinese burp to show their appreciation of a meal, don't they?

Every half-hour or so, Glaak would excuse herself to go to the ladies. Burt said she splashed water on her face to 'rejuvenate her complexion' or some such twaddle. Probably summat she'd read in a magazine. First time she left the table, I caught a glimpse of her ankles. There was quite a bit of retention going on down there. The water had to go somewhere, I suppose. It should've been her Achilles' heel, but I really fancied those chubby fins. Pins, I mean. Now that were odd. Millicent were built like a blocked drainpipe, always had been, and I've never been one for lasses what were broad in the beam.

THE FISHERMAN'S CATCH

Glaak had me in a right lather, I tell you. Pheromones. Must of been. Or some cheap Asian perfume. There were summat fishy going on, but I couldn't quite put me finger on it.

"Bit of a siren ain't she, Burt?" I said when Glaak had gone to the loo for the eighth time.

"You should see her in the bedroom, Jim. All over me like a rash." Burt scratched his particulars. I chuckled. She'd stuck him proper; what were happening in his petri dish was anyone's guess.

"'Course, Millicent will want to see her," I said.

"Aw, Christ. Do we have to, Jim?"

Burt and our Millicent didn't exactly get along. Not since Millicent broke Elsie's nose over a pilfered creamcake recipe what won Elsie the crown of Mrs. Cream '82. But I'd already told Millicent that Burt had a new lady-friend, and her nose were longer than her resentment was deep.

"Millicent's happy for you, Burt," I lied. "She wants to make Glaak feel at home." Glaak had just returned to the table. She got busy licking her plate. Then Burt's. Then mine. But still, that throbbing gullet had me hot under the collar.

Stick to the here and now, Jim. The river, the line, the bait. Don't let your mind wander. Mm, it's not the bait. Shouldn't be. It's quality stuff. So what is it? What am I doing wrong? Am I feeding out the line too far? I can't see two feet in front of me without the torch. I'm new to this night-fishing malarkey. Still learning the ropes. Give it time, Jim old boy.

The big night arrived and me and Millicent was standing outside Burt's house, all glammed up in our Sunday best. Millicent had even had her hair done, though I couldn't say it'd done nuthin for her. No hairdresser's *that* good. We was arguing as usual, but as soon as the door opened we put on our happy-smiles. After thirty-five years of marriage we had our act down pat. God, but Burt looked a sight in his corduroys and moth-eaten tie. Elsie had knitted him that tie. We shook hands as if we hadn't seen each other for donkey's years and

Burt planted an awkward kiss on Millicent's over-powdered cheek. Then he led us through to the living room. Glaak were sitting on the sofa and I went over to give her a peck as Burt made the introductions. There were that smell again, a hot musky whiff like summat fermenting, but tear me a new blow hole if it didn't smell *good*. Burt were one lucky sailor, I tell you.

But when I turned back to Millicent she were just standing there, ogling Glaak like she were a beached whale. She didn't respond to me questioning eye, or me subsequent none-too-subtle nudges and Burt were looking a bit embarrassed, like, so I took her by the arm and led her over to the other sofa. It were the first time in all our years together I'd seen her lost for words. I weren't going to pass up the opportunity to bask in that blissful silence. So when Burt said he were going into the kitchen to fix us some drinks I said I'd stay with Millicent and Glaak. What with Glaak not understanding English, I asked Millicent what were up and she blanked me completely. She had the sort of thousand-yard stare me dad used to wear. She took a pack of *Silk Cuts* from her handbag, lit a cigarette between trembling fingers, and took one long drag, almost all the way down to the tip. When I gave her a poke in the ribs she started whispering hoarsely, and that were the end of me brief dalliance with peace and quiet. "Can't you see it, Jim?" she said. "Look at her. *Look at her.*"

I looked, all right, and Gorgeous Glaak were sitting there looking all sultry and enticing, which I thought were right decent of her under the circumstances. But then I looked again, and I thought I saw... I rubbed me eyes real hard. It were just a trick of the light. Whatever was going on between these two, I were starting to feel seriously out of me depth. I turned to Millicent and me mouth opened and closed like a fish. I didn't know what to say.

"*Can't you see?*" she said. The poor dear was getting hysterical. "She's not even hu—"

"Hummus and olives anyone?" Burt said as he came through from the kitchen. He put the tray of drinks and nibbles on the coffee table.

THE FISHERMAN'S CATCH

"You didn't say what you wanted, Millicent, but I know you've always been partial to a G and T. A Thai beer for you, Jim."

"Bit fancy, Burt," I said, grateful for the intervention. Before I could pause to think, I'd popped one of the olives in me mouth. I spat it out and stuffed it down the side of the sofa. I hate olives. Then I stood up and put an arm round Burt's shoulder. "Let's us blokes talk next door," I said. "Leave the girls to have a natter, like."

As I steered Burt back into the kitchen, I looked over me shoulder and Millicent and Glaak was sitting there in stony silence. There were more chance of a pair of flounders down the fish-market having a good old natter. Two fag butts in the ashtray now, and Millicent were already reaching for a third smoke.

"What's up, Jim?" Burt said when we were round the corner.

"You tell me, Burt," I said.

"Aw, Christ..." He rubbed his hand down his face. He looked as tired as Millicent's wig. "It's Glaak."

"She cheating on you or summat?" I'd like a bit of that action, I thought.

"What? No! She's... Well... You ever heard of the Night Fishermen?"

I'd heard of them, all right. One of them tall tales people liked to bandy about down at the pub. Legend had it there was this spot on the bank of the Severn where devil-worshippers used to gather long ago. At the witching hour, they'd bugger each other and animals and stuff, and all that mischief and merriment and what-not in the dark would call up weird tentacled entities from the depths of that ancient river.

Burt suddenly put his arms 'round me and let out an anguished sob. I pushed him back, a bit disgusted like. His face were dripping with sweat. He looked like he'd just been for a dip. "I were lonely, Jim," he said. His eyes were those of a drowning man. "You don't know how lonely I've been these last few months. I swear, I would've tried *anything*. Maybe even one of them Thai Brides you hear so much about. But then I read this book from the library. This local author, and I—I did what he said and I...I—I *caught* summat, Jim. Summat...*wrong*. I took it home with me and put it in the sink, but soon it outgrew the sink, so I put it in the bath and then it grew *legs* and... It gets inside your head. You know what it can do, Jim. What *she* can do."

Part of me thought he were having me on. Then it occurred to me. "You put her in Elsie's old clothes, didn't you?"

"Don't she look lovely in 'em?" he said, and his smile were so sickly I knew he were beyond hope. He were sinking without a trace.

"Couldn't you have made do with the Adult Channel?" I said, ever so gently.

Then there was this horrible scream from the other room. We raced through to find Glaak busy gnawing the wife's face off. She looked like she were enjoying it, too. Glaak, I mean. Not the wife. Millicent... Well here I'd probably make a joke about how it had improved her looks, like, but it hadn't. It really hadn't.

Glaak had her pinned at close quarters, stretched across the coffee table, and she were tucking into her cheeks like they was hot fillet steaks. And Millicent, she were screaming me name, over and over. Last time she'd put that much effort into it, it'd been our wedding night and I thought her eyes were going to pop out. Now, one of them did. It bounced off the coffee table and rolled lumpenly under the sofa.

Well I had to come to her defence, didn't I? Thirty-five years, I owed her that much.

I grabbed the ashtray and gave Glaak a good clonk on the noggin with it. She fell back and off Millicent, and then I were on Burt's lover like a white squall. I hit her again and again with that ashtray until her face fell in like one of Millicent's notorious sunken cakes. All these maggots wriggled up to the surface and looked at me like I'd disturbed their beauty sleep. I have to say, for me that were the clincher.

THE FISHERMAN'S CATCH

"Bloody hell, Jim," Burt said.

The living room were a mess. There was gristle and fag butts and broken glass and olives all over the place. And the blood: we was practically swimming in it. Millicent had leaked out all over the carpet and there were this fixed snarl on her face where Glaak had bitten off half her top lip.

That's how I'll always remember her.

So really, it were all Burt's fault. If he hadn't of tried to one-up me on Millicent we'd both be sitting pretty at home about now, instead of sitting on our sore arses in the middle of the dark. At this rate I'm more like to catch a cold than anything else.

I've let me mind drift again, haven't I? I bet Burt hasn't. I bet that's his secret. Focused as Captain Ahab is old Burt, when he wants to be.

I switch on the torch and let the beam slide along the bank. There he is. About fifty yards up from me with all his tackle and his chillbox. He's even got his waders on. He's pretending to ignore me. After Glaak we sort of fell out. He reckons I overreacted or summat. Left him high and dry. And there was me offering to clean up the mess and everything, the gett! Well, he'll get his in the end. And with a bit of luck I'll get mine and all. See, I've got me own secret weapon. These big fat juicy maggots what look like Burt? I picked them right out of Glaak's face.

Second time 'round, me and Burt will have us both a decent catch.

One More Song
Eliza Chan

After Mira closed the door, the selkie shed her skin, leaving the mottled grey fur in a heap like stepped-out-of work clothes. Mira handed her one of the many robes hanging on the hat stand and kept her eyes on her blue and green rug, only catching glimpses of the woman's bruises. There were purple marks the size of fingers on her legs, and red, raised lines across her back. Mira blinked rapidly, her hands already clenched into tight fists as she tried to keep her rising anger from bursting its banks.

"How can I help you, Ms...?" Mira asked.

"Iona, just call me Iona," the selkie said, knotting the robe tightly at her midriff. She winced visibly and her eyes darted up. Mira moved to her drink cabinet, deliberately turning her back so the other woman didn't have to look her in the eye.

"I need help. I, my husband, well you can see his handiwork. I asked for a divorce, I tried to go to the police. They wouldn't listen. Said I was only on a spousal visa so..."

Mira handed Iona the mug. She clasped her hands around the porcelain like it anchored her.

"I assume he has some leverage?"

The client nodded, tucking her hair back so Mira could see a ragged hole where her right ear should have been—a void of darkness, as if that part of her had simply ceased to exist. "He cut a patch out of my skin. I can't swim far, not out of the city at any rate, or I'll drown."

She was smart, Mira mused. Selkie skin couldn't heal like most, but others had tried, even with pieces missing, to escape their partners. Their bodies washed up against the buildings, water-logged and drowned.

"Iona, I'm afraid you may have misunderstood my services," Mira began. "I'm a private investigator. I watch, find things, report back. I don't take direct action."

Mira leaned back in the brown leather armchair and waited for her client's reaction. In the pause she could hear the seawater lapping just below her window sill.

"I've heard otherwise. You're the one who'll get things done."

Iona's grey eyes were staring at her with hope. She would have been beautiful when she was young but now her silver-grey hair and eyes were concealed beneath weary dark circles and rippling wrinkles around her mouth. No laughter lines.

Mira had vowed she was done with all that. It was dangerous work, and those who came pleading to her door rarely had the money to pay. Shell necklaces and a side of salmon didn't keep the landlord from yelling obscenities about stinking fish wasting his time. Even a submerged studio apartment caked in coral cost more than she was bringing in these days.

"I'm sorry, I got out of that business years ago," Mira started. She reached for the box of business cards on the side table. "I suggest you run. I know a kelpie with a small delivery business. He can get you a new ID card and hide you in the van, take you somewhere to hole up."

"I can't run. I ran before and he paid a seawitch to find me."

Mira looked up and saw the blue tattoo on Iona's hand. She had been tagged. The seawitch's magic was impossible to remove without the marine courts. And Iona couldn't get to them without her skin.

"He's going to kill me," Iona said, "I know it. Maybe not today, or tomorrow, but he'll do it. You are the only one that can help me."

Mira swore as she used the ladder to drag herself out of the water and into the biting wind of the tram platform. Already regretting the selkie's tears and cash payment, Mira slid into the tram just as the doors slid shut. Tired mums with hybrid prams, businessmen in partially unzipped wetsuits, and shoppers with bags that knocked haphazardly against everyone's knees filled the carriage.

A bunyip offered his seat to an elderly woman, water dripping from his protruding tusks as he inelegantly flopped from the chair onto all four webbed feet. Looking at him suspiciously, and at the muddy puddle he left pooling on the plastic chair, the elderly lady gripped her handbag tight to her chest and shuffled away without meeting his eyes. The air was damp and stagnant, not just because of the sea water dripping from the bunyip's whiskers. He sighed and rolled his eyes, catching Mira's glance as he did. They nodded in mutual understanding.

"It's not fair though, you've got four legs," a school boy complained to his friend as they recounted a football match.

"So do you," the other boy quipped as he nickered under his breath.

"I'd beat you in a wrestling match, mind," the first boy said as he started to put his scuba apparatus back over his head.

The kelpie boy didn't answer, but turned into horse-form and snatched up his school clothes in his mouth. The doors slid open at the next stop and Mira saw the boys dive into the water, jostling good-naturedly as the mildewed glass slid back and hid them from sight.

In ten years, the human will be a manager and the kelpie will work on the factory floor until his back gives out, Mira thought bitterly.

"Tell me," a voice said, the reek of alcohol assailing Mira's senses. "Why do you do it?"

"Excuse me?"

A middle-aged woman leered up at her, clinging to the tram pole. She stabbed one finger against Mira's arm to punctuate her speech.

"All that hair and big eyes, reeling them in like stupid fish. He might just be a piece of meat to you, but he was someone's husband!"

Mira's arm started to hurt under the repeated jabbing. "You've misunderstood—"

"You are all the fucking same. Siren songs and false promises."

Mira started to move down the carriage, but the woman's words carried and everyone was staring at them.

"I wish you'd just slept with him! At least then he'd have been satisfied," the woman shouted. Her voice was breaking and despite herself, Mira stopped. She knew this woman's story as well as many others. The suicide rate for unrequited fixations on sirens was as high as the number of restraining orders that had been issued.

Mira walked back and put a hand awkwardly on the drunk woman's shoulder. "I'm sorry, but that is not our intention. Despite popular belief, we don't just…switch it on and off."

The woman's eyes widened, then her mouth pursed and she pushed the hand away. "Bullshit! You are all the same!"

Mira's good intentions crumbled in the face of ignorance, and she leaned in close so only the woman could hear.

"Maybe if you hadn't been such a wet fish, he wouldn't have been tempted."

Mira was smug as she exited, satisfied to have had the last say until she turned and saw the window as the tram rolled away. Faces of frightened women watching her with narrowed eyes, clutching their boyfriends and husbands close. The water pooling on the raised platform began to seep into her shoes.

"Shit," she said under her breath. She had only made things worse.

The sushi place at the corner was completely underwater, with only the carp-shaped windsocks and ornamental dragons on the tiled roof showing. Mira moved along the raised walkways and dove down to find the entrance. There was an artificial air pocket inside the restaurant doors. A small red bridge and a waterfall graced the entrance. A kappa stood under the water, a look of pure pleasure on its face.

"Welcome, patron. Please hang up your wet suit and breathing apparatus, and avoid falling in the water!" he said without opening his eyes.

Mira burst out laughing.

"Oh, it's you. Kai won't be happy," the kappa said as he shuffled out from the stream. His skin was tough like turtle shell but he waddled awkwardly. The whole look was rather comical, even though Mira knew his beak could pierce flesh and he had the strength to carry off an adult human if he was so inclined. The kappa puffed out his chest and frowned at her, but being no higher than Mira's waist, it just made her laugh even more.

"What if I'm not here to see Kai? I might be here to see you!" she said in her brightest voice.

The kappa picked at the webbing between his hands, inspected it, and then ate the pickings. "Those tricks don't work with me, Mira."

Mira feigned innocence as she winked and walked on. As she passed through the enchanted tori gate, her clothes dried instantaneously. Kai was behind the sushi counter, the knife glinting in the dim light as he sliced raw fish onto a platter. His blue-grey hair was pulled into a topknot and he wafted the smell of the ocean across the room. Not for the first time, Mira felt her heart sing and wondered if the pain was the same that men felt for her song.

"Are you going to say hello, or were you just planning to watch?" he said.

"The view isn't too bad," she admitted, crossing the room.

"And yet I get the distinct feeling this isn't a social call," Kai said. He wiped the edge of the platter and turned it to check from all angles.

"There's nothing wrong with a bit of business and pleasure," Mira said, putting a slight melody into her words.

Kai raised an eyebrow then took the platter to the nearest table and started eating. Mira sat next to him and dropped the act.

"Okay, you win. I need something from you."

"I'm not allowed to disturb the balance, Mira."

"Yes, all you can do is make sushi and do calligraphy," she retorted. It was both the attraction and the curse of knowing a water dragon. His premises were a safe zone—many of her clients had found a moment's reprieve from all the arid crap of the world within its walls—but Kai wouldn't lift a finger to change the equilibrium. They had fought about it more times than she cared to remember, until she had finally had enough and left him.

"You don't need to know anything," she continued, touching his wrist gently. "Just give me a blindspot. A few hours is all I need."

"You are kidding?" The sushi fell from his chopsticks. "Mira, I thought you packed it in? You know I can't keep doing this. After last time—"

"I'm not like you. I can't just sit by and watch our people being hurt." She regretted her words as soon as she had said them. Mira knew that Kai had no choice—he had been sent as their ambassador and for right or wrong, he had to stick to the rules.

"That's not fair. Integration is our only hope, and if they think we are using our powers to directly harm humans then all you'll do is save one person and screw the rest." Kai rubbed his temples and slumped back wearily.

Mira pushed her chair back and stood behind Kai. She traced a finger around his right ear tenderly and then leaned in close, her arms draped over his shoulders. "He cut her, right here. Cut her ear clean off."

Kai's shoulder stiffened and he pushed her away. He raised a hand and soft bamboo flute music filled the room. Mira recognized the melody as a glamour, shielding their words whilst it played.

"Give me two days. I can get you an hour, two at most, from

noon. And that's it. Then we have to talk about this, Mira. Properly."

He looked at her, and Mira could see flickers of see his dragon form superimposed over his features. She had started to forget what he looked like as a dragon. For a decade now, he had been forced to live as human because his sheer size alone was deemed unsuitable, frightening, monstrous.

"Mira," he said softly, shaking her from her thoughts. "You know if you get caught even I won't be able to protect you."

Mira smiled grimly. "I'm not the one who needs protecting."

The aquarium Iona's husband owned was a monstrosity by sea-dweller standards. It took up the whole sixth and seventh floor of an old office block, the floor to ceiling glass windows turned into tanks. With the city half-submerged, there was marine life everywhere and the aquarium was a grotesque carnival of cruelty, needlessly entrapping the animals in squat boxes to be peered at.

Mira did her groundwork in the bar beside the aquarium, listening to the workers gossip and vent after work. The men respected Iona's husband. Hard-up after losing jobs in fishing and tourist boats, they drank rum and talked about what they would like to do to his selkie wife. He simply laughed along with them.

At noon on the second day, Mira threw on a glamour: young, human, coffee-coloured skin and dark hair, wide frightened eyes and a backpack bulging with possessions, as if she had run away from home.

"I," she said at the door, tilting her head towards the camera in the corner so he would see her pretty face. "I need a job."

"We aren't hiring," the man at the ticket office said, leafing through an old newspaper.

"Please I, I really need the money. I'm...desperate."

As if on cue, the phone rang. The ticket officer answered it, frowning a little before reaching into his desk and printing off a complimentary ticket for her.

"He'll meet you at the stingray exhibit."

Mira didn't have to act terrified as she walked around the maze of decrepit tanks. Tanks were piled on tanks, with the fish all clustered near the top of the water, gasping for air amongst the bodies of their dead comrades. Green algae coated the glass on both sides and there was a thick film of scum on every surface. It was nothing more than a morgue. Mira had seen fishmongers who kept their animals in better condition than this.

Around the corner there was a room made of glass. Floor, ceiling, and four walls were joined into one seamless tank. Kite-shaped stingrays soared around them and underfoot like ripples in the water. A middle-aged man stood at the centre. He had thinning hair, a shirt that had once been white but was now yellowing at the collar and underarms, and gold-rimmed glasses that looked like fish tanks. There was something sallow about his whole appearance. He approached her and smiled with the geniality of a predator.

"I'm the aquarium owner, Steve."

"Levi," Mira answered.

"So you are looking for work? Industrious of you," he said, looking her up and down with an appraising eye.

"I—I'm new in the city," Mira said. "And I've worked on a fish farm before, so I just thought…"

"You'd use your skill set to find a job. Impressive. I like that. There aren't many young girls in the city that would be smart enough to think of that."

"It's—I just needed the money," Mira said, looking down at her feet.

She heard him open his wallet and a wad of banknotes was pressed into her hands. It was more money than the average unskilled worker made in a month. Steve's hands lingered over hers. "Call it an advance," he said.

"Oh, but that's too much, I mean, I wasn't expecting so much…thank you, but are you sure?" she said.

His hands moved up her arm and tilted her chin up so she was looking at him. "We'll make sure you work it off."

Mira tried to look flattered and confused, resisting the disgust crawling all over her skin. She turned away, hoping it would look as if she was overwhelmed. In silence she stood staring at the stingrays, waiting for his next move.

"They are a member of the shark family," he said.

"Oh?"

"But everyone thinks they are so much friendlier. See that happy face on its underside? Looks can be deceptive. Those aren't eyes, they are gills."

"Amazing."

"Mermaids swim with stingrays, keep them as guards," he said. His hand had somehow made it to her shoulder. Mira grimaced under the glamour and pretended not to notice him smelling her hair.

"I'd love to meet some seafolk," she said. "I mean, of course I've seen them in the streets and stuff, but I've never been friends with one of them. I've got so many questions, you know, stupid things really. How do they breathe out of water and stuff."

"I could answer your questions. My, um, late wife was a selkie," he said.

"No, really? I don't believe you, however did you get a selkie to fall for you?" Mira said, setting the net.

"I have captured many sea creatures. Seafolk? Well, they aren't much different. They might look more like us, yes, but we both know they are nothing more than fish. And, well, you should know how to catch a fish. With some bait and a hook. Easy as that. Just don't expect to have an intelligent conversation with one of them," he said.

"Then why did you marry her?" Mira asked before she could stop herself. Luckily he took her vehemence for naïve enthusiasm.

"I have a reputation. I mean, how do people know I'm any good at rearing the creatures if I don't have proof of it? And a selkie…well they are easy enough to seduce, we all know that. All you need to do is buy them a couple of nice dresses and compliment their hair. But do you know the average length of a human-selkie marriage? Six months. I have been married for eight years. That makes me, unofficially of course, the leading expert in seafolk around these parts."

Kai's words echoed in her head. She couldn't do harm to a human unless in self-defense, but the nape of her neck was tingling from the desire to. She had a seawitch tattoo there, same as all the other seafolk who lived in the cities, that would burn her if she used any of her magic illegally.

Mira pretended to be in awe as he beamed and then suddenly she laughed curtly. "No! I believed you for a moment there. You are pulling my leg! How could someone like you get a selkie for a wife?"

His face dropped, along with his cloying goodwill. "I am most certainly not! In fact, I have proof!"

He rummaged in his pocket, flustered as strands of hair fell across his forehead. Pulling out his keys, he brandished them inches from her face. "See, proof!"

Attached to a jangling set of boat and house keys was a scrap of grey fur, ragged and dirty with lint from his pocket.

"You keep it on your keys?" she said.

"Yes, um, to remind me of my dear departed—"

She snatched the keys from him. "You keep it on your keys!" she repeated, no longer holding back the rage.

The stingrays had gathered into a dark mass above Steve's head, their happy underbelly faces swimming before her eyes over and over. Her neck started to burn. Mira moved over to the glass and put her hand on it.

No direct harm.

"I could do with a drink," Mira said.

Steve's eyes widened and she knew the glamour had faded in her anger. He grabbed her arm and pulled her away from the glass as she started singing. Mira let herself fall on the ground without interrupting the song. Her voice spiraled higher and higher, the tune of waves and whale song. Steve shoved his hand roughly over her mouth, but it was too late. The glass began to reverberate and splinter around them.

"Siren bitch," he spat as he let go of her and groped around his neck. Mira realized belatedly he must have a protective charm. She shouted out her last note as the glass smashed around them and the room flooded with water and stingrays and fresh blood.

Once Mira returned her pelt, Iona went straight to the marine courts under the protection of some of Mira's contacts. She would be immune from the seawitch's spell until the court had come to a decision, and Mira was confident of what side they would fall on.

Steve, on the other hand, had gone missing.

Pouring herself a drink, Mira sat in her office armchair and decided not to let it bother her—she deserved one night off before she started worrying about him. She dozed off, but woke with a start when the phone rang. It sounded like pounding on her skull at first and took Mira a while to answer it.

"Mira? Mira, are you okay?" Kai asked.

"It's going swimmingly, what's up?"

"The lines have gone crazy. I've had half a dozen reports of a man who has approached every seawitch in the city to learn how to kill a siren. If this goes down, the balance is screwed!"

"The balance? Always about the balance! It's already screwed. You are about the only one who has stuck to the letter of the amnesty agreement. We were fools to ever agree to curtail our powers when they were the ones who polluted our waters!"

"I think you should come here for a few days, until it blows over. I would just feel better if—"

The pounding started again. But it was different this time. Someone was trying to break down her door.

"Eh, I need to go Kai. Someone is knocking."

"Don't open the—"

She hung up the phone and rubbed her temples. She didn't have a head for alcohol anymore and confrontations were a huge annoyance.

Steve smashed in the glass of her window with a huge fish hook. He was carrying a fishing net in his other arm. "So," he said, as he unlocked the door through the broken glass, "this is where the harpy lives?" The stingrays had had some revenge. Barb punctures riddles his arms and face.

"You honestly thought my own animals could kill me? I'm not that stupid. And all for Iona? Really? She has nothing to do with you. She's my wife!"

"It's called domestic abuse. Holding someone against their will. There are laws," Mira said as she slowly stood up.

"Screw the laws, no human jury has ever taken the side of seafolk. You are all asking for it."

"And that's why I still have a job," she said, realising her words rang true.

He threw the net towards chair, but she moved easily away. Too easily. A second net wrapped around her head, tightening immediately so that the mesh pressed against her face in stinging lines. He wrapped the fish hook around her neck.

"Try to sing now, you mermaid whore," he said smugly.

Mira's voice would not come. The net had choked her breath, like drowning. But he had forgotten she had tools other than her voice. She grabbed at an ornamental conch and smashed it hard against his leg so the spike dug into his flesh. Steve swore and let go.

"You slag! I'm going to make you pay!" he shouted and flung the conch to one side.

Mira peeled the net off her head and grabbed the hat stand—even Kai would consider this one self-defense, she thought grimly. Her voice was still hoarse and numb and Mira could only hope the enchantment would wear off quickly. As Steve sliced down toward her with his weapon she whipped the hat stand in the way. The hook cut the bathrobes into shreds, but became entangled in curved arms of the stand. Steve screamed and pushed with his shoulder, forcing Mira back against the wall, pinning her there.

"Make me want you so badly I drown myself? That's your game, right?"

Nothing would've revolted her more. Mira kicked him as hard as she could, but she didn't have the physical strength to do any real damage. Steve laughed cruelly and seemed to be enjoying himself. She saw the violence in his eyes and knew that whatever happened, it was worth it to save Iona from this. Mira let herself go limp so that Steve leaned in closer, and then cracked him hard with a headbutt.

Then her voice came back.

She sang a single note, higher and louder than she had done in years. The power pitched through her and slammed Steve to the ground. Right now if she told him to stop breathing, he would.

"You wouldn't dare," he hissed through the enchantment. "The amnesty forbids you from harming me."

Mira sang a simple refrain and watched the blood drain from his face and his conviction falter. Her body ached so much she barely registered the heat from the nape of her neck.

"Oh? Really? But I'm not doing anything, you are," she said. "I want you to relive it. Every hurt you gave your wife: every emotional, physical, and sexual piece of shit you subjected her to, you are going to do it to yourself with this lovely fishhook." She picked up the hook from the rug and put it reverently in his hands.

Then she turned her back on him, humming her song under her breath, and put the kettle on to drown out the noise. She tidied the charmed net into a drawer, wondering if she could use it against the mercenary seawitch—she would have to deal with that little problem sooner rather than later.

When she checked on Steve, he was holding the fish hook in both hands, fighting her song for control. And losing. He looked shocked every time his own hands opened up another cut. Trails ran down his body and pooled in bloody footprints on her rug.

Mira remembered why she had stopped doing these jobs. And how many rugs she had gone through. She remembered how the power made her feel, and she wasn't sure if she liked it.

"Go. Go and get cleaned up," she said.

Steve screamed at her, but he could not control his body. It pulled him over to the window, yanked it open, and he stepped off the edge into the raging sea below. The tide was low, and he fell two floors before he hit shallow water. The water blushed with the flow of his blood, and as he thrashed, Mira could already hear the carnivores of the sea honing in on him. His protection charm wouldn't work this time.

"No direct harm," Mira reassured herself. She looked at her bloodstained rug and the cooling mug of seaweed tea in her hands. She shook her head and headed for the door, reaching it just as it was flung open. It was Kai.

"Are you okay?" he said, breathless and dripping wet.

Mira smiled and pushed them both out of the room, closing the door firmly behind her. She slid the brass door sign to "closed" and put her arm through Kai's.

"No rescuing needed today. But it won't affect the balance if we eat, right?"

"What happened?" Kai said.

Mira pulled out some very damp cash and waved it under his nose. "No questions, I'm paying."

"Mira…"

She smiled back at him once as she walked to the stairs. With a brief pause, Kai followed.

HOMECOMING
Tabitha Lord

Penelope

I dreamt of him last night. But my dreams are shadows, whispers. Texture, form, and color unravel into nothingness. They are the shreds of my tapestry strewn across the cold stone floor of the salon. He slips from my grasp as the sun rises over the water and invades the darkness of my imaginings.

I hear the household awakening below and emerge from beneath the warm embrace of the coverlet. I will remain in the bedroom until I know the men have taken themselves off for the day. My appearances are calculated, always impeccably timed. I must drift just out of reach—the doe dashing between distant pines, barely outside the arrow's range. It is a dangerous game I play. My husband is not dead. This I know with certainty. But he has not returned. He may never return.

Eurykleia enters, her feet padding softly across the floor. She pours warm water into the basin for me to wash. We exchange pleasantries and I clasp her hand in thanks before she leaves with the chamber pot. She is my one true ally. Our beginnings were auspicious, hostile even, but after the birth of my son, whom she loves above all others, her heart softened toward me. Our alliance was forged while protecting that son, and his inheritance, over all these long years.

The smell of fresh bread wafts through the room, and I hear scraping benches and boisterous, masculine voices. Eventually, all is quiet and I venture down the stairs. Peering into the large room, I watch my servants as they tidy bedding, scrape dishes, and sweep out the dirt from a dozen boots, and I swallow my rage. The women

HOMECOMING

pause and look at me. My face remains impassive. I nod at them before unlocking my salon.

Always, the first moment is a shock. My work of the previous day, precious and exacting, lies in ruins, a tangle of thread and intentions. But it is as it should be. The shroud hangs unfinished on the loom.

I startle as a large, calloused hand grips my arm. When I turn, my breath catches in my throat.

"Penelope," he says, his eyes narrow and his voice low.

I stand mute, my heart racing.

He traces his thumb along the pulse at my neck and when I shudder softens his grip.

"Penelope," he repeats. "Almost as clever as your ill-fated husband." He grins as he gazes over my shoulder at the loom. "But not quite."

He knows, and it will be useless to deny it. Instead, I lower my eyes and allow my lip to tremble when I whisper, "Please, I am not ready."

"Faithful, steadfast Penelope," he says with some admiration, but then his voice hardens. "You will choose. And you will do it soon. My patience wears thin."

The threat hangs between us. Still staring at the floor, I nod and he turns to leave.

When I am certain he is no longer in my house, I slam the salon door so hard that I rattle my own teeth, and then I lock it shut. My hands shake as I stare at the mess of yarn by my feet. I pace the room, clenching and unclenching my fists. I am furious, and now I am also desperate. My plan, carefully laid with Eurykleia's help, has failed. Antinous will force my hand and make me choose a husband from this self-serving, insolent band.

I sink heavily into the chair at my loom. I kept our household together throughout the long war, and during the ensuing years of peace. I raised our son, and held those who threatened him at bay, but an end is coming—I can feel the future pressing in on me, constricting my chest as if a vice.

The air is too thick to breathe.

I'm running out of time.

I must bring my husband home.

Hurrying to my bedchamber, I pass Melantho outside the kitchen, dusting. A beautiful girl, her dark hair tumbles wildly down her back and the pink tint of her cheeks contrasts strikingly against her porcelain skin. I know she beds Antinous, just as I know he believes I will choose him as my next husband. She stares at me, her lips parted into the smallest of leers, and with sudden clarity, I know it is she who has betrayed me to Antinous. She who has divulged that each night, Eurykleia unwinds the work I have spent hours toiling over; revealed that my promise to wed when the work is finished has always been a ruse. I stare back at the girl, my face expressionless, and continue toward my room.

Once inside, I click the lock into place. My propensity towards cloistering myself is well known to my household—it will not surprise them when I remain hidden away for the next few days, claiming some malady or other.

An ornately carved chest sits by the foot of the bed, a wedding gift to me from Odysseus. A blanket rests on its lid. I remove the soft wool and open the box, inhaling the undertones of rose beneath its earthy wooden scent. Tucked inside is a small handloom that belonged to my mother. Next to it, sorted into a rainbow of colors, my best threads. As I remove the loom, my hand brushes a smooth wooden box—ancient, passed from mother to daughter over the eons. *For later.*

I begin to weave the most exquisite piece I will ever create. While I thread the loom and pass the shuttle back and forth in a steady rhythm, a memory, vivid and fierce, pulls me into its potent embrace. I am trapped as it plays before my mind's eye.

Odysseus is in the field. His long, unkempt hair frames his sunburned skin. He mumbles incoherently to himself, and to the oxen and horse

HOMECOMING

lashed to the plow. No crop grows in the salt-filled ground. Only dusty clots of dirt billow from behind him as he trudges hour after hour in the blazing sun.

He does not want to go to war. His king has commanded him, but it is a deadly folly, he tells me, a disastrous undertaking from which most will not return. So he pretends madness. He pretends that his clever mind has disintegrated, wasted, just as our once-lush fields have transformed into seas of dust.

The king sends his messenger, Palamedes, and a contingent of foot soldiers to investigate. They quickly tire of watching Odysseus, unwashed and incoherent, wander the halls of our home and the fields of our property. They are impatient to secure his commitment, and his resources, for their king's pleasure. They dismiss his madness as a deception.

Without warning, Palamedes rips my infant son from my arms and carries him outside. I chase in panic, but a soldier catches my arm and holds me back. I watch in horror as Palamedes places Telemachus in the field, directly in the plow's path. The animals advance, unwavering. And the wildness in Odysseus's eyes does not lift. It does not lift until the moment before he will crush our son under the hooves of the ox and the blade of the plow. My screams finally die in my throat when he stops, throws down the reins, and stalks into the house, slamming the door behind him. He leaves for war the next day, and I am left with the echo of his madness.

I shudder as the memory fades, and hesitate before returning to my task. Steadfast, loyal, faithful Penelope, they call me. I am all these things. And none of them.

The ocean breeze is damp against my face. I carry no torch, fearing even the smallest glow will give away my presence. The path is well known to me, though, and my feet tread easily over the rocks. Water crashes below and the salty tang of it fills my nostrils. Moonlight dances off waves.

When the mouth of the cave yawns before me, I enter and allow my eyesight to adjust to the dim interior. I have much to do this night, under the cover of darkness. Setting my basket on the ground, I remove a clay bowl, my newly-crafted silk shawl, and a tiny bottle. The fresh, icy water running through this cave originates inland and flows out to join the sea. Filling the bowl, I crack the wax seal off the bottle and empty its fragrant contents into the water and soak the scarf in the mixture.

My blood is not pure. My father was a mortal. But the mysteries have been passed to me from my Naiad mother, and our magic comes from water. Not seawater, but fresh. While my iridescent scarf floats in the bowl, I fill the tiny bottle with more of this pure water and set it carefully on the ground.

I remove a final object from my basket. It is a shell, beautifully curved and gleaming white. Kneeling at the water's edge, I begin to chant. Dipping the shell into the edge of the sea, I call her name. Then I wait.

Kalypso

She stares at his still form. His breath against her neck is warm and rhythmic in sleep, his arm heavy across her chest. Carefully, she moves out from underneath him and gently tucks the blanket back in.

When he awakens, she offers him spiced wine. He smiles and takes the bowl from her hands. They are matched in height, but his powerful build could crush her as easily as if she were a twig under his boot. She shivers with delight at this thought, and then at her next thought: for all his strength, his skill with sword and bow and knife, his cleverness, it is *her* power that rules here.

When he paces the stony floor of the cave like a caged animal, she sings, and the change comes over him. First he stares at the horizon, at some distant memory. Then he sways on his feet, catching himself against a wall. Finally, with a predator's eye, he sees her. Energy and desire ripple off of him in waves. He pushes her onto the bed and has her with such ferociousness and greed that she feels as if she is drowning, as if that were possible. Sometimes he calls her by the wrong name. She never corrects him. Later he cries, his shoulders wracking with sobs while she embraces him and licks the tears from his cheek. *Mine*, she thinks.

She believes she is in love, but it is an obsessive, savage love. She feels the madness of it lurking within her—it infiltrates the crevices of her mind, seeps between her thoughts, and weaves its tendrils around her heart.

And then she feels something different. Something altogether foreign. There is an urge, a tenacious whisper, compelling her into the sea. She fights the burn of it, shrugging it off like a cloak weighing too heavily in the hot sun.

What is wrong? he asks.

Nothing, my love, she answers and rolls away from him. She stares beyond the draperies, now tied neatly to the bedposts, and into the dimly lit room beyond. He sees this palace, this prison in all its splendor, as she wishes him to. At times, even she confuses the illusion with reality, but for just a moment, a dirty rock wall stares back at her instead of silk tapestries.

The strange, nagging hunger persists, compelling her out of the bed. Her skin crawls and she pulls at her own hair. A shriek boils up from her belly and she cannot stifle it. Alarmed, he is next to her. I must go, she says.

I will come, he offers.

No!

The moon highlights the stillness of the water and she turns, panicking. His boat sits unfinished upon the cradle, its seaworthiness as yet untested. He must not try to follow.

Turning back to the ocean she raises her face to the sky and shrieks a cry filled with ecstasy. Arms outstretched, she summons the violence of the sea and feels it heed her call. Waves rise up and crash onto the shore, wind howls, sand whirls. This is her birthright.

Without a backward glance, she dives into the water, her sleek body disappearing under the black depths.

She is pulled forward to some unexplained place. Yet, in the way a bird must when migrating home, she knows she will find it. She swims for hours and recognizes her destination when the longing to come ashore becomes urgent, immediate. The rocks are jagged, but she is adept at navigating this terrain, as sure of her motions on a beach or cliff as she is underwater.

The cave is a dark blot against an even darker sky. Dripping, she enters. A woman stands silently, close enough to the entrance that her face is reflected in the light of the full moon. Dark hair, streaked with white, cascades down her back. She is petite in form and her face is beautiful, if careworn. You, she says.

Kalypso, the woman answers. Cousin.

The two stand in silence, taking the measure of one another. Finally, the woman speaks. My husband must come home now. Her voice is steady, melodious, but unyielding.

He will not, Kalypso answers.

The woman takes a step forward and Kalypso, wide-eyed, steps back. Unintentionally, she places a hand over her belly.

The woman stills for a long moment, then nods slightly, unsurprised. A gift for your trouble then, the woman says, unraveling the shawl from her own shoulders and presenting it. An offering. *A surrender*, Kalypso thinks.

Kalypso is taken aback by how easily the woman has acquiesced. She reaches for the scarf. A voice in her head warns her not to touch it. But it is exquisite. It calls to her, insistent, seductive. She aches to feel the silk caress her skin, and even in the dim light it shimmers as if woven with pure silver.

Kalypso snatches it from the woman and presses it to her face, inhaling the musky, floral scent. An indiscernible pattern rims the edges, so complex and intricate that Kalypso becomes lost in it. Minutes go by. Finally, she winds it around herself and looks back at the woman.

Go to him, the woman whispers. But it may be only the wind speaking.

Penelope

Always, the visions appear to me in water. I am a voyeur while a great city burns and Odysseus, covered in dirt and blood, wields his sword. Later, I watch him command his ship as it pitches violently in a raging storm. Men scream in terror and disappear into the vast blackness of the deep. Still later, I see *her* drag him ashore, and I watch in rapt horror when he awakens in her arms.

I am shaken by our encounter. Although I have seen her reflected in shimmering pools of water, I am stunned by her beauty in the flesh, and by the sheer *otherness* of her. My husband has been with this woman for seven years.

The visions are fickle, though. They come as they wish, not as I wish. Now, staring into the clay washbasin in my bedchamber, only my own countenance stares back. It is possible nothing has changed, but I refuse to contemplate my fate if that is so.

I hear the suitors below, demanding to be fed. Their jovial tone of evenings past is gone. Antinous has informed them all of my deception and they are smug in their wounded hypocrisy.

I summon Eurykleia and she helps me dress. This evening, I take care with my hair and clothing. I will not be covered in layers of mourning, but instead I will appear every bit the lady of the house. We dust powder on my cheeks, redden my lips, add a touch of kohl around the eyes. When we are satisfied, she holds the silver-plated mirror up for me to examine the results.

"He will return, my lady," she assures me.

"He must," I agree.

We make one stop before entering the great hall. I hand Eurykleia a heavy burden concealed in cloth, and she follows behind me.

When I step into the room, there is a moment before they notice me and I am able to survey them. Suitors, they call themselves, all wishing to take my husband's place. But thieves, leeches, and pompous fools are what they truly are. This home will belong to my son after his father, not to one of these lazy, self-serving braggarts.

I compose myself as silence falls and all heads turn in my direction. Sweeping toward the front of the room, I position myself at the fireplace and prepare to deliver my performance.

"Noble gentleman," I begin, my hands outstretched, beseeching. "For many long years I have held out hope that my husband, Odysseus, would return. I have remained faithful and true to him—my beloved." At this I lower my gaze.

"I was unprepared to face the truth," I whisper so softly that the men must collectively lean in to hear me. Then, as if summoning my courage, I continue in a bold voice, "But I must accept that he is gone forever."

The crowd murmurs—nodding, approving. "These lands are vast and this household well-appointed. Enemies threaten to take it from me, and though I have done my best, I fear I cannot stand alone any longer."

The men taste victory, and their excitement grows palpable. "My son is young. Although he wishes to be master of this house, he is yet unready."

Pausing, I gesture toward my salon in wordless acknowledgement of my failed pretense. "Please forgive a woman's faithful heart, and her excessive grief."

I summon my household staff, ready with a lavish spread of food and drink, and they stand poised to serve. "But gentleman, how do I choose from among you? You are all worthy—fine, well bred, distinguished." I smile at them with appreciation and then shake my head as if confused.

I have their rapt attention. "Tonight, let us feast together, as friends. And tomorrow, befitting my late husband's memory, we shall have a competition!"

Cheers fill the hall. I summon Eurykleia forward and together we remove a gleaming, deadly bow from under its wool protection. Odysseus's bow.

The crowd falls silent once again. I caress the curve of its handle and let my hands slide along the lower limb. Then I hold it aloft, my arms quaking from the strain of it. "In three days' time, whoever shall restring this bow and shoot an arrow through the target, that man shall be my husband!"

Kalypso

He is asleep when she returns. She tips her face toward the glow of the rising sun and exhales her relief.

She knows she keeps him through trickery and magic. Perhaps his obsession for her has grown into something resembling love, but she has never put that premise to the test. She understands she stole him from another. But now, his wife has yielded him.

Humming softly under her breath, she enters the cave and begins to prepare a meal. The aching hunger that drove her to Penelope has now been transformed into a true need, and she sets to cooking. Her voice becomes haunting, rapturous, and the song crescendos into a bold melody. She turns and her breath catches in her throat.

He is there.

Already, heat emanates from his body as he advances toward her, when suddenly he stops. His gaze drops to her neck and he reaches for the silk shawl, caressing the material between his fingers. He pulls it from her shoulders and raises it up to his face, inhaling deeply.

In an instant everything changes. His eyes clear and he stumbles backward, away from her, and falls to his knees with a guttural, anguished groan. Penelope, he cries.

When he looks back at her, there is rage in his eyes. He surveys the room and she knows he sees it for what it is. A cave, a dark dungeon. And he sees her for what she is. Beautiful, terrible, his captor.

No, she screeches at him. You are mine now! She flings the cooking pot and all its ingredients across the room.

His eyes blaze as he rises and stalks toward her. Her fury rapidly transforms into panic and fear. The air leaves her lungs and icy dread creeps up her spine. Please, she begs, stepping backward and away from him. It can be as it was.

His expression is unchanged. Now it is she who falls to her knees, sobbing. Please, she says again. There is a baby.

He stops. The violence leaves his eyes, but a cold horror takes its place. You are a monster. The child will be a monster.

He works tirelessly on his boat. It is nothing more than a raft really. She suspects it will be reduced to twigs when the inevitable storm rages over the sea. *You will not make it home in this*, she says.

Then I will die trying, he answers.

During the journey, she swims next to him, and if she tires and needs rest, he allows her to lie on the deck of the craft. When the etesian wind erupts from the northeast and tears at the makeshift sail, she stands solid and unmoving on the bow, arms outstretched, face like stone.

He watches her, his expression unreadable. Out of habit, out of desperation, she begins to sing. No! he roars, and she is silent. He pulls the scarf from under his shirt, moves away from her, and holds it to his face again. She turns back to the abysmal loneliness of the sea.

On the third day, they sight shore in the distance. Childlike, at first he only stands and stares, and then he begins to paddle, laughing with delight, as the land grows larger. It is further than he anticipates and soon he is sweaty with exertion, and from years spent idle. But he keeps on, grim determination in the set of his jaw.

She calls the gentle south wind and the sail billows, propelling them landward. When they are close enough to the port that figures appear, bustling in the marketplace, she knows it is time. She reaches a hand toward him as tears stream down her cheeks, but he is already home. He does not notice when she slips silently into the waves.

Penelope

The bow leans against the chest in my chambers. This weapon will know its master. Arrows will fly steadfast and true for Odysseus alone.

Seated on the floor of my bedchamber, I open the lid of a stone box and remove a lock of his hair, long preserved. I add these strands to the bottle filled with sacred water from the cave. As they swirl about in a tiny vortex, I speak his name. Finally, strand-by-strand, I add them to a pot of melted wax.

To make the bowstrings I use three separate strands of linen thread, twisted and sealed together with this melted wax. It is taxing work, and though my fingers are nimble and my eyesight keen, I am not a young girl who can labor for hours at her task. But I am determined, and soon it is finished.

Just as I stand to stretch, there is a knock at the door. Eurykleia enters her eyes alight with fevered excitement.

"My lady, your son, Telemachus, has returned!"

My heart leaps into my throat at this news. We embrace and I choke back a sob. "He is well?"

"Yes," she assures me. "He is with Eumeaus, dear old friend, likely resting and learning the state of affairs here before he comes." Pausing, she adds, "There is talk of a stranger with Eumeaus."

We hold each other's gaze, afraid to hope. A moment later, her tone becomes disdainful. "I have also overheard Antinous speaking to Melantho, asking her to seek out Telemachus and let slip to him about the archery competition. He wants to lure him here to witness it."

She pauses again and her face contorts with anger. "He intimated that there may be an accident with the bow during the competition, and that he would finally be rid of Telemachus for good."

I shake my head. "Do not fear. Telemachus is safe." And while I know this to be true, my hatred for Antinous burns in my chest, a scorching ember.

"We must follow Melantho," I say.

Eurekleia dresses me in worn, coarse clothing, and shrouds my head in a scarf. She brings us two market baskets from the kitchen and we slip outside. I spy Melantho weaving briskly through the crowds, her raven hair floating after her. She is making her way toward the town center, where at this time of day, merchants, shopkeepers, ships' crews, and statesmen will be congregating to conduct business and share the day's news. My son will most likely be here somewhere.

Melantho sees him before I do. Her demeanor shifts and she pretends interest in a colorful array of fresh produce, all the while edging her way toward Telemachus. He is seated with a small group of men, Eumaeus among them. And there is another. He faces away from me.

Eurykleia and I position ourselves, hidden from view, near a baker's stall, and watch as Melantho approaches the group. She feigns delighted surprise when she nearly runs into Telemachus. He greets her politely, if stiffly.

"My lord, you have arrived just in time!" she exclaims. At his puzzled expression she continues, "For the competition. Surely you have heard?"

HOMECOMING

When he admits that no, he is unaware of any competition, she explains, "Your mother has finally decided to choose a husband from among the suitors. She has devised a brilliant contest using your late father's bow. The winner of the contest wins her hand." She claps her hands in feigned excitement.

The stranger chooses this moment to stand and speak. I am still unable to see his face, but when I hear his voice, I know. I recognize the deep timbre, the softness of tone disguising power, the subtlety of his inflection. "A contest for the lady's hand, you say?"

I can see that this stranger's presence confuses Melantho. She tilts her head as if trying to get the measure of him. "A contest with bow and arrow," she repeats, nodding slightly.

"In my day, I was rather adept with bow and arrow. Perhaps I should enter this contest? Telemachus, what do you think?" He laughs and claps Telemachus on the back.

My son grins broadly, and in that moment I understand he knows he is with his father. "Certainly," he answers.

Melantho's stiff smile shows me she cannot determine if this man is serious or teasing her. But then he pulls a silk scarf from the folds of his tunic. I gasp and squeeze Eurykleia's hand. "I am newly arrived here and have not had the pleasure of courting your lady. Perhaps you could give her this token, so she may think favorably upon me and allow me to compete for her hand?"

The girl takes the scarf and stares at it, her gaze darting between Telemachus and Odysseus. Telemachus nods. "Please, do take this to your lady," he orders.

The morning of the contest dawns clear and bright. I have not slept since I saw my husband in the marketplace, and Eurykleia must labor with dusting powder to hide the dark circles under my eyes. Today, I will wear the finest of my clothes—finer even than when I announced the contest to the suitors. Today, Odysseus will come home. And he will be well met.

Once again, Eurykleia carries the heavy bow into the great hall, while I hold the meticulously wound strings draped over my arm. The room is filled with laughter and boisterous posturing, but they fall into a reverent silence when I enter. Surveying the crowd, I do not see Telemachus or Odysseus, but I know they will come.

"Noble guests," I greet the men. "I present to you Odysseus's bow." Eurykleia sets it down on the ground, leaning it against the stone wall.

I gesture behind the crowd. "Whoever shall string this bow and shoot an arrow through twelve axe heads—he shall be my husband!"

Amidst the cheering, there is a commotion at the entryway. I hear one of the housemaids exclaim, "Telemachus has returned!"

The tenor of the suitors' banter shifts subtly, but they are careful not to offend me, and so they welcome Telemachus with forced good humor. My son enters the room followed by Eumaeus, and then Odysseus.

For the first time in twenty years, I look upon my husband's face in the flesh. I was but a young girl, and he a young man, when we were wed. A lifetime has been lived in his absence, and yet it seems as if no time has passed. His eyes meet mine across the room. Although he is bearded and his hair streaked with gray, I would know him among many thousands.

I keep my expression carefully neutral but give a small nod in his direction, and receive his in return. My heart thuds loudly in my chest, and I hold back a gasp as my body remembers the feel of his touch before my mind can censor the thought.

The suitors must not become suspicious, so I turn my attention to Telemachus and greet him with the true affection of a mother for her long-absent son. He embraces me, and whispers in my ear, "Clever mother."

"Finish this," I whisper back.

HOMECOMING

He smiles and steps up onto a long table. In his youthful strength, he towers over the suitors. "I shall try out this bow." He gestures for the weapon and Eurykleia hands it up to him. I place one of the strings in his hands and hold my breath, for he almost succeeds, but at the last, it is too much for him to wield. Ruefully, he says, "Clearly I have not yet mastered my great father's strength."

The men magnanimously clap him on the back as he leaps down from the table and hands the bow off to the first suitor in line. I notice that Antinous has positioned himself apart from the others, as if he will be jurying this competition, or perhaps saving his own turn for last. He fancies himself the leader of this pack of jackals, but he is neither the youngest nor strongest of their lot, and I suspect he is concerned that if Telemachus struggled with the bow, he will as well.

When Eurymachus, considered by Antinous to be a close rival for my hand, fails miserably, Antinous's eyebrows knit with concern. He stops the competition with his hand held high and says, "Friends, perhaps we have not given the Gods their due and they are displeased." Nervous voices lend their assent. "Let us make a sacrifice tonight to Apollo and resume this contest tomorrow."

The suitors cede to his authority immediately. As they begin to disperse, another voice thunders above the rest. "I would have a turn."

All eyes turn toward the stranger, still poised near the entryway. Telemachus moves to pick up the bow and hand it to his father, but Antinous interrupts. "You look a beggar," he accuses insolently. "Do you dare to enter the lady's home and compete for her hand? We will not have it!"

The others grumble their agreement and begin to hurl insults of their own. I see Telemachus, ready to argue, so I call them to attention myself. "Noble gentlemen!" Surprised silence falls over the room. "This stranger is a guest in my home, as are all of you." I pause and look directly at Antinous—a challenge. His face contorts with anger.

"What harm can come of giving this poor man a chance at the bow? Should he have any success, he would be welcome to a warm meal, some fresh clothing." I smile out at the crowd benevolently, and most of them forgive the tender heart of a woman.

I find Melantho in the back corner of the room, standing with the other housemaids, and catch her eye before continuing. "Besides, he sent me a lovely gift as a token of his friendship and goodwill. I cannot, in good conscience, turn him out." Melantho's face drains of color and she looks to Antinous, who does not see her. She knows full well she did not give me the scarf, and by now she must suspect something dangerous is unfolding.

I gesture at Telemachus, who brings the bow. In my hands I clutch a fresh string. We both converge on Odysseus. My husband's eyes never leave mine as I hand him the string. "May your arrow fly true, my lord," I say softly, so that only he can hear.

His eyes glisten with unshed tears, but his grip is steady when he takes the string from me. Our skin touches and he inhales sharply.

Telemachus leans next to me. "Mother, you must go. Leave with Eumaeus," he orders gently. I look from my husband to my son—so alike in stance, in coloring, in the shape of their face that I cannot fathom why others do not see it. Finally, I nod.

Eumaeus and I leave the hall, barring the door securely behind us.

The screams are terrible. I stand mute. I know my husband's rage, his madness. I have seen it reflected in the enchanted waters of the cave while he battled enemies on all sides. I've watched him stare into the deep abyss of the sea, scream at unseen demons, slay monsters.

I know, too, my husband's love, his passion. I have felt it lavished upon myself. Felt the heat of his touch, the warmth of his breath. And I have watched him love another, completely, mercilessly.

I have known him mostly from afar. And in this moment, between

HOMECOMING

horror and relief, between freedom and submission, I understand why I have only now called him home.

About The Authors

Kelly Sandoval's fiction has appeared in *Asimov's*, *Shimmer*, and *Best American Science Fiction and Fantasy*. Because she hates free time, she edits the online short fiction magazine *Liminal Stories* with Shannon Peavey. She lives in Seattle, where the weather is always happy to make staying in and writing seem like a good idea. Her family includes a patient husband, a demanding cat, and an anarchist tortoise. You can find her online at kellysandovalfiction.com.

Amanda Kespohl is an appellate judicial clerk who writes bench summaries by day and fantasy novels and short stories by night. She lives in Tallahassee, Florida with her beagle, Bailey, and spends her spare time reading fairy tale retellings and Marvel comic books. Check out her website at amandakespohl.wordpress.com or find her on Twitter at @amandakespohl.

L.S. Johnson was born in New York and now lives in Northern California, where she feeds her four cats by writing book indexes. Her stories have appeared in *Strange Horizons*, *Interzone*, *Long Hidden*, *Year's Best Weird Fiction*, and other venues, and she has been nominated for a Pushcart Prize and longlisted for the Tiptree Award. Her first collection, *Vacui Magia: Stories*, is now available. Find out more about her at traversingz.com.

Pat Flewwelling is an Oshawa, Ontario-based author of non-fiction, science fiction, fantasy, and horror. When not working full-time for a major telecommunications company, and not working part-time as an editor and ghostwriter, Pat is an avid blogger and reader, who also dabbles in painting and playing guitar. Pat's fifth book, *Helix: Plague of Ghouls*, is forthcoming in 2016.

Gabriel F. Cuellar lives under a maple tree with a husband, two cats, two dogs and a truckload of rats, who graciously allow her the time to write a bunch of nonsense every day.

Randall G. Arnold is a well-traveled engineer and designer now leveraging years of technical writing experience, and passion for environmental and social causes, in speculative fiction writing. He enjoys listening to and composing music and discovering quirky hangouts. "The Dolphin Riders" won honorable mention in the 2015 Texas Observer fiction contest and is his first story to get past an editor. His website is at http://unsettled.space

Michael Leonberger is a writer, a filmmaker, and a horror movie enthusiast. A graduate of the VCUarts Cinema Department, he is responsible for the short film "Hair Grows In Funny Places" (the tragicomic love story between a werewolf and a dominatrix) and the feature length romantic comedy "Goodish" (a movie he co-directed that premiered at the 2014 Virginia Film Festival in Charlottesville, VA). He recently published his first book, Halloween Sweets, about a teenage girl who can raise the dead, and has since published several short stories. He also writes a column for the website Digital America.

V. F. LeSann is a co-writing team presently living in Lethbridge, Alberta, Canada, comprised of Leslie Van Zwol and Megan Fennell. Court clerks by day and writers of myriad strange tales by night, they enjoy adding a touch of grit to fantastic worlds and believe that most things can be improved by adding 'in space' to the initial idea.

Tamsin Showbrook lives in Manchester, UK, where she taught English in secondary schools until she had her two kids. Now she tutors part-time and writes a variety of stuff into the depths of night most days. She loves reading—can't get enough Margaret Atwood, Neil Gaiman or David Mitchell—as well as hiking and running. Her best ideas do tend to come to her while she's exercising, which means she has to make frequent scribble-stops and will never achieve marathon-level fitness, but she's okay with that.

Simon Kewin is the author of over 100 published short and flash stories. His works have appeared in *Nature, Daily Science Fiction, Abyss & Apex* and many more. He lives in England with his wife and their daughters. The second volume in his Cloven Land fantasy trilogy was recently published. Find him at simonkewin.co.uk.

Cat McDonald lives in an eighth-floor apartment in Edmonton with a baby tortoise and at least a dozen tarot decks. She's studying Investigations at Macewan and Tarot at Northern Star college, and makes better choices now than she did five years ago. Eli is two years old and loves strawberries.

Sandra Wickham lives in Vancouver, Canada with her husband, toddler son and two cats. Her friends call her a needle crafting aficionado, health guru and ninja-in-training. Sandra's short stories have appeared in *Evolve, Vampires of the New Undead, Evolve, Vampires of the Future Undead, Chronicles of the Order, Crossed Genres magazine, LocoThology: Tales of Fantasy & Science Fiction, The Urban Green Man* and *Luna Station Quarterly*. She blogs about writing with the Inkpunks, slush reads for *Lightspeed Magazine* and promotes the Creative Ink Festival for writers, artists and readers.

K.T. Ivanrest wanted to be a cat or a horse when she grew up, but after failing to metamorphose into either, she began writing stories about them instead. Soon the horses became unicorns and the cats sprouted wings, and once the dragons arrived there was no turning back. When not writing, Kate can be found sewing, cosplaying, and drinking decaf coffee. She recently completed a PhD in Classical Studies, which will come in handy when aliens finally make contact and it turns out they speak Latin.

Adam L. Bealby writes weird fiction leaning heavily into fantasy, horror and arch satire. His short stories and comic work have been published in numerous anthologies, including *Spooked* (Bridge House

Publishing), *Dragontales* (Wyvern Publishing), *Pagan* (Zimbell House Publishing), *Darkness Abound* (Migla Press), *Once Upon A Scream* (HorrorAddicts.net), *World Unknown Review Vol. 2* and *Murky Depths* magazine. He lives in Worcestershire, UK with his wife and three children, and a harried imagination. Catch up with his latest ravings at @adamskilad.

Eliza Chan writes about East Asian mythology, British folklore and madwomen in the attic, but preferably all three at once. She has work published in *Fantasy Magazine, Lontar* and recently in the Fox Spirit anthology *Winter Tales*. She is currently writing a novel set in the world of 'One More Song', alongside working as a Speech and Language Therapist and completing a Masters. When not in front of a screen, Eliza can be found playing board games and cosplaying whenever possible. Find out more at www.elizawchan.wordpress.com and @elizawchan.

Tabitha Lord currently lives in Rhode Island. She is married, has four great kids, a spoiled cat, and lovable lab mix. She holds a degree in Classics from College of the Holy Cross and taught Latin for years at an independent Waldorf school. She also worked in the admissions office there for over a decade before turning her attention to full-time writing. You can visit her author website at www.tabithalordauthor.com, and follow her on www.bookclubbabble.com where she posts author interviews, reviews, and more. *Horizon,* her first novel, was released December 2015, and she is currently at work on the sequel.

About the Anthologist

Rhonda Parrish is driven by a desire to do All The Things. She founded and ran *Niteblade Magazine*, is an Assistant Editor at World Weaver Press and is the editor of several anthologies including, most recently, *Sirens* and *C is for Chimera*.

In addition, Rhonda is a writer whose work has been in publications such as Tesseracts 17: Speculating Canada from Coast to Coast, Imaginarium: The Best Canadian Speculative Writing (2012 & 2015) and Mythic Delirium.

Her website, updated weekly, is at www.RhondaParrish.com

TURN THE PAGE TO LEARN ABOUT MORE
ANTHOLOGIES IN
RHONDA PARRISH'S MAGICAL MENAGERIES

More Magical Menageries Anthologies from Rhonda Parrish

Fae
Rhonda Parrish's Magical Menageries, Volume One

Meet Robin Goodfellow as you've never seen him before, watch damsels in distress rescue themselves, get swept away with the selkies and enjoy tales of hobs, green men, pixies and phookas. One thing is for certain, these are not your grandmother's fairy tales.

Fairies have been both mischievous and malignant creatures throughout history. They've dwelt in forests, collected teeth or crafted shoes. *Fae* is full of stories that honor that rich history while exploring new and interesting takes on the fair folk from castles to computer technologies to modern midwifing, the Old World to Indianapolis.

Fae bridges traditional and modern styles, from the familiar feeling of a good old-fashioned fairy tale to urban fantasy and horror with a fae twist. This anthology covers a vast swath of the fairy story spectrum, making the old new and exploring lush settings with beautiful prose and complex characters.

Corvidae
Rhonda Parrish's Magical Menageries, Volume Two

In Corvidae birds are born of blood and pain, trickster ravens live up to their names, magpies take human form, blue jays battle evil forces, and choughs become prisoners of war. These stories will take you to the Great War, research facilities, frozen mountaintops, steam-powered worlds, remote forest homes, and deep into fairy tales. One thing is for certain, after reading this anthology, you'll never look the same way at the corvid outside your window.

Featuring works by Jane Yolen, Mike Allen, C.S.E. Cooney, M.L.D. Curelas, Tim Deal, Megan Engelhardt, Megan Fennell, Adria Laycraft, Kat Otis, Michael S. Pack, Sara Puls, Michael M. Rader, Mark Rapacz, Angela Slatter, Laura VanArendonk Baugh, and Leslie Van Zwol.

Scarecrow
Rhonda Parrish's Magical Menageries, Volume Three

Within these pages, ancient enemies join together to destroy a mad mommet, a scarecrow who is a crow protects solar fields and stores long-lost family secrets, a woman falls in love with a scarecrow, and another becomes one. Encounter scarecrows made of straw, imagination, memory, and robotics while being spirited to Oz, mythological Japan, other planets, and a neighbor's back garden. After experiencing this book, you'll never look at a hay-man the same.

Featuring all new work by Jane Yolen, Andrew Bud Adams, Laura Blackwood, Amanda Block, Scott Burtness, Amanda C. Davis, Megan Fennell, Kim Goldberg, Katherine Marzinsky, Craig Pay, Sara Puls, Holly Schofield, Virginia Carraway Stark, Laura VanArendonk Baugh, and Kristina Wojtaszek.

Equus
Rhonda Parrish's Magical Menageries, Volume Five

There's always something magical about horses, isn't there? Whether winged or at home in the water, mechanical or mythological, the equines that gallop through these pages span the fantasy spectrum. In one story a woman knits her way up to the stars and in another Loki's descendant grapples with bizarre transformations while fighting for their life. A woman races on a unique horse to save herself from servitude, while a man rides a chariot through the stars to reclaim his self-worth. From steampunk-inspired stories and tales that brush up against horror to straight-up fantasy, one theme connects them all: freedom.

Featuring nineteen fantastic stories of equines both real and imagined by J.G. Formato, Diana Hurlburt, Tamsin Showbrook, M.L.D Curelas, Laura VanArendonk Baugh, V.F. LeSann, Dan Koboldt, J.J. Roth, Susan MacGregor, Pat Flewwelling, Angela Rega, Michael Leonberger, Sandra Wickham, Stephanie A. Cain, Cat McDonald, Andrew Bourelle, Chadwick Ginther, K.T. Ivanrest, and Jane Yolen.

Also Available
from World Weaver Press

FROZEN FAIRY TALES
EDITED BY KATE WOLFORD

Winter is not coming. Winter is here.

As unique and beautifully formed as a snowflake, each of these fifteen stories spins a brand new tale or offers a fresh take on an old favorite like Jack Frost, The Snow Queen, or The Frog King. From a drafty castle to a blustery Japanese village, from a snow-packed road to the cozy hearth of a farmhouse, from an empty coffee house in Buffalo, New York, to a cold night outside a university library, these stories fully explore the perils and possibilities of the snow, wind, ice, and bone-chilling cold that traditional fairy tale characters seldom encounter.

In the bleak midwinter, heed the irresistible call of fairy tales. Just open these pages, snuggle down, and wait for an icy blast of fantasy to carry you away. With all new stories of love, adventure, sorrow, and triumph by Tina Anton, Amanda Bergloff, Gavin Bradley, L.A. Christensen, Steven Grimm, Christina Ruth Johnson, Rowan Lindstrom, Alison McBain, Aimee Ogden, J. Patrick Pazdziora, Lissa Marie Redmond, Anna Salonen, Lissa Sloan, Charity Tahmaseb, and David Turnbull to help you dream through the cold days and nights of this most dreaded season.

Beyond the Glass Slipper
TEN NEGLECTED FAIRY TALES TO FALL IN LOVE WITH
Some fairy tales everyone knows—these aren't those tales.

Kate Wolford, introduces and annotates each tale in a manner that won't leave novices of fairy tale studies lost in the woods to grandmother's house, yet with a depth of research and a delight in posing intriguing puzzles that will cause folklorists and savvy readers to find this collection a delicious new delicacy.

KRAMPUSNACHT: TWELVE NIGHTS OF KRAMPUS
EDITED BY KATE WOLFORD

For bad children, a lump of coal from Santa is positively light punishment when Krampus is ready and waiting to beat them with a stick, wrap them in chains, and drag them down to hell—all with St. Nick's encouragement and approval.

Krampusnacht holds within its pages twelve tales of Krampus triumphant, usurped, befriended, and much more. From evil children (and adults) who get their due, to those who pull one over on the ancient "Christmas Devil." From historic Europe, to the North Pole, to present day American suburbia, these all new stories embark on a revitalization of the Krampus tradition.

Whether you choose to read Krampusnacht over twelve dark and scary nights or devour it in one nacht of joy and terror, these stories are sure to add chills and magic to any winter's reading.

HE SEES YOU WHEN HE'S CREEPIN': TALES OF KRAMPUS
EDITED BY KATE WOLFORD

Krampus is the cloven-hoofed, curly-horned, and long-tongued dark companion of St. Nick. Sometimes a hero, sometimes a villain, within these pages, he's always more than just a sidekick. You'll meet manifestations of Santa's dark servant as he goes toe-to-toe with a bratty Cinderella, a guitar-slinging girl hero, a coffee shop-owning hipster, and sometimes even St. Nick himself. Whether you want a dash of horror or a hint of joy and redemption, these 12 new tales of Krampus will help you gear up for the most "wonderful" time of the year.

Featuring original stories by Steven Grimm, Lissa Marie Redmond, Beth Mann, Anya J. Davis, E.J. Hagadorn, S.E. Foley, Brad P. Christy, Ross Baxter, Nancy Brewka-Clark, Tamsin Showbrook, E.M. Eastick, and Jude Tulli.

OPAL
FAE OF FIRE AND STONE, BOOK 1
by Kristina Wojtaszek

White as snow, stained with blood, her talons black as ebony…

In this retwisting of the classic Snow White tale, the daughter of an owl is forced into human shape by a wizard who's come to guide her from her wintry tundra home down to the colorful world of men and Fae, and the father she's never known. She struggles with her human shape and grieves for her dead mother—a mother whose past she must unravel if men and Fae are to live peacefully together.

Trapped in a Fae-made spell, Androw waits for the one who can free him. A boy raised to be king, he sought refuge from his abusive father in the Fae tales his mother spun. When it was too much to bear, he ran away, dragging his anger and guilt with him, pursuing shadowy trails deep within the Dark Woods of the Fae, seeking the truth in tales, and salvation in the eyes of a snowy hare. But many years have passed since the snowy hare turned to woman and the woman winged away on the winds of a winter storm leaving Androw prisoner behind walls of his own making—a prison that will hold him forever unless the daughter of an owl can save him.

CHAR
FAE OF FIRE AND STONE, BOOK 2

Fire is never tame—least of all the flames of our own kindling.

Raised in isolation by the secretive Circle of Seven, Luna is one of the few powerful beings left in a world dominated by man. Versed in ancient fairy tales and the language of plants, Luna struggles to control her powers over fire. When her mentor dies in Luna's arms, she is forced into a centuries-long struggle against the gravest enemy of all Fae-kind—the very enemy that left her orphaned. In order to save her people, Luna must rewrite their history by entering a door in the mountain and passing back through time. But when the lives of those she loves come under threat, her rage destroys a forest, and everything in it. Now called The Char Witch, she is cursed to live alone, her name and the name of her people forgotten.

Until she hears a knock upon her long-sealed door.

World Weaver Press, LLC
Publishing fantasy, paranormal, and science fiction.
We believe in great storytelling.
worldweaverpress.com

Made in the USA
San Bernardino, CA
02 September 2017